BLUE COLLAR FOLKS

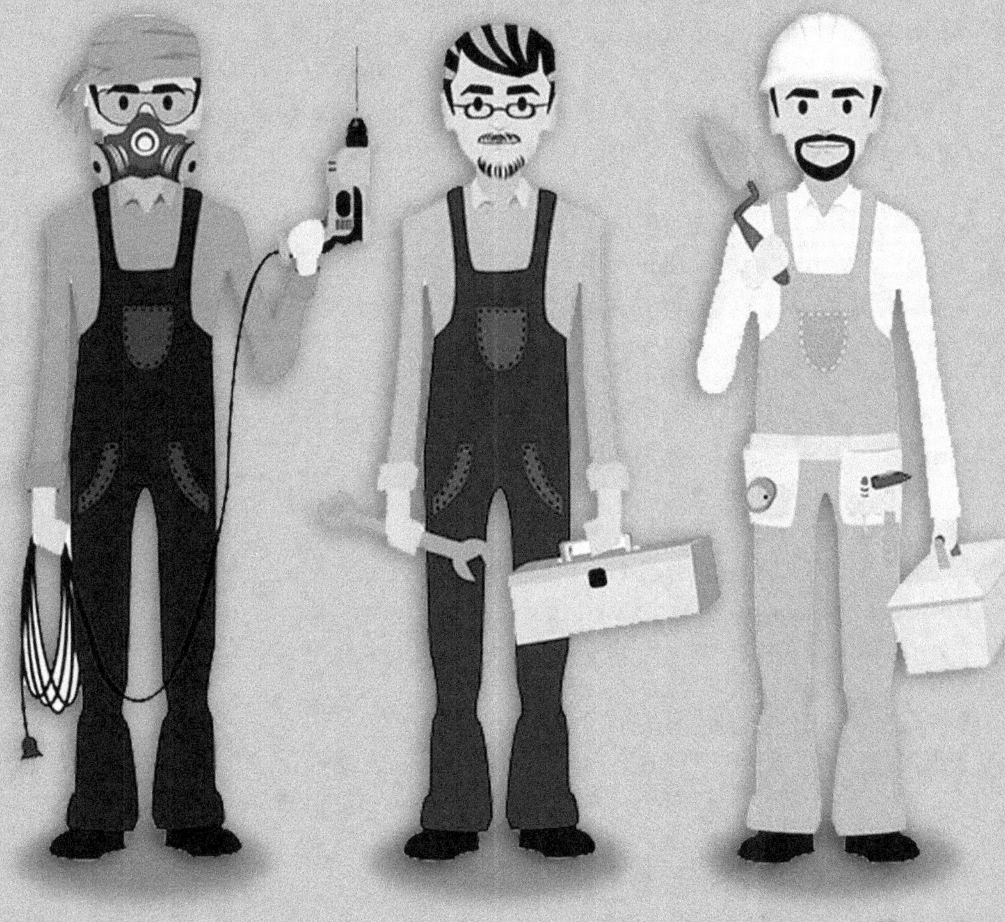

TODD DALEY

WORKBOOK PRESS LLC
187 E Warm Springs Rd,
Suite B285, Las Vegas, NV 89119, USA

Website: https://workbookpress.com/
Hotline: 1-888-818-4856
Email: admin@workbookpress.com

Ordering Information:
Quantity sales. Special discounts are available on quantity purchases by corporations, associations, and others.
For details, contact the publisher at the address above.

Library of Congress Control Number:
ISBN-13:   978-1-956017-81-6 (Paperback Version)
                978-1-956017-82-3 (Digital Version)

REV. DATE: 14/10/2021

"Those who love work, love life." -- Fay Slimm

Table of Contents

Chapter 1 – Pretty Invalid

Walking along the shaded sidewalk towards St. Vincent's Hospital, Tom felt anxious about his girlfriend, Joanie. Like Staten Island's autumn weather, the pretty young woman's health was variable. There were good days and bad days, with the threat of stormy days just over the horizon. It was a new decade, the 1980s, and everything appeared to be in a state of flux. There were now 226 million people living in the good old USA. Japan had surpassed America as the number-one auto producer in the world. GM no longer made Pontiacs – Tom's car. And Congress had recently raised the minimum wage to $3.35 an hour. Tom remembered earning $1.25 an hour working for the A & P in the early 1960s.

He also noticed a decline in decorum and service in the country. Profanity was common in bothmen and women. His mom asserted that a reliance upon swearwords reflected a limited vocabulary. After filling your car, gasoline attendants no longer cleaned your windshield. Of course, there was much discord and strife during the 1960s – especially over the Vietnam War. But that was then, and today it's now. As the existentialists say – life is temporary, precarious, and risky. All we experience is the existential present – for better or worse.

Staten Island, bursting at the seams, had more cars, more pedestrians, and more crime. Even the hospital was beset by change – a series of unanticipated renovations. Looking up at the sky, he saw a flock of geese flying overhead. Instead of sparrows, robins, and blue jays, people now saw those big ungainly birds squawking in the sky. The entranceway to the looming hospital was framed by two-by-fours patched together in a makeshift archway. Tom hurried through before strong wind could send them tumbling down on his head. He noticed that the other pedestrians also walked quickly into the busy reception area.

Joanie had been plagued with chronic headaches – off and on for several years. She lived with Tom in Elm Park on the second floor of his mom's house on Pulaski Avenue. Almost from the start, it was a star-crossed romance. When Joanie's family moved to Indiana, Tom had no choice but to focus on school – channeling his sexual impulses into getting an education. Thus, a good example of Freudian sublimation was manifested by the overachieving student during his high school and college years.

Years later, separated from her husband back in Indiana, Joanie hadn't bothered to finalize her divorce. It had been a short unhappy marriage, which the young woman seldom talked about. Not one to inquire into a person's past, Tom was happy to be reunited with Joanie. The two high school sweethearts lived as husband and wife under the aegis of English common law – an accepted condition in the Haley family, though frowned upon by Joanie's folks, the Gardellos.

Rushing into Joanie's room, Tom pulled up a chair and kissed her on the lips and cheek, which felt feverish and damp.

"How are you feeling, sweetie?"

"Pretty good today," she replied with a wan smile.

Tom understood the enormous toll the illness exacted on the pretty invalid. It must have taken a lot of psychic energy for her to project optimism and well-being.

"I had a nice dream. Amon was touching my forehead and saying a prayer."

Tom recalled the day six years ago when the charismatic young man had placed his hand on Joanie's forehead while murmuring a prayer. The immediate effect was to alleviate her pain – propelling her towards a miraculous recovery.

"He did help you. Just as he helped Dick Grimsby, that woman Evette, my mom, and so many others. I was there when he lifted that car off Evette while I slid her out."

"But it didn't last. How come?"

"That's not entirely true. Dick walks better than he used to and my mom's face still looks good."

But Tom had to admit that her facial asymmetry had reappeared. It seemed that his faith healing was only a temporary phenomenon. There was a reversion to the previous state for many of his cures. After Amon had saved a young man who jumped off a ferry boat, he had been given given the appellation Mariners Harbor Messiah by the press – including the Daily News and the Staten Island Advocate.

"Faith healing requires faith. So if it doesn't work – it must be our fault."

"No Joanie. It's not that. Maybe the effects of his powers are diminished because he's no longer with us."

Amon Dakota, the so-called Mariners Harbor Messiah had been killed in a drive-by shooting near his tugboat in the Kill Van Kull. He had been rehabilitating a Victorian house on Simonson Avenue for the homeless. This endeavor had run into opposition from the neighbors. It was the typical "not in my backyard" syndrome. At the moment of Amon's passing, gray clouds overhead parted and the sun's rays burst through – shining light and warmth upon them.

"Thanks for your scientific explanation. I feel so much better now."

At this point, a nurse entered the room and asked Tom to leave. They were going to wheel her down to another floor for some tests. Tom kissed Joanie goodbye, holding back his tears, and leaving the room with a lump in his throat.

On the way back from the hospital, Tom stopped at Kaffman's bar on the corner of Morningstar Road and Walker Street. The smoky sour-sweet smelling saloon had been the site of Tom's reunion with Joanie after an absence of several years. He recalled his then girlfriend, Martha's fury upon seeing Tom's excitement with the appearance of his high school sweetheart. In an instant, Tom landed on the floor, Joanie rushed to his aid, and Martha swept past the two huddled on the floor, as the stunned bar patrons looked on in disbelief. Someone uttered the well-known line that "Hell hath no fury like a woman scorned."

Tom's musings were interrupted by the entrance of Harry the Horse. Years ago Harry would walk down Pulaski Avenue, toting a glove, a broomstick bat and a high-bouncing Spalding, yelling "Who wants to play stickball?"

Instantly, Tom, Joey Caprino, Mike Palermo, Gene Munski, and others clamored onto the street. Soon a boisterous running-bases stickball game was underway. The rollicking, high-scoring game occasionally ended when a hard-hit Spalding landed on a roof or in a neighbor's living room. Those were the days kids played on the sidewalks and in the streets all day long. Tom's first sight of Pulaski Avenue was Joey Caprino throwing a rubber ball against his front porch stairs and catching the rebound in an endless game of stoop ball. During the 1950s, Willie Mays of the Giants used to play stickball with New York City kids. The Dodgers' Duke Snider didn't care for the game – trying to hit a small rubber ball with a skinny broomstick bat. During that era, there were disputes over who was the best centerfielder: Willie Mays, Duke Snider, or Mickey Mantle.

Chapter 2 – Only the Good Die Young

"How's the Pied Piper of Elm Park? Remember when I hit a line drive that broke Mrs. Egger's window?"

"Yeah. It was always a shot off your bat. You even hit a pop fly that landed in a tub of cement. That woman hated my guts. Called the cops on me once."

"Remember Granny Schmidt? She was a real fan of yours," Tom asked with a smirk.

"The crazy old lady that used to sit in her window, cursing me out?"

"The one and only Granny Schmidt. She passed away a couple of years ago. I think Dooley's liquor store went out of business soon after. She alone kept them going with her daily trip to buy booze there.

Tom ordered a Ballantine beer for himself and Harry from the bartender, Rudy Kaffman. The red-faced bartender had known Tom's dad, Thomas Haley, a hard drinking loyal customer back in the 1950s. Tom's mom, Claire Haley had once entered the dimly lit saloon to chastise Kaffman about serving liquor to her alcoholic husband. She used the term "blood money" to describe his barroom proceeds. His mom was known as a "tough cookie" in the neighborhood. Once the school year was underway, Tom's street games were severely restricted. Homework had to be done first. The existence of rules governing work and play, as well as the balance existing among life's activities, were common phenomena of the 50s and 60s.

"Ain't it late for you? Your Curtis students deserve a teacher who's awake and not hung over."

"I'm off from teaching. I'm on a six-month sabbatical to finish my master's degree. I'm doing a project with laboratory rats. It's on the effects of nutrition on learning."

"Rats? I hate those animals. I was working on an old house that had a family of rats living there. I set of bunch of traps. Must have killed a dozen of them. Big bastards with long tails – some of them a foot long!"

"No, these are white rats. Mostly tame. Although one of the females is a biter." Tom showed Harry a bandage on his wrist. Their teeth grow all the time – that's why they're constantly gnawing at stuff."

"That figures. Watch out for the females. Speaking of females, how's your girlfriend doing?"

"Joanie's doing OK. Getting better, little by little.

"I thought that Amon guy cured her? I'll never forget how he lifted that heavy beam off me. It must have weighed 250 pounds. He was a pretty good stickball player too. Hit a shot off me that must have gone 300 feet."

"Amon was awesome. He left us too soon," Tom said sadly.

"Only the good one die young. Anyway I got to get out of here. Time flies when you're in a ginmill. Say hello to Joanie for me. And watch out for those rats -especially the two-legged ones!"

As Harry exited Kaffman's, Tom thought about time – the grinding gears of the universe turning and grinding up people and places – all the stuff of the world. The adage time is money had become popular in the 1980s where everything had a dollar sign attached to it. Leaving the bar, he saw an elderly man in a corner who looked like his father, Thomas Haley. Stopping to stare at the man, the latter felt Tom's eyes on him and looked up puzzled. Barroom boozers all looked alike – bleary-eyed, red-faced, and dazed – using up that precious commodity called time. The stale, smoky air pickled your skin, fermented your stomach, destroyed your liver, and fried your brains. Yet the social pull of bars was undeniable.

Entering the cellar of his mom's house via the backyard metal door, Tom checked on his twelve laboratory rats – housed in four cages of three rats each with males and females separated. Rats were notoriously fertile. The last thing he wanted was a rat population explosion. They were Wistar-Lewis albino rats, known for their docility, homogeneity, and intelligence. For eight weeks the young rats had been separated into two groups with respect to diet. The control group had a high-protein diet, while the test group had a low-protein diet. The two groups were easily distinguishable because the low-protein group were smaller and more nervous than their well-fed peers. Joanie had assisted Tom with the rats, handling the rodents more confidently than Tom.

The feisty protein deprived female never bit Joanie. That particular rat seemed to have it in for Tom – apparently aware that she was in the low-protein group because of him. Once, Tom had seen Joanie giving the low-protein group some cheese to boost their diet. When caught, she smiled and promised her boyfriend not to tamper with the rats' diet again. In science good data outweighs good ethics. Witness the atomic bomb developed by the U. S. during the second world war and dropped on the Japanese cities of Hiroshima and Nagasaki.

Tom was aware that extrapolating his results to people was risky, despite the similarity between human and rat anatomy with respect to nutrition and learning. Rats were intelligent and resourceful animals. It was estimated that New York City had nearly as many rats as people residing in its confines. Rats quickly learn to avoid rat poison, forcing exterminators to utilize chemicals that render rats infertile – rather than killing them directly. There were also problems with the small sample size of twelve rats. He would have to use Gossett's t-distribution rather than the normal distribution to analyze the data. But his thesis advisor at C.C.N.Y. had approved the project after Tom brought in one of his white rats plus pictures of his elaborate wooden maze as evidence he wasn't "faking" the research.

Tom constructed the maze made out of plywood and two-by-fours, covered by a wire screen. This prevented the rats from escaping the maze and enabled Tom to observe their progress though the elaborate maze. To induce the rats to travel through the maze from starting point to ending point, Tom used both positive and negative reinforcements. The negative reinforcement was an ultrasonic whistle sounded while the rat traversed the complex maze until the end point where a piece of cheese provided the positive reinforcement. Tom used the number of wrong turns as the index of the rats maze-learning performance. The rats maze running experiment would be conducted over thirty days. Then the rats would be set free, except for Tom's favorite – a friendly alpha male with extraordinary testicles.

Chapter 3 – Saturday Morning Games

With Joanie in the hospital, Tom spent Saturday mornings in his mom's kitchen as she pored over the Advocate, Staten Island's hometown newspaper which featured a mix of local and national news. The major news on the Island was its increased development – particularly on the South Shore. The new Staten Island Mall had been built on odiferous landfill, where layers of topsoil covered a sprawling garbage dump site. For many years, Staten Island represented the locale of choice for the other four boroughs to deposit their discarded stuff – including the bodies of folks bumped off by violent New Yorkers. But that was the shady past. Urban renewal in the form of a shopper's paradise – a spacious indoor mall – was living proof of Yogi Berra adage – "It ain't over 'til it's over."

"Mom, have you tried that new Mall? It has Macy's at one end and Sears at the other, and everything else in between – including book stores, clothing stores, bakeries, pizza places, ice cream stores, and even Chinese restaurants."

"I prefer Port Richmond. It's just two stops on the number three bus. To get to the Mall, I have to walk down Richmond and Forest. And then get the bus that goes out towards Mid-Island to reach the Mall," she replied, rustling her paper.

"And it's better to support the small shopkeepers, instead of the big capitalists who own Macys, Gimbels, and Sears."

"Listen McGee, you're not so idealistic yourself. Torturing those poor rats so you can get a raise from the Board of Education. By the way, make sure those rodents don't get loose. The last thing I want is a white rat crawling around in the kitchen."

"They're locked in their cages – safe and sound. What's wrong with getting a raise? You're the one always talking about your brother Jack's success at Macys. Wasn't it George Bernard Shaw who said that at age thirty communists with brains become capitalists?"

"Don't throw your obscure literary references at me. I've read a book or two in my life," Claire replied petulantly.

"Indeed you have. My friend Amon was a big reader. He had stacks of books in his tugboat."

"Speaking of Amon, I see where the local politicians have decided to put a plaque honoring him in Mariners Harbor, whom they call the Mariners Harbor Messiah."

"Yeah, now everybody is on the bandwagon, praising the guy after they labeled him as a foolish do-gooder at best or a crackpot at worst," Tom muttered, sipping his coffee.

"Before you run off to the ball field, see if the hedge needs trimming and sweep up the leaves in the backyard. You're a do-gooder – except when it comes to this house."

Tom was warming up, tossing overhand and sidearm fastballs. The Spalding pounded against the concrete wall of the P. S. 21 schoolyard with a loud thud that echoed off the paved walls and stairs of the spacious ball field. On the paved portion of the school yard were nine-foot baskets with metal backboards mounted on thick steel poles. All of Tom's Elm Park pals were at work or gone from the neighborhood, hence Tom was used to playing solitary games of stickball and basketball. The current generation of teenagers seemed to be into sex, booze, and pot. Like all folks down through the ages, Tom thought his generation was the best.

Walking over to the basketball court, Tom started taking some of his patented high-arching jump shots along with his sweeping hook shots, plus some banked layups. He recalled that Amon was a fast learner when it came to sports. The young man had quickly developed a deadly jump shot, along with his tenacious defense and aggressive rebounding. Suddenly, Tom noticed a short, wiry teenager walking into the schoolyard – someone he hadn't seen in the neighborhood before. Soon the two of them were taking shots at the nine-foot rims. Unlike Tom, the kid (whose name was Billy) was making nearly every shot. They played a few games of "horse" which Billy won easily. Then they played a couple of one-on-one games which had the same results, although the margins were narrower, thanks to Tom's height advantage.

Resting awhile the two of them sat down, leaning against the concrete wall, which blocked the wind. Tom remarked that his opponent was very good. Billy responded that he played JV basketball for Port Richmond. He, in turn, asked if Tom had played basketball back in his high school days.

"No. I was never that good and I just focused on my school work at Port Richmond. I made the permanent honor roll there."

At that point, Tom noticed a familiar face entering the schoolyard. It was none other than Joey Caprino, the stoop ball champ of Pulaski Avenue, toting a gym bag and a stickball bat.

"Hah! You're just in time for a basketball contest against this guy here, Billy, star of Port Richmond's junior varsity," Tom yelled out, greeting his old friend and shaking his hand awkwardly, but warmly.

Joey looked taller and thinner than in his street game days. He also sported a thin mustache, which gave him a sinister look until he smiled his familiar smile of days gone by.

"OK. We'll show these young guys how the game was played in the old days," Joey said in his nasal voice as he grabbed a rebound on took a shot, which was his patented sweeping hook shot. The ball hit off the front of the rim and catapulted towards the other basket.

"You look a little rusty. I betcha you forgot how to play stoop ball," Tom observed. "Don't worry about it. I always missed the first few shots." Joey took a second shot which also clanged hard of the rim. But the third shot, a wheeling hoot shot from ten feet out went banked into the basket.

Without further preliminaries, the threesome starting playing basketball with the swift, quick handed JV star opposing the slow moving, easily winded Elm Park duo. Double teaming did not deter the slashing and leaping youngster who scored at will. Tom found that driving on Billy was ineffective because he often stole the ball. So Tom was forced to shoot his high arching jump shot from way outside. Joey scored occasionally with outside one-handed set shots. The oddly matched contestants played three games with the same result: hard-contested victories by the JV star.

"Well, Billy I look forward to seeing your name in the Advocate in the near future. You're a rising star, " Tom commented.

"Let's see what you're made of. How about some stickball?" Joey asked getting his glove and a Spalding out of his duffel bag.

Again it was the two Pulaski Avenue denizens against the high school wunderkind. Joey pitched while Tom played the field. The stickball proceeded uneventfully with Tom and Joey unable to hit the deceptively fast youngster. Joey used a mixture of curve balls and fast balls, plus his dancing knuckle ball to hold Jimmy to a couple of hits but no runs.

Then in the final inning, Tom hit a line drive home run that barely cleared the fence, to give the two oldsters a 1 – 0 lead. The former Pulaski Avenue street players celebrated their apparent victory. But Joey's arm gave out after the kid hit a ground single past him. So Tom took over, throwing sidearm to protect his aching shoulder. With two strikes on him and the game on the line, Tom tried a blooper pitch, hoping to catch the kid off-balance. But Jimmy was not fooled. He smashed a towering fly ball that landed in the cemetery across the street.

Tom, always the good loser laughed, while his competitive friend spat on the pavement and yelled: "Son of a bitch!"

When Tom went to retrieve the ball, he found it sitting on the bench where, years ago, he and Joanie had spent many romantic interludes of kissing, hugging, and talking about obscure topics like the early Dutch settlers of New Amsterdam – before it became New York City. He noticed the inscription carved on the bench: Tom and Joanie inscribed within a heart. Despite all the changes in the world their bond had remained unbroken over the years.

Chapter 4 – A Request from Joanie

Tom walked through the tree shaded entranceway way to St. Vincent's Hospital. Joanie appeared to be making progress and gaining strength each day. Entering the room, Tom was surprised to see Joanie on her feet tethered to monitors that continuously recorded her vital signs, she beckoned to her boyfriend.

"Come on, walk with me. I'm going for a stroll down the hallway."

Tom complied, holding her hand as they strolled slowly down the long corridor. As they walked along, Joanie took his hand humming the Carpenters' song "Superstar" which had been playing when they met and danced a Kaffman's bar so long ago. The two high school sweethearts had survived lengthy separations and societal barriers to become reunited. Now a serious illness that was on-again and off-again presented a further obstacle in their longtime romance. Oblivious to the nurses, patients, and other onlookers the star-crossed lovers danced to the Carpenters' haunting melody that echoed in their minds.

"I think I'm getting dizzy. Let's stop," she whispered, as Tom held her hand and gently guided her back to her room.

As Tom tucked her into bed, Joan murmured something about Amon.

"What about him?"

"I saw him standing next to me last night. He put his hand on my face and said a prayer. He's still with us, helping us. We just have to believe."

"It's the power of positive thinking. Research has shown that a person's attitude is key to recovery," Tom replied, holding her hand and kissing her febrile cheek.

"Tom. I want you to pray for me at St. Roch's every Sunday."

Tom started to object, but he agreed. After all, prayer couldn't hurt and it might just help. The French philosopher Blaise Pascal said that God does not mark his presence in the world with indelible footprints. So he proposed Pascal's wager. Even if the probability of God's existence is low, the potential reward of infinite happiness is huge if God does exists. Thus, the expected value (the product of probability and reward) of such a wager is extremely high. Therefore, Pascal urged people to take the religious wager – be kind, humble, generous, and sincere. English physicist Isaac Newton postulated the existence of God, because the motions of such celestial bodies as the planets around the sun and the moon around the earth were explainable under his law of gravity. He rejected the notion of randomness and attributed causality to God's eternal dominion of the universe. Similarly, Einstein expressed the fundamental laws of physics in the form of complex mathematical equations. This mathematical conception of the universe was an indication of the existence of God, according to Einstein.

The Dutch philosopher, Spinoza, who had been excommunicated by both the Jewish and Christian religious authorities, stated that the universe and God were one and the same. He was a determinist – asserting all actions and events occur as a result of absolute, logical necessity. Tom recalled that the Scottish philosopher, David Hume, actually did away with physical substance and the cause-and-effect laws of science. It seemed to the skinny science teacher that the more a person learned, the less he actually knew about the concrete world. The trend in modern philosophy was to remove matter from the world and turn it into a diaphanous network of abstract propositions. Similarly in physics, the concrete world of objects and forces was transformed into systems of equations. It almost seemed like a good argument to stop reading and forsake the world of ideas, which his cousin, Rusty Haley, referred to as "pointy-headed book learning."

As Tom went upstairs in his lonely second floor Pulaski Avenue apartment, he heard the phone ringing. The sound of the phone always brought a chill down in his fine. Could it be bad news about Joanie?

Fortunately, a familiar over-confidant voice exclaimed: "Tom I need you to come in tomorrow to come in and cover a class."

Before Tom could demur, Lou Stout, Curtis High School principal said he'd pay Tom $150 per diem — off the books. Cover Mrs. Murray's history classes on unions — just for the day.

"You'll earn some cash and plus her enduring gratitude. She might even give you a little, as her way of saying thank you."

"Yeah sure. Rosie Murray is married to a burly detective who'd put me out of my misery within ten seconds."

"She has prepared lesson plans and notes. Just follow the recipe, collect your money, and wait for Rosie's unique way of showing gratitude. Just drop her notes and she'll bend over to pick them up."

"Rosie bending over is an awesome sight. She should have a sign on her backside: look but don't touch."

"If I write out the sign, you can stick it on her ass," the burly administrator quipped. "Any way, there's a grade advisor's position opening up in the fall. You'll be first on my list."

"No thanks. I know my limitations. I'm a classroom teacher — first, last, and always."

"By the way, how's Joanie doing? She's in the thoughts and prayers of me and the missus."

Tom agreed to cover the classes. After all, he could use the dough and it would take his mind off Joanie's medical issues and his rat experiment. That thought reminded him to go downstairs to the cellar and run the white rats through the maze. He noticed that the differences in mistakes made by the two groups of rats narrowed as time progressed. Apparently, even protein deprived rats mastered the complex maze with fewer and fewer wrong turns.

The granite walled cellar needed a paint job. It had been last painted by his dad more than twenty years ago — in pink and white with festive patterns and fancy cutwork. On the walls were curious narrow pipes with funneled openings. Someone had told him that they were gas lights used in the era before electric lighting became prevalent. The house had been built by its first owner in the early 1900s. America owed so much to blue collar workers, both black and white, who built this country with blood, sweat, and tears. There were down-to-earth folks who had the common sense not to question cause-and-effect and material substances. Even Joanie teased Tom about his "weird ideas" and regretted that he wasn't grounded in everyday reality. She even teased him with his mom's favorite dictum: "Life must be lived on a basis of realtiy."

Chapter 5 – A Lesson on Unions

Approaching the limestone façade of Curtis High School with its formidable gargoyles that had intimidated students and teachers for more than seventy-five years, Tom missed the ups and downs of the classroom. Despite the hassles with rambunctious teenagers and the boredom of treading over familiar academic turf, Tom got a kick out of teaching. It was akin to going on stage to perform in front of a lively, restive audience. At the front door, the redoubtable Lou Stout greeted him with a slap on the back – handing him Rosie Murray's notes on unions.

"Did she drop them in front of you?" Tom inquired, visualizing her bent-over ample derriere.

"Not today. She was unusually sure-handed today. I think she saves that awesome sight for you. You're her favorite, Tom."

"That's because I'm always saving her wonderful ass by covering her classes," Tom replied unhappily.

"Here's her schedule and her rooms. By the way she's showing films in her two of classes, so you got an easy day ahead of you. Stop in my office at the end of the day for the $100."

"What do you mean $100? You said $150 over the phone," Tom said petulantly.

"Just wanted to see if you were paying attention. You'll get your $150 off the books as promised. I take care of my super sub."

"One hand washes the other," Tom replied with the husky administrator's favorite cliché.

"Speaking of hands. Where did you get those cuts? Were you attacked by a rabid dog?"

"Nah. One of my rats, a nasty female, likes to take a bite out of my fingers."

"Why don't you feed them?"

"That's the point of the experiment. The one that bites is in the group that is malnourished. In other words, she's protein deprived. It's the idea of the experiment."

"Just don't bring them around here. I have enough trouble with this crew here," Stout answered as he headed down the long dark hallway, eyeballing students for any signs of hassles or mischief.

Entering Rosie Murray's class, Tom braced himself for the usual chorus of Bronx cheers, vented whenever high school students had an anticipated free period taken away. Swiftly moving to the blackboard, Tom wrote the aim of the lesson: "Who needs unions?"

"Nobody needs them. End of lesson, so give us a free period," said Kenny, a lanky black kid who was a rising Curtis basketball star. Tom wondered how he'd fair against Billy from the P. S. 21 schoolyard.

"Put a lid on it, Superstar. Unions are necessary to protect workers," replied Pam, a chubby redhaired girl, who was as bold as her dyed red hair.

"Isn't he the guy who does those crazy experiments that blow up?" somebody called out from the back of the classroom.

Glancing at his notes, Tom asked: "How did unions get started in this country?"

"Workers got together to protest low wages and long hours. Before that unions were illegal," George answered. He was a short kid who took school seriously – a rarity at Curtis High School, which was on the downside of its academic trajectory.

"That's correct. Under the New Deal, workers were given the right to form unions and bargain collectively for higher wages and better working conditions," Tom concurred.

"He's always right – a freakin' nerd," Kenny observed.

"Let's try to be positive folks."

"Yeah. If you can't say something nice, don't say anything at all," Kenny piped in with a highpitched voice.

Tom realized he had a comedian on his hands. Hence, he did not react. Moving on, he again read from Rosie's notes: "What happened in 1911 at the Triangle Shirtwaist Company?"

"There was a big fire which killed 148 workers, mostly young girls sewing dresses and shirts at a big factory in New York City," George answered.

"That's right. After that terrible fire, there was an effort to improve working conditions for factory workers – greater worker safety and shorter hours."

"Those friggin' factory owners didn't give a shit about the workers," Kenny exclaimed.

"You sound like a Commie," Jerry, a short kid who sat by the windows

"You want a knuckle sandwich?" Kenny snapped, getting out of his chair. A jester meant to show who's boss.

"Let's keep the discussion civil. We can disagree without yelling or threatening each other," said Lulu.

She was a perky Hispanic girl with a silver necklace and bracelets that jangled whenever she moved. Lulu reminded Tom of Lora, a student of years gone by who would jangle her copper bracelets to ward off the bad vibrations of her classmates.

"Well said. We can disagree on issues without turning violent," Tom concurred.

"If you look at the early union movement in this country, most of the violence was perpetrated by the company bosses and the mine owners. That guy John D. Rockefeller brought in scabs to run the factories and goons to beat up the workers," Hank called out from the back of the classroom.

"I think you're right on that point," Tom replies, checking his notes.

"At about that time, John D. Rockefeller owned the largest oil company, as well as many coal mines. It was a common practice for the owners to employ scabs to thwart striking workers and to use force to intimidate them," Tom stated, reading from Rosie's notes.

"We all know what a goon is," said Pam, pointing at Kenny. "But what is a scab?"

"Do want a fat lip?" Kenny objected.

"Try it Superstar. My brother will kick your ass!" the feisty coed replied.

"Now settle down both of you," Tom interjected as he moved down the aisle where the two hostiles sat. Later Tom learned that Pam had a big brother, who was a senior on Curtis's formidable football team. "

"A scab is a person hired by the company to replace the workers who were on strike. It's a union-busting tactic that is illegal in most states nowadays," Tom reiterated from Rosie's notes.

"Wasn't there a man, Henry Ford, who made cars on an assembly line for the first time?" inquired Susan, who was as smart as she was pretty.

"You go girl!" Kenny replied, smiling warmly at the demure teenager.

Tom had long understood that there was a pecking order in high school classrooms: looks and athletic ability trumped all other qualities – especially brains.

Again, perusing Rosie's notes, Tom mentioned strike of the 1890s when President Grover Cleveland sent army troops to break the strike. Soldiers fired into the crowd of strikers, wounding and killing scores of people. As a result the strike failed and the union leaders were jailed. One of them was Eugene Debs, a socialist, who said: "The capitalists own the tools they do not use, and the workers use the tools they do not own."

"Sounds like a Commie to me," Kenny called out half-seriously.

"Did you know the Communists came out for Blacks in baseball before anyone else?" Jerry asked his loquacious classmate.

"Only you would know something weird like that," Kenny replied.

"You probably don't even know who Jackie Robinson was," Jerry continued.

"How 'bouta punch in the nose?" Kenny rejoined, getting out of his seat.

"Calm down the both of you. You're one angry bunch of kids. How about a little love and understanding? Now where were we? Who was Henry Ford?"

"Henry Ford made his cars cheap so that the average Joe could buy them. Which was good for the country," Hank, a husky boy called out from the back of the classroom.

"Way to go Hank," Lulu yelled, jangling her silver bracelets.

"What happened to unions under Franklin Roosevelt's New Deal?" Tom asked.

"They were given legal status so workers could go on strike to get more money," George answered, Tom noticed that he, along with Susan took notes, which prompted Tom to write the key points on the board.

Tom was surprised that the students laboriously copied the notes into their notebooks – including the troublesome Kenny – after he borrowed a pen from Lulu. Mercifully, the bell rung ending the class.

"I'm glad to see that you guys keep a notebook in social studies.

"Mrs. Murray checks our notebooks and gives us extra credit for keeping good notes," George explained.

"Sounds like a good idea," Tom observed, making a mental note to do that himself.

Then, Kenny apologized for getting into a hassle with Jerry. "I know about Jackie Robinson and Larry Doby – the first two Afro-Americans in baseball, Mr. Haley."

"You're absolutely right. And there was a pitcher named Satchel Paige. He was the guy who said don't look back – something might be gaining on you," Tom added.

"I like that. Don't look back 'cause somebody will catch you," the high-strung youngster said.

"He also said think cool thoughts and avoid running at all times."

"Can't disagree with that either," Kenny nodded his head and left the room.

Lulu then came up to the front and complimented Tom on his teaching the history of unions.

"You should thank Mrs. Murray. I used her lecture notes for the lesson."

"Sometimes this stuff is confusing and the class gets so noisy that I can't think straight. But you never lose your cool," the youngster replied.

"The trick is to remain calm in the midst of a storm. The way you shake those bracelets reminds me of a student named Lora, who did the same thing when things got out of hand."

That seemed to please Lulu, who smiled. Turning, she marched down the hall jingle jangling   her silver bracelets and anklets. Like life itself, teaching was filled with déjà vu moments.

Chapter 6 – A Walk to Mariners Harbor

One chilly morning in early December ,Tom walked down Morningstar Road, moving briskly an if impelled by the brisk wind. Turning left, he trudged along Richmond Terrace towards the harbor. Gone were the decayed hulks, abandoned ships, and rotting wharfs where Amon had lived on an abandoned tugboat. As a result of the city's urban renewal program, the Kill Van Kull was a bordered by a park-like region dotted with shrubs and evergreens, and paved walkways cutting through trimmed marshy weeds and grasses. On the very utility pole that Amon had once fell, attempting to connect a wire to his tugboat, was a plaque commemorating him – the Mariners Harbor Messiah – for his good work in the neighborhood. Further down on Simonson Avenue was the big Victorian house that Amon had rehabilitated for a residence for the homeless, down-and-out alcoholics, and ex-drug addicts. It was still maintained by community volunteers, including Tom himself, and Amon's widow, Mary. The latter, though careworn and melancholy, carried on his good work. This selfless, noble woman was truly a modern day saint, who taught at St. Mary's in Port Richmond for whatever meager salary she was paid.

"How is it going Mary? The house looks pretty good. Are the residents behaving?"

"Things are going well. I have Jose helping me with the needed repairs, which are constant for an old house like this," she replied with a weary smile.

Tom observed the short stocky custodian, who was busy repairing the front porch. He stopped to say hello and resumed his hammering. Then he reached into his overall pockets to extract another nail. Tom realized that he had never worn pants like that and made a mental note to buy a pair at J C Penney's.

Mary inquired about Joanie's health, to which Tom hastily responded that she was making slow but steady progress.

"Amon said she would be getting well. And he inquired about your rat experiment."

"You communicate with Amon?" Tom asked incredulously.

"Everyday. He knew about your project on nutrition with white rats before I even mentioned it to him."

"That's amazing. I recall Joanie saying she had a dream about Amon and felt his presence in her room in the middle of the night," Tom replied in an offhand manner.

"I sense you're a doubter. Amon often said that you were too much the scientist. There are other ways of knowing besides observation and reasoning."

"I never doubted Amon's unique powers when it came to healing and clairvoyance. He amazed me with his recounting of past events in my life. The things I myself witnessed defied logical explanation. And he was an awesome athlete to boot."

"I miss him everyday. He was so kind and gentle. There will never be another person like him," she said, her eyes filling with tears.

Noticing the leaves and trash on the front sidewalk, Tom got hold of a rake and a garbage bag. He swept the sidewalk and raked the leaves from the sidewalk as well as the back yard. When Amon was around, he pitched in with these chores and saw to it that the residents of the big 19th century house did their part. The charismatic young man was able to recruit the reluctant residents, many of whom were reformed alcoholics, drug addicts, and ne're do wells, to pitch in with cleanup and maintenance.

Such chores are the vital essence of life. Once you plunged into them, a person felt real satisfaction. There was something to be said for physical labor. Unlike teaching, where the results of your pedagogical efforts were seldom evident, a person could see the fruits of his manual labor. The lack of verification in teaching, along with rampant discipline problems, were critical in   teacher burnout. Without holidays, summer vacation, and sabbaticals there would be a mass exodus from teaching – regardless of salaries and benefits – which were barely adequate. Of course, extensive patience and a fondness for children and adolescents, are essential ingredi ents in the constitution of teachers. In addition, that old fashioned word – idealism – cannot be forgotten when considering the intrinsic rewards of the profession.

Walking back along Richmond Terrace, Tom passed the apartment house where Cara and himself had spent a few summers in the 1950s. This was before their mom and dad had resumed custody of the two youngsters. They had spent many hours looking out at the ship and tugboat traffic on the dark choppy waters of the Kill Van Kull. The gray outline of the Pulaski Skyway and the dingy buildings of Newark were visible in the distance. Ships moving in opposite directions appeared to be on a collision course, until they miraculously passed each other unharmed. At the time, Staten Island seemed like a crowded metropolis, compared to rural Bloomington with its open fields, seldom trafficked roads, and quaint little farms.

Even the manner of speaking of Staten Islanders had been strange. Words were jumbled together, suffixes dropped, and sentences poured out of people at breakneck speed. Years later, when Tom returned to South Jersey, he found their colloquialisms quaint and peculiar. And it seemed to take South Jersey folks forever to complete a thought. It's a blessing that no one is quite as adaptable as children. And it's a truism that some misfortune in the lives of children is not necessarily a bad thing. Hemingway said it best: We are stronger in the places that have been broken.

Tom recalled reading an essay by Bertrand Russell on the question: Is life a dream? He asserted that it's not illogical to suppose that all life is a dream. The problem is that the sense-data in our dreams is not the sense-data of our waking world, because the later corresponds to physical objects. Another philosopher, Bishop Berkeley, said material objects only exist when you perceive them. Material objects are just combinations of sense-data – hot, cold, shape, color, texture, odor, weight – that exist only in our minds when we see them. Russell refuted this absurd idealist notion by using a cat to represent the material object. A cat is able to move around the room when we're not observing it. In addition, cats tend to get hungry and thirsty over time — something an abstract sense-datum is incapable of.

All this philosophic speculation could not alter the harsh facts of reality: Joanie was very ill, Amon was gone from the earth, change is ever present in the world, and we're all mortal. His mom had a ready answer to the life-is-a-dream issue: The reality of living boiled down to food, clothing, and shelter — all of which must be earned through hard work. Claire Haley had come of age during the Great Depression and was down-to-earth. She was always hitting Tom with her old standby of food, clothing, and shelter — the rest was just material greed and the desire for luxuries. Even the automobile, the mainstay of the American economy, was ideologically suspect to his mom. A car is a luxury, she'd proclaim in her sisng-song voice.

Occupied by these philosophic thoughts, Tom walked eastward on Richmond Terrace — heading towards a large grassy field. He tread along a narrow dirt pathway which led to the abandoned where a strange red-bearded hermit had lived. He had been a customer of Tom's when he had a Herald Tribune paper route as a youngster. Years later, Tom was walking in through the field near the hut. Upon peering through the window, he had seen the unfortunate man lying on the floor dead. The police were summoned and the poor man was determined to have died a few days earlier. What particularly disturbed Tom was the attitude of the police. It was just another routine fatality for them. We live alone and die along. A grim reality that analytic philosophers like Russell and Berkeley would likely agree about.

Peering into the windows, Tom observed that there were no occupants of the ramshackle hut. The door was ajar, so Tom walked into the abandoned hut. Strewn on the wooden floor were beer cans and potato chip bags presumably discarded by teenagers over the years. In one corner was a dripping sink and a slimy toilet bowl. Tom pushed the lever and to his surprise, it flushed. There seemed to be a universal reluctance to flush public toilets in the country. People talked about the dumbing down of America, but Tom believed it was actually the idling down of America.

Nobody wanted to lift a finger – work was to be avoided no matter what.

Tom remembered the time he had taken Amon to the shack. He told him about his experiences as a newspaper boy delivering the Herald Tribune paper before school seven days a week. He had delivered the paper to the occupant of the shack for a week. Knocking on the door to collect his money, Tom waited for a response. When the door to the shack was opened, Tom was so startled by the man's scary red-bearded appearance, that he ran away and never returned. Amon surprised him by his knowledge of the red-haired hermit's fate – he had died alone in the shack. Amon's awareness of the tragic life and death of the hermit seemed to indicate ESP.

On the other hand, Tom knew that the story of the Hermit's death had been widely publicized publicized in several stories appearing in the Advocate. Tom had observed stacks of Staten Island's local paper in Amon's tugboat. Maybe he had seen stories about this strange red-haired man in the paper. As time progressed, Tom's opinion changed about his gifted friend. He had witnessed additional instances of the charismatic young man's psychic abilities. Gradually, Tom became a believer. As with many events in life, there were occurrences which could not be explained through logical reasoning. Indeed Bertrand Russell's analytical reasoning did not totally dispel the quaint notion after all, that life may very well be a dream.

Heading back up the long gently sloping hill of Morningstar Road, Tom exclaimed: "Life us just a never ending dream. But supposed you had a dream in which you were sleeping and had a dream. That's it! Maybe life's just a dream within a dream. So dying is just a matter of unwrapping layers of dreams."

An old man walking in the opposite direction accosted him. "Hey dreamer. Can you spare me a few bucks for a meal?"

Tom recognized the man as one of his father's old drinking buddies. He was much worse for the wear and tear of a lifetime of drinking. He reached in his pocket and gave him a five-dollar bill, plus some spare change.

Tom had read the biography of Bill Wilson, the founder of Alcoholics

Anonymous. He was struck by Wilson's assertion that each alcoholic has his own drinking story and his own road to sobriety. Fundamental to recovery was individual anonymity and group conscience. A group of alcoholics was more effective than the lone alcoholic, in a moment of remorse, promising never to drink again. Claire Haley had dragged her husband to AA meeting to no avail. He would be on the wagon for a few months – working as a house painter and returning each night sober as a judge. Then came the unhappy night when he burst into the house singing, laughing, and yelling – as drunk as a skunk.

"Thank you, sir." Then pausing a moment, the old man did a double take, "Why your Tom Haley's son!"

"That's me. Carrying the Haley name forward – for better or worse," Tom replied grimly.

"You used to play stickball. Your dad bragged about that. Said you were the best stickball player on Pulaski Avenue."

"I wouldn't go that far, but I still like to whack that Spalding when I'm not teaching."

"You're a teacher? Your dad would have been proud to know you made good."

"Well, my mom gets the credit for that. She saw to it that I went to school and did my homework. Schoolwork, not stickball, was the priority. Hanging out on the corner was forbidden."

"Yup. Your mom was a tough cookie," the old man growled, and resumed his unsteady walk down Morningstar Road.

"Tough Cookie" was the description of nearly everyone in the neighborhood – in describing the redoubtable Claire Haley.

"Easy Going", "Laidback", "Flakey", "Big Kid", "Brainiac", and "Book Worm" were the most frequent labels attached to Claire and Thomas Haley's scholarly son when he was a teenager. The tag "Klutz" was also applied when he sat down on painted chair and wore the evidence thereof on the backside of his dungarees. Lately, the term "Barfly" had been used to refer to the Curtis science teacher. This tag Tom determined to shed by spending less time in neighborhood bars like Kaffman's and K. C.'s. Promising to spend his time more constructively, Tom realized he hadn't run his white rats through the maze in a few days. He missed Joanie's help with the experiment because she was more adept at handling them. And like everything Joanie engaged in, she made it a fun activity.

Soon he was in the dingy but familiar confines of his cellar, putting the rodents through their paces. With each passage through the twists and turns of the wooden maze, the rats made fewer and fewer mistakes. He noticed that the protein-deprived rats were mastering the maze with only a few more mistakes than their well-fed peers. He hoped that the implications of his project would not be jeopardized by results which weren't even statistically significant. The whole point of the experiment was to extrapolate to human beings. Tom was attempting to demonstrate that an inadequate diet was a factor in the subpar academic performance of poor children in the U. S. and in third-world countries. With the rise of conservative candidates in Washington, there was mounting pressure to reduce government spending on food stamps for welfare recipients, as well as for the working poor.

Chapter 7 – Saturday Morning Headlines

A chilly Saturday morning in his mom's sunny kitchen was the setting for a mother-son tete-atete, as the former pored over the Advocate, searching for tidbits that provoked her interest or anger. Any article about President Reagan provoked her. The only compliment she ever bestowed on America's 40th President was that he looked good in a business suit. Initially, Claire Haley was suspicious about Amon's motives, but was persuaded of his good intentions after reading an article about him in the Advocate. His efforts in rehabilitating a Victorian house in Mariners Harbor to provide a residence for down-and-out alcoholics and the homeless had impressed the hard-nosed but compassionate survivor of the Great Depression.

"I see Reagan is cutting federal aid to the cities, but is spending billions on jet planes and atomic bombs. The damned fool will start a big arms race with Russia. And that rat-faced Casper Weinberger reminds me of Dr. Strangelove. He wants to bankrupt the Russians by outspending them on armaments. We'll wind up in a nuclear war with Russia and then what?"

"Not to worry. The cellar will make a good bomb shelter," Tom replied, slurping his coffee.

"I'm not going into that cellar with those horrible rats of yours!"

"If things get bad, we can fry them for food. And there are lots of old newspapers to read."

"Reagan's getting senile. I noticed when reporters ask him questions, Nancy whispers the answers for him," Claire asserted in a matter-of fact manner.

"That's why there won't be any nuclear wars. Nancy wouldn't be able to have those lavish parties at the White House where half of Hollywood attends."

"Yeah. She's very friendly to Frank Sinatra, Jimmy Stewart, John Wayne, and Jane Wyman."

"Wasn't Jane Wyman his first wife," Tom inquired.

"Doesn't matter. Those Hollywood stars have no morals," she replied angrily.

"Now you sound like one of those holier-than-thou church ladies."

"And you sound like one of those head-in-the-sand people who don't want to face reality."

"Maybe life is just a dream where there's no difference between the waking world and the world of dreams."

"That sounds like bar talk to me. Stop spending so much time in saloons."

"No. That a philosophic proposition proposed by Bertrand Russell."

"Russell should focus on his antiwar campaign instead of idle talk about life being a dream," she responded, rustling her paper.

"See that snow falling outside? It's just a dream," Tom retorted.

"Fine. Go out, shovel the snow, and follow your dreams," she snapped.

Working steadily, Tom cleared his sidewalk. He noticed his new neighbor, Burt maneuvering a gas-powered snow blower next door. He missed the old Italian man, Antonio, who had lived there years ago. Like Tom, Antonio favored hand shoveling to remove snow from the pavement. The latter was a hard-working immigrant from Italy who did masonry – laying down sidewalks and patios. America had been blessed with such immigrants from all parts of the globe, who knew how to work with their hands doing honest labor.

Unfortunately, the use of elbow grease was being replaced by mechanization everywhere. No wonder there was an epidemic of obesity in the country. Even the autumnal rite of raking leaves had been replaced with those noisy leaf blowers. In addition, hand hedge clippers were disappearing in favor of electrical hedge clippers, for which the danger of severing the extension cord was ever-present. He had recently read a proposal to install moveable sidewalks in cities to move pedestrians from point A to point B. For Tom, walking was more than physical exercise. It was the chance to enjoy nature and to reflect about the events of day in a calmrational way. He was convinced his best decisions were made while walking. Whether it was doing household chores or yard work or simply walking the streets, Tom was definitely old school. Even as a classroom teacher, Tom was continually on his feet – moving from his desk to the blackboard and seldom sitting except to take attendance.

Walking quickly along the shaded sidewalk on Castleton Avenue which lead to St. Vincent'sHospital, Tom nervously checked that patched two-by-four archway above him. He felt hisusual anxiety about Joanie plus guilt because he had forgotten to go to St. Roch's to pray for her. Joanie projected a forced cheerfulness – hiding the pain emanating from an inoperable brain tumor. Extensive Xray treatment and chemotherapy had reduced the size of the lesion, but it had not been eradicated. Since the brain is the seat of a person's thoughts, emotions,and memories the effects of such invasive treatments could not be predicted. Because ofJoanie's youth and spirit, doctors were optimistic about her ultimate recovery. On the elevatorto her floor Tom recited a prayer – hoping to make up for his ecclesiastic negligence. Had theshoe been on the other foot, Joanie would have gone to church everyday to pray for him.

"How you feeling today?" Tom asked, as he rushed to her bedside to give her a hug and a kiss.

"Pretty good all-in-all. Although those chemos knock the shit out of me," she replied with herlabored cheerfulness.

"That's encouraging. You look good, Joanie," he responded untruthfully.

Actually, she had an ashen pallor and looked thinner than when he last visited her. He understood that the effects of chemotherapy were sometimes more devastating than cancer itself.

Xray and chemotherapy destroy both normal cells as well as cancer cells.

The "bad" cells aremore vulnerable to those treatments than the "good" cells, but the latter are affected by the application of these powerful toxins notwithstanding. Fighting cancer was still a new science and America was more interested in building bigger bombs and deadlier missiles than in finding cures for deadly diseases like cancer, diabetes, and cardiovascular anomalies. Lyndon Johnson was the last President to invest big time in scientific research and in public schools and and colleges. Ronald Reagan always settled the guns vs butter debate in favor of the former. Maybe the Reagan presidency was just a bad dream, from which America will awake with Bobby Kennedy as her President.

"Tom, are you there? Lately you seem off on cloud nine when you're with me."

"No I'm here. I was thinking about the notion that life is a dream. Bertrand Russell had argued against it. But it's a pretty appealing idea with all the bad stuff going on in the world."

"Well I am all for that. Maybe this awful illness is just a dream and tomorrow I'll wake upfree of pain. Did you go to church for me?"

"I pray for you all the time, Joanie. You don't have to go to church to pray for somebody," hereplied defensively.

"Fine. You rather think about ridiculous stuff like life is a dream, than to go to St. Roch's and pray for me."

"I'm sorry. I'll go to church tomorrow. It's been hectic with running the rats through the maze. I wish you were home to help me with it."

"How's Miss Feisty – the female who bites you? "

"She's OK. As long as I wear my thick leather gloves there's no problem."

"So how's your mom doing?"

"She's fine – just keeps rolling along."

"Your mom's a tough cookie. I wish I had her strength. You should be able to handle the maze running yourself now. Try to sweet talk her Miss Feisty. Like you used to do with me," she said, irritated with him.

"Joanie that's not fair. I love you — all I want is for you to come home," he said emotionally.

"Hold my hand. Let's not fight. Who knows how much more time we have?"

"Joanie, don't talk like that. You're getting better everyday. I can see it for sure."

"Remember the day we first met?"

"Sure do. It was a softball game in that little league field near Forest Avenue. You were part of that peanut gallery watching the game and you kept on yelling at me," he observed.

"You kept on looking over at me. And then you ran into a teammate — like the Klutz you've always been. So I ran over to you and the rest is history."

"It was your fault. You distracted me with your loud voice and your cute ass."

"Your nose was bleeding. I should have let you bleed to death, you big jerk!"

"You know, Joanie. It's a nice story and I've told it to many people over the years."

"It's our story, Tom. Every couple has their own story. Whatever happens to me, never forget our story."

The phone was ringing as Tom entered his lonely apartment on Pulaski Avenue. Picking it up, Tom said. "OK. Who's AWOL this time. Rosie Murray's used up her personal days, unless you're giving her special dispensation."

"Jesus! You have ESP like that Amon fellow from Mariners Harbor. No, it's not Miss Big Ass. Dick Grimsby is having trouble with his bad leg. So you we need in a pinch."

"Same deal as before? Remember I'm supposed to be on sabbatical."

"One hundred fifty off the books just like before. You know I take care of my super-sub," the unflappable administrator replied.

"What's Dick doing tomorrow?" Tom asked, realizing that his colleague's leg problem was more evidence of Amon's lack of efficacy. Whether it was Joanie, his mom, or Dick Grimsby – theMariners Harbor Messiah's healing powers were short-lived – now that he was no longeramong the living.

"Your favorite topic – photosynthesis. Do pretty much what you want. Set off one of yourrockets. Just don't aim at me when I'm walking by your class."

"Not to worry. I'll dust off my lesson on green plants. My match head rocket days are over."

Years ago Tom had set off one such rocket to demonstrate Newton's 3rd law of motion. Instead of heading towards the ceiling, the rocket had veered off and struck Lou Stout in his ample backside as he was passing Tom's room – to the joy of the students. Another effect of this"practical home experiment" was spewing sulfur fumes that filled the second floor of the old building. Unfortunately, there were more and more bureaucratic rules governing in-class experiments conduct nowadays. In all levels of education, academic freedom was under fire. America had become a litigious society where laws regulated every aspect of one's waking life.

Chapter 8 – A lesson on Photosynthesis

Tom held two green bean plants, one with a sprouting stem twined around a long stick and the other with a shorter stem and wilted leaves that clumped at the bottom of its stick. As the students filed into the class, Kenny detoured at the front desk.

"What did you do to that poor plant? Breathe on it or sneeze on it?" the pesky student exclaimed.

"Everybody get settled and we'll find out exactly what happened to the plant."

George raised his hand: "One plant was watered, while the other one was not. All living things require water to survive."

"Any other ideas?"

"The dying plant didn't get sunlight. Plants need sunlight in order to grow," Jerry called out.

"Is that why you sit by the windows? You look like one of those scrawny pea plants," Kenny remarked, as his classmates snickered.

Jerry started to reply, but thought better – muttering under his breath.

"There so many bad vibrations in this room," Lulu declared, rattling her silver bracelets and fidling with her necklace.

"I'm picking up good vibrations. She's giving me excitation. Good, good vibrations," Kenny sang In a high-pitched voice that was actually on-key.

"Jerry's right. Green plants need sunlight as well as water to survive," Tom said, as he pointed to Susan who had politely raised her hand.

"The process is called photosynthesis in which plants manufacture their own food and give off oxygen in the presence of sunlight," the pretty honor roll student answered. Tom turned to the blackboard and wrote the equation for photosynthesis:

$$\text{Carbon Dioxide } + \text{ Water } \longrightarrow \text{ Carbohydrates } + \text{ Oxygen}$$

"I understand Mr. Grimsby checks your notebooks regularly. So it might be a good idea to jot this down, along with the other key outcomes of the lesson."

"That's all we do in high school – copy notes in our notebooks," Lulu complained, shaking her silver bracelets.

"What is the catalyst for photosynthesis?"

Kenny raised his hand: "It's chlorophyll, the stuff in toothpaste to keep you from having bad breath. Remember that Lulu."

"Want to check how sweet my breath is, sir?" the feisty girl replied, fiddling with her silver necklace.

As soon as Kenny got up from his seat, Tom signaled him to stay put. "How about maintaining some decorum here folks. I'm sure you wouldn't pull these antics with Mr. Grimsby or Mrs. Murray."

"She just yells at us or sends Kenny to the dean," Lulu observed.

"Yeah, that woman's got some temper. Makes me want to jump out the window," Jerry added, looking outside, perhaps for a place to land in such an emergency..

"And she hates it when I rattle my bracelets," Lulu chimed in.

"How do plants help the environment?" Tom asked, anxious to prevent the lesson from becom Ing a critique of a fellow teacher.

Susan, always the serious student, raised her hand: "Green plants take in carbon dioxide exhaled by people and produce oxygen which we need for breathing. "

"How else do plants help us?"

"They provide us with food and their roots absorb excess water during floods," George replied.

"Don't coal and oil come from plants buried under the ground from the time of dinosaurs?" Hank called out from the back of the class.

Hank seldom spoke out in class, but was right on target when he chose to do so. He was a husky boy who was recruited by the football coach because of his obvious size and strength. However, he quit the team to work afternoons in the A & P on Richmond Avenue. This was the same supermarket that Tom had worked at during the summers of his junior and senior years at Port Richmond High School. The difference was that Tom's mom did not allow him to work year round while in high school.

Nevertheless, Tom did deliver the Herald Tribune newspaper daily before school from the 7th grade until the end of his junior year. Those five years of bicycling in all sorts of weather paid off for Tom in good health and superb endurance. In addition, he became an avid reader of the Trib – developing a keen interest in current events during the 1960s. Had he been allowed by Claire Haley to play sports in high school, Tom believed he would have made the basketball team as a useful sixth man. Whether his academic performance would have been impaired was a moot question. It didn't matter because his mom's word was the law in the Haley household. And it wasn't bad to be remembered as a member of the permanent honor roll. One of these days, he'd get around to finding his name on the school's wall for the year 1964.

Tom was occupied by those thoughts as he transcribed the major points of the lesson on the board. The students were surprisingly conscientious about copying their notes from the blackboard. The trick in teaching was to keep them occupied. Lou Stout had said it many times: Busy hands are happy hands. With time running out, Tom asked the class what would happen when mankind runs out of coal, oil, and natural gas.

George raised his hand: "We could use solar power and wind energy, which don't pollute the way fossil fuels do."

"Why don't we burn wood like they used to do in fireplaces?" Lulu inquired, rattling her silver bracelets.

"That girl wants to tear down all the forests just to feed her fireplace. Did you ever think that most folks don't have fireplaces?" Kenny replied in a sarcastic tone.

"What about biomass? Burning green plants," Jerry suggested. "You may have a point there. Did you ever see how fast dandelions grow? They seem to sprout overnight – it's amazing," Tom concurred.

"Mr. Haley, only you would pay attention to dumb plants like dandelions," Kenny snapped.

"Nothing grows faster than crabgrass. They could make fuels out of crabgrass," Jerry replied.

"Someday you'll start a company called Jerry's Crabgrass Corp," Kenny exclaimed as the bell rang and the students headed for the door.

Lulu came up to Mr. Haley's desk disconcerted. "This stuff on green plants is so confusing and there are so many bad vibs at Curtis. Sometimes I don't know whether to eat shit, chase rabbits, or bark at the moon."

Before Tom could urge her to refrain from any of those actions, she turned and left the room. The long dark hallway resounded with the jingle-jangling of her silver bracelets and necklace. Some of Lulu's fellow students made disparaging remarks about her noisy passage as she promenaded along Curtis's narrow hallways. Pausing before gathering Dick Grimsby's notes on photosynthesis, Tom recalled a student from the past who wore copper bracelets and neck laces, which she continually rattled. What was her name? Lora ! Lulu was Lora all over again . Except she rattled silver bracelets and anklets as pranced down the halls. As with everything In life, teaching was filled with déjà vu experiences.

It was curious how prone to complaining today's students were in the 1980s. The capacity of people to endure hardships and look on the bright side of day-to-day living was quite limited. His own high school days were the happiest of his life. What could be better than to be young, humming along at the peak of your abilities, acquiring knowledge and meeting new friends, and anticipating a bright future. Maybe it was just the heady optimism of the early 1960s as reflected by America's youthful president – John Kennedy. So much had happened to the country since the New Frontier – assassinations, racial strife, and a protracted, bloody war in Asia.

Driving back from Curtis on Richmond Terrace, Tom stopped at the St. George Tavern, a dingy bar not far from the sprawling U. S. Gypsum plant. The plaster manufacturing factory had tall smokestacks and huge pillared bays with dusty dump trucks filled with calcium sulfate – the raw materials upon which the plant depended. Disembarking from his old gray Pontiac, Tom inhaled the dusty fumes that permeated the area. No wonder islanders referred to the neighborhood as emphysema alley. The prevailing philosophy with respect to manufacturing was that pollution was the price to be paid for economic prosperity. Even his students were not overly concerned with environmental pollution. It appeared to be accepted as a necessary evil of the twentieth-century America – along with congestion, crime, poverty, and the Cold War.

Chapter 9 – Rusty Haley

Ordering a Ballantine beer, Tom sat at the bar and helped himself to some stale pretzels in a large bowl. The saloon had the typical stale odors and hazy air of the neighborhood bars which dotted the landscape of Staten Island's North Shore. Prohibition's failure back in the 1920s had demonstrated alcohol's powerful grip on American culture. Certainly local and state governments benefitted from the tax revenues accruing with the sale of these intoxicating beverages. Tom's musing about America's ubiquitous liquid was interrupted by the entrance of a burly red-haired man in overalls, Rusty Haley.

His cousin was much the same easy going man – the years had added a few pounds, a sprinkling of gray hairs, the thickening of of jowls – that Tom fondly recalled from his childhood. Family lore had given him the undeserved nickname "jailbird" as a result of a bungled liquor store heist, in which the proceeds – contained in a canvass bag, had inexplicably wound up in his mom's possession. She promptly called the police and his red-haired cousin was arrested for robbery. Claire Haley was furious about the front page story plastered in the Advocate. This was at a time when the police had often made visits to the Pulaski Avenue house intervening in alcohol-fueled domestic disputes between Tom's mom and dad. During the late 1950s, Elm Park had its fair share of heavy drinking dads who rendered a heavy toll on the welfare and wellbeing of its blue-collar families.

Plopping himself on the next rickety stool, Rusty was surprised to see his school-teacher cousin sipping a beer besides him. "Well I'll be damned, if it isn't Curtis 's favorite science teacher! How you doing?" "Pretty good. I'm on a six-month sabbatical now doing some research with white rats," Tom replied, ordering Rusty a Ballantine.

"Shit, I hate rats. There's a lot of them at the plant."

"These are the tame ones. They don't bite except for one mean female," Tom said, showing his cousin a scar on his right hand.

"Better you then me. How's your mom doing? She's some tough cookie."

"You'r e about the fourth person to say that recently. My mom was strict, but she wasn't Attila the Hun."

"She's the reason you're teaching at Curtis instead working in that shit-pot factory across the street," Rusty replied, taking a big gulp of his beer.

"What's in those big concrete silos with the ladders running along the sides?" Tom asked, looking across the streaky windows across Richmond Terrace.

"You mean the big boys? We call the silos big boys. That's where the selenite is stored until its ground up and heated and purified into plaster and wallboard."

"Selenite is a mineral. It's the source of gypsum, which is calcium sulfate ," Tom observed.

"They mine in different places of the country. It's shipped here for processing."

"It's always dusty around here. I wouldn't want to be breathing those gypsum particles all day long," Tom remarked.

"Just try working in the plant for an eight-hour shift. Some days it's worse than others. I'm coughing all day and half the night," Rusty replied, draining his glass in a second gulp.

"Don't you wear some kind of mask?"

"Yeah. But after a couple hours I toss mine. It gets wet and it's in the way. You can't breathe good with It on – especially when pushing a heavy wheel barrel or lugging something across the floor."

"I'd keep it on. You don't want to be inhaling that dust all day," Tom advised his hardnosed cousin.

"Now you 're starting to sound like my wife. She's got the twins bugging about the friggin' mask."

"By the way, Jill and Jennifer are doing well at Curtis. I had them in

General Science last year and they aced every test."

"Good. I tell them to hit the books, so they don't wind up at a dump like U.S. Gypsum."

"I read something about OSHA investigating the plant in the Advocate."

"Yeah. The government's always snooping around the place. We're only allowed 5 milligrams per cubic meter of gypsum in an eight-hour day. If they close it down, where am I gonna go?"

"I used to work as a guard at the big Con Ed plant in Travis years ago. City inspectors used to visit every once in a while. We'd call the plant engineer to warn him. Within minutes, the black smOKe pouring out of their big chimney turned into white smoke," Tom related.

"They have an electrostatic filter, just like the one we got. Nobody wants air pollution, but companies have to operate. Otherwise, there's no jobs. Not that U.S. Gypsum is a great outfit to work for."

"You're fortunate to have such great kids. They're smart girls and well-behaved. Didn't let on that we're cousins – first or second," Tom said, munching on a stale pretzel.

"So does your sister still paint? I remember that art show we went to at Sailors' Snug Harbor."

"That was a long time ago. She's got the painting bug like my dad did," Tom replied, ordering another round of beers as the bartender replaced the pretzels with peanuts.

"I heard something about a possible strike at Gypsum," Tom continued.

"Shit! Staten Island is like a one-horse town. If a guy has a fight with his wife, half the Island knows about It the next day."

"That might have been true in the 1950s and 60s, but not today. When I worked at Con Ed, the guards were talking about a strike Some big shots came around to talk to the part timers. I played dumb. Pissed off, they left the plant. One of them said not to worry about me because I was just a big easygoing kid."

"A strike might happen. The men are unhappy with the pay. They're talking about a wildcat strike. The company says they'll move the whole operation down south. There's no unions down there and the pay is lower and with no environmental regulations," Rusty declared.

"Years ago I had a job offer to teach in Maryland, but I turned them down. I have no interest in living or working in the South. It's redneck country."

"So how's Joanie doing? I hear she's at St. Vincent's."

"Maybe you're right about Staten Island. Everyone knows everybody else's business!"

Laughing, Rusty got up from his stool. "Thanks for the beer. I'll have my wife pray for her. She's a better Catholic than either of us."

Chapter 10 – A Plea to Amon

As they left the bar chuckling, Tom suddenly felt a cold chill. Heading for his car, he addressed a plea to his buddy, Amon, the Mariners Harbor Messiah: "Don't forsake us – Joanie really needs your help. Nothing 's the same since you left us. I beg you – make Joanie well again."

Feeling the nostalgia of a person who reached their 36th year—roughly the midpoint of a person's life, Tom drove west on Richmond Terrace. He slowed down as he passed under the Bayonne Bridge and the gray, choppy water of the Kill Van Kull came into view. The quaint array of old docks, rusted hulks, and abandoned ships of bygone days had been removed replaced by a park-like setting of benches, shrubs, trees, upon neatly trimmed grass. There were no traces of the defunct Bethlehem Steel shipyard where warships and freighters had been built during the Second World War.

A similar process had been occurring of urbanization throughout the North Shore, in which grand old Victorian houses were being knocked down in favor of duplex homes. Fewer wooded lots existed on the Island as population growth inflated the value of real estate. The current frenzy to maximize profits had changed friendly neighborhoods into congested aggregates of estranged inhabitants. Drug use, street crime, and gun violence were on the rise. Back in the 1950s, the children were looked after and monitored by all the adults in the neighborhood. Tom recalled playing stickball on Pulaski Avenue in front of the grownups who acted "in loco parentis". In the 1980s, neighborly bonds had been severed with alienation and anonymity as the inevitable result.

Slowing down on the Terrace, Tom stopped his old gray Pontiac near the utility pole that Amon had climbed years ago to draw electricity into his tugboat. At what point Con Edison became aware of Amon's draining their amperage free of charge, Tom never determined. Nonetheless, any objective weighing of the Mariners Harbor Messiah's plusses and minuses would point to the preponderance of good deeds done – particularly in providing shelter for alcoholics, ex-drug addicts, the homeless, and and lost souls down on their luck. Naturally, his good work raised the ire of the usual vigilantes who didn't appreciate the influx of "undesirables" into the neighborhood. Amon's untimely death in a drive-by shooting was almost inevitable as the local newspapers began to criticize his endeavors as misguided and self-serving. The country had a tradition of tearing its heroes down after praising them as wunderkinds. Walking along the freshly paved sidewalk, Tom found the plaque mounted a small granite column. He read the inscription on the plaque: "The borough of Staten Island commemorates the work done by Amon Dakota in providing housing for the homeless and helping the downtrodden of our North Shore community."

"So what do you think? That's a nice memorial – not too shabby. You're probably embarrassed by all the acclaim. Yet it's nice to be remembered after we leave this veil of tears. Amon, I'm asking for one last miracle – heal my Joanie."

Stopping for one last look at the murky Kill Van Kull, Tom heard a soft moaning. At the same time, the gray sky brightened as the sun burst through the clouds. Stunned by this sudden change, Tom saw these phenomena as signs that his plea had been answered. As Pascal stated long ago, God does not mark his presence in the world with irrefutable evidence. Time alone would tell if the almighty had responded.

Tom was awakened by the jarring sound of his phone. Groggily picking up the phone, he heard the familiar voice of his boss, Lou Stout.

"I got another job for you, buddy. Alan Katz has a big union meeting tomorrow in the city and I need you to cover his class."

"Oh shit! How much?"

"The usual – $150 in cash. Alan's the guy that busts his ass to get you guys a nice raise every couple of years."

"I'm well aware of that. What's it on?"

"The origins of democracy," the Curtis Principal said in a matter of fact manner.

"Oh shit!"

"Is that all you can say? How about thanks for the extra dough off the books. His notes will be in your mailbox. Or do you want Rosie Murray to hand them to you?"

"Only if she drops them and then bends over to pick them up," Tom snapped.

"See you bright and early tomorrow. No late night boozing tonight."

Chapter 11 – A Lesson on Democracy

Walking into Alan Katz's history class, Tom got the usual mixed reception of cheers and boos. Turning to the blackboard, he wrote the aim: The Origins of Democracy. He noticed some familiar faces in the class.

"Democracy has its roots in ancient Greece and Rome," George answered. He was a studious kid who was not well-liked by his peers.

"That's correct. Does anyone know what the Magna Carter was?" Tom asked, checking his notes.

"A paper signed by King John of England granting the noblemen the right to govern and giving people certain rights," Susan replied. She was a popular girl who had looks and smarts.

"Very good. This event occurred in the year 1215 AD. It was the first time that the power of the king was limited anywhere in the world."

"What about the Greeks? I thought they were the first," Hank called out from the back of the class.

"Well, in Greece and Rome only the noblemen could vote. Women could not vote," Tom replied.

"That's cool," Kenny commented, to which Lulu rattled her silver bracelets.

"Also the ancient Greeks and Romans had slavery," Tom read from his notes.

"That's not cool," Kenny replied.

"In the Magna Carter there was also a provision for habeas corpus. What's that?"

Jerry, who sat by the windows raised his hand. "It means that if a person is arrested, he must be notified of the charges against him. And he has a right to a trial by jury."

"Wow Jerry. You're really up on the law. You must have been arrested," Kenny observed to the amusement of the class. Kenny's humor usually came with jabs aimed at his peers.

"You're so quick with the putdowns. How about saying something nice," Lulu chimed in, rattling her silver bracelets and necklace.

"You have a very nice – personality," Kenny answered with a smirk.

"Oh go fuck yourself!"

"Mr. Haley, send her to the dean for profane language."

"How about everyone maintaining their cool," Tom said, vexed with the constant bickering in the class.

Moving on, Tom asked some questions about the Bill of Rights. Raising his hand, George responded.

"It was written by James Madison in 1787, giving people certain basic rights like freedom of speech, press, and religion, the right to a speedy trial, and no searches of your house without a warrant."   Checking his notes, Tom stated that slavery existed in the early days of the republic.

"That's messed up," Kenny responded.

"And women did not have the right to vote."

"That's cool," Kenny responded, as Lulu shoOK her silver bracelets.

"Also, you have the right to bear arms," Hank called out from the back of the room.

"Good! I'm gonna get me a gun right after school," Kenny said gleefully. Fortunately, the garrulous youngster said outrageous things for effect.

"Only if you're of sound mind and body," Jerry quipped.

"Want a fat lip?' Kenny responded, getting up from his seat.

"Sit down, Kenny. We ought to have a civil discussion of ideas without flying off the handle."

"Yeah. Just like Hamilton and Burr who settled their differences by trying to put a bullet in each other's noggin," Pam responded, fluffing her bright red dyed hair.

"Didn't Aaron Burr live in Port Richmond?" Susan inquired.

"You're right about that. There's a house on Richmond Avenue with a plaque on it stating that fact," Tom stated, recalling the day years ago, when he showed Amon that very house. Pausing, he felt a surge of nostalgia for his deceased friend. Death was so final. Like time itself, it was irreversible.

"Mr. Haley. You seem preoccupied today. Is everything alright?" Lulu asked, shaking her bracelets.

Nodding, Tom transcribed the Bill of Rights on the blackboard:

The Bill of Rights (James Madison, 1787)

1. Freedom of speech, press, assembly, and religion

2. Right to bear arms

3. No quartering of soldiers

4. No searches of house without warrant from a judge

5. No self-incriminating and no double jeopardy

6. Right to speedy trial by jury

7. For claims more than $20, right to trial by jury

8. No cruel and unusual punishment 9. Other rights retained by the people (right to privacy)

10. Powers not given to federal government retained by the states

"So in the old days, persons settled arguments by shooting at each other?" Jerry inquired, shifting his attention from the window to the matters at hand.

"Shit! It still goes on. You've never heard of drive-by shootings?" Kenny exclaimed.

"There's too many guns around. Why don't the police take away guns from the troublemakers?" Lulu asked, strOKing her silver necklace thoughtfully.

"People have the right to bear arms – it's the second amendment of the Constitution," Hank called out.

"Actually in New York City, there are very strict gun control laws. But the fourth Amendment prevents he police from searching your house without probable cause or a search warrant, " Tom read from his notes.

"I think the laws are tipped in favor of criminals rather than law abiding citizens," Jerry responded.

"That's right! What we need now is more law and order. Lock up all the troublemakers," Kenny called out half-seriously.

"You sound like that southern sheriff, George Wallace," Hank called out.

"That's not funny, guys. What the world needs now is more love and less hatred," Lulu responded, shaking her silver bracelets.

"What the world needs now is love sweet love. That's the only thing there's much too little of," Kenny sang in his unique high pitched voice.

At that moment, Lou Stout walked by – amused by the glib youngster's antics. Fortuitously, the bell sounded ending the class. As Tom prepared to leave the class, the sound of Lulu's jangling necklace and bracelets made him smile. If you didn't see the humor in teenagers, you'd never survive as a high school teacher. Tom recalled Dick Grimsby's sage advice when he first started teaching: "Roll with the punches and don't take yourself too seriously. Someday he would remember the crazy antics of Curtis students with a smile, as well as the jingle jangling sounds of Lulu, and her predecessor Lora, as they walked down Curtis's long dark hallways. If only those hallowed halls could talk – what a story they'd tell of the students and the times they were witness to.

Chapter 12 – More Saturday Games

Another Saturday morning rolled around with Tom and his mom sharing coffee and breakfast on a chilly morning in January. The latter had her usual breakfast of a soft boiled egg and toast, while Tom munched on Wheaties with banana. Spread out on the table was the Advocate, which Claire Haley perused between bites of her buttered toast. Tom patiently waited for her comments on the events of the day, as he had done since his high school days. Despite her hard earned cynicism, his mom was politically liberal – supporting the left wing of the Democratic Party. She had discarded her allegiance to Communism when it became apparent that Russia would never achieve her cherished ideal of a classless society. The Marxist ideal – from each according to his ability and to each according to his needs – would never be realized anywhere in the world unless there was a fundamental change in human nature. Tom thought of himself as democratic socialist, despite his hope to attain a salary in which he could spend money on Joanie without any second thoughts.

"Guess who I saw the other day? My cousin Rusty. He works at that U.S. Gypsum plant on Richmond Terrace. They might go on strike. The pay and working conditions suck."

"Your jailbird cousin. Where did you meet him? At a bar?"

"Mom, that incident with the bag of money occurred twenty years ago. He has a wife and children now. People make mistakes and they learn from their mistakes."

"You're right. Next time you see him, say hello for me. So how is the rat experiment going?"

"Pretty good. I need just another few weeks of collecting data on their maze learning ability and I'll be done. Then, I'll do the statistical analysis and write the whole thing up," Tom replied matter of factly.

He realized the writing of the thesis included an extensive review of the pertinent literature plus the rationale for the study. He had done much of writing already – surprising himself with the alacrity of his progress. At a certain point, the thesis had begun "to write itself." Even though he had majored in math and science at City College, his English professors there had praised his writing – urging him to take more humanities courses. And of course, like his mom, he had always enjoyed reading.

"Once I finish my thesis, I'd like to get back to reading books again," he declared.

"Of course. But your school work comes first, McGee."

"Mom. Don't you think I'm aware of that?"

"So how's Joanie doing?" she asked, putting her newspaper down.

"She's OK. I believe Amon will help her," Tom replied, waiting for his mom to disagree.

"That's ridiculous!" Claire snapped, but seeing her son's distress, she changed her tone. "I mean he's not even around anymore."

"I was down by the Harbor the other day and I felt his presence. It was a gut feeling. Amon will heal Joanie."

His mom looked out the kitchen window, noticing some snowflakes fluttering from the sky. As the flakes meandered to the ground, the sun abruptly disappeared behind the clouds – darkening the kitchen. Suddenly, she felt a haunting loneliness. When did these feelings of loneliness and sadness become so prevalent in her life?

Turning to her son, she said, "Why don't you take a nap in the living room? You look tired."

One mild Saturday in January, Tom decided to play some basketball at the P. S. 21 schoolyard. Arriving at the site of so many contests in his youth – basketball, stickball, and softball – Tom was surprised to see the schoolyard deserted. The current crop of adolescents were loath to venture outside during the winter. Tom remembered bringing a snow shovel to clear the snow around the nine-foot baskets in order to play a game with like-minded youngsters. The Greek ideal of a sound mind in a sound body was no longer in vogue. Slowly warming up, the Curtis teacher took an assortment of high-arching jumpers, sweeping hooks, and driving layups. He recalled playing basketball with Amon, who was a gifted athlete even with unfamiliar sports. There was an effortless grace at everything he did – from fishing to carpentry, to house painting, to basketball, to stickball, to bowling, to public speaking, to just walking with a friend. When one spoke to Amon, he listened with an unusual intensity. Tom always had the feeling that Amon was genuinely interested in other people's opinions and that he learned something from everyone he encountered in his life. Would that contemporary American politicians had those qualities, instead of closed minds and strong aversions to new ideas. Tom recalled Bobby Kennedy's famous quote: "Some men see things as they are, and ask why. I dream of things that never were, and ask why not."

As Tom paused to mull over his own thoughts, he was astonished to hear someone call out his name.

"Mr. Haley, you playing basketball or thinking about your lessons?

"I'm doing both, Kenny. What are you doing in this neck of the woods?"

"I got family in the Elm Park, near Morningstar Road. My cousin, Sherifa, goes to Port Richmond."

"That's cool. Are you up for a game of HORSE?" Tom called out.

"I'm always ready to compete. The rumor's out that you're not a bad athlete – for an old guy," Kenny replied as he took a bounce pass from Tom and buried a long jump shot.

"I'll take that as a compliment. Not bad for a bench warmer."

"I ain't no bench warmer. Coach Kramer has been starting me since the middle of December."

"Very impressive. And you're not a bad student when you stop clowning around."

"My mom's kind of strict about school. But you know how it is. I don't want to act like that nerd George."

"Heaven forbid."

They played a few games of horse in which Tom had to replicate shots taken by the talented Curtis unior. The latter connected on long jump shots from every part of the court, which Tom was unable to do consistently. And then Kenny turned it up a notch by shooting driving layups right handed and left handed. The kid was very fast, starting and stopping abruptly, darting and leaping about as if his legs were made of steel springs instead of flesh and bones.

"How about a game of one-on-one"? Kenny asked with a smirk.

"Just one game. I'm running out of steam," Tom agreed reluctantly.

"Tell you what. I'll just take outside jump shots – no layups."

The game began with Kenny blocking one of Tom's sweeping hoOK shots. Something that only Amon was able to do regularly. Driving against the quick-handed high schooler was out of the question and most of his fifteen-foot jump shots were tipped or blocked. Consequently, Tom was forced to take long jump shots which were mostly off the mark. Kenny was deadly with his jump shot inside or outside. It was no contest, until Kenny allowed Tom a few side jumpers and a couple of long hoOK shots which went in to both player's surprise. Then going into high gear, Kenny nailed five jump shots just beyond the foul line to win the game 21 to 9.

"Great game. You're going to be a star," Tom exclaimed, gasping for breath.

"You're not so bad for an old guy. Did you play high school ball?"

"No. The basketball coach asked me to come for the team. He had seen me playing in the gym. My mom wouldn't allow it. She wanted me to focus on scholastics."

"Man. You're mom must have been a tough cookie."

"You're about the sixth person to say that about my mom. It was a different era. Your mom's word was the law," Tom replied grimly.

"Well I'm gonna see my cousin Sherifa now," Kenny said shaking his teacher's hand.

"Is she really your cousin?"

"Sherifa's my kissin' cousin. If you get my drift," Kenny replied with a wide grin.

Arriving home, Tom hurried down to the cellar to run his rats through the extensive maze. As in previous trials he observed that the difference in errors between the malnourished rats and the control group had narrowed. Apparently, the protein deprived rats had mastered the maze – with fewer and fewer errors as time progressed. Thus the difference average number of errors for the two groups had barely reached statistical significance at the .05 level. It was clear that the maze-running experiment was just about finished. Prolonging the experiment further would produce ever diminishing returns. "I gotta wrap it up guys and set you free. Except this guy, Mu Alpha with the big balls," Tom said as he picked up the large rat, who was the friendliest of the group. He already figured out where he would release his white rats – an area relatively uninhabited and free of alley cats. Just as he entered his apartment two floors above, the phone rang.

Knowing his caller, Tom spoke: "Just tell me the rooms and the lesson."

"It's right up your alley. Bill Lawler wants you to cover his general science classes. He's doing a lesson on the elements."

"Lawler, he's that new guy. Why is he out?"

"Hell, I don't know. Maybe he's got the clap – like you used to get."

"Never happened. I led the league in attendance as a teacher and as a student," Tom replied, feigning annoyance. But the extra money off the books was nice.

"Same deal. You get $150 cash. Just don't blow it on booze and broads,"

Chapter 13 – A Lesson on the Elements

Tom walked into a class of Curtis freshmen he didn't know, carrying Mendeleev's periodic table which He hung from hooks above the blackboard. He also had samples of various elements, compounds, and mixtures. The class settled down after the usual hassling that freshmen are prone to. Lawler, who was referred to as the rookie by his colleagues, had trained them well. Most of the students got out their notebooks, with the exception of a heavyset kid who was flirting with a cute girl with a long pony tail that twitched as she turned her head from side to side. Apparently, she wasn't buying whatever her neighbor was selling.

"That's Mendelson's periodic table," a red-headed boy called out from the back of the room.

"No, it's Mendeleev's periodic table," said Kelly, the girl with the pony tail.

"That's correct. What is the key feature of the periodic table?" Tom asked.

"It shows the elements in order of increasing weight," Ronnie answered. He was the younger brother of Kenny, Curtis's promising basketball star, whom Tom had played against at the P. S. 21 schoolyard.

"That's also correct. Notice the vertical columns of elements. What's true about them?"

"They have similar physical and chemical properties," said Robert, who wore thick glasses and was purportedly very smart.

"Right again. Notice that elements to the left are metals, while those elements to the right are nonmetals, and in between are the transition elements which have properties of both metals and nonmetals."

Robert raised his hand. "What about the heavy elements at the bottom of the table – Radium, Uranium, Thorium, and Plutonium?"

"Those elements are radioactive, emitting radiation. They are used in nuclear reactors and nuclear bombs," Robert answered.

"He's a brainiac," Ronnie declared.

"That's OK. Nothing wrong with being smart. And you know what? We all have smarts. It's just a matter of applying ourselves," Tom responded.

"But some people are smarter than others," Ronnie persisted.

"No. Some students study harder than others," Tom replied.

Tom showed the class samples of elements: iron, copper, aluminum, sulfur, iodine, and bromine. He also showed them samples of compounds: salt, sugar, chalk, and rust. Next he displayed samples of mixtures: salt water and sugar water. Turning to the board, he asked the class to define elements, compounds, and mixtures .Through a series of questions and answers. Tom arrived at the answers he sought and wrote the following definitions on the board. To his amazement, the students carefully copied the definitions on the board. This novice teacher, Bill Lawler had taught the youngsters well.

Mixture – two or more substances physically mixed together; Ex: saltwater, tincture of iodine. Compound – two or more elements chemically united in definite proportions; Ex: salt, sugar, rust, Element – pure substance that cannot be brOKen down chemically; Ex: carbon, oxygen, iron, gold.

Checking his notes, Tom asked: "Who was Jacob Berzelius?"

"He was the person who came up with chemical symbols for the elements," Kelly responded, as her ponytail twitched.

"That is correct," Tom responded as he went to the board and began copying the elements with their respective chemical symbols. Once again he was pleased to see the freshmen copy, with the exception of the heavyset kid, who was named Roy. From his build, Tom assumed he'd become a lineman on Curtis's formidable football team.

"Roy, kindly get your notebook out and start taking this down," Tom commanded.

"Yeah, Meats. You're no better than us common folks," Ronnie exclaimed. He had his big brother's boisterous ways.

Roy grimaced at his classmate, but took his tattered loose leaf and a thick stub of pencil. Slowly and laboriously, he began copying the notes from the blackboard.

Symbols of the Elements

Carbon – C	Hydrogen – H	Oxygen – O	Nitrogen – N
Sulfur – S	Phosphorous – P	Iodine – I	Fluorine – F
Helium – He	Calcium – Ca	Chlorine – Cl	Iron – Fe
Aluminum – Al	Gold – Au	Silver – Ag	Lead – Pb
Sodium – Na	Uranium – U	Copper – Cu	Zinc – Zn
Mercury – Hg	Silicon – Si	Radium – Ra	Lithium – Li

"How come the symbols of elements like gold, silver, lead, and sodium don't begin with the letters of their names?" Robert inquired, taking his glasses off.

"Some of the symbols come from their Latin names. Latin was the language used by scientists in the Middle Ages," Tom replied.

"What do you want, everything to be easy four-eyes?" Ronnie snapped.

"That wasn't very nice," Kelly declared, wagging her ponytail.

"Nice guys finish last," Ronnie rejoined.

"Do you know who first used that line?" Tom asked.

"The ugly bear, Sonny Liston, who Muhammad Ali knocked out," the pesky freshman answered.

"No. It was a baseball manager – Leo Durocher."

"How come teachers know all these weird facts that normal people don't even care about?" Ronnie remarked.

"Yeah. The other day we had to learn about electrons, protons, and neutrons. Who cares about that stuff," Roy complained.

"I heard that the smallest particle of all is the Higgs-boson," Robert asserted.

"You're absolutely right. There was an article in the Advocate about it. Scientists are calling it the God particle because it's the ultimate building block of all matter," Tom said. "So we're all made of the same stuff. And we're all part of God," Johnny, a red-haired boy, who spoke up for the first time.

"I wouldn't go that far. Red hair is a sign of the devil," Ronnie snapped as the class drew to a close.

Tom noticed some material on acronyms Mr. Lawler wanted him to go over. He quickly wrote them on theblack board for the students to record in their notebooks.

PEMDAS – the order of operations in arithmetic – Parentheses, Exponents, Multiplication, Division, Addition, and Subtraction

My very eager mother just served us nine pizzas – Mercury, Venus, Earth, Mars, Jupiter, Saturn, Uranus, Neptune, and Pluto (the nine planets)

Mother has some extra oranges – Michigan, Huron, Superior, Erie, and Ontario (great lakes)

Brinclhof –   Bromine, Iodine, Nitrogen, Chlorine, Oxygen, and Fluorine (diatomic elements)

Remembering the mnemonic for spelling "ie" and "ei" words – from his own school days – Tom hastily wrote the following rule on the board. If it sounds like "e" – its i before e, except after c.   Ex: believe and receive If it sounds like "a" -its e before i. Ex: neighbor

As luck would have it, the bell rung just as the students finished copying the acronyms. It always amazed him that high schools were so dutiful about copying notes from the blackboard. Wearily, Tom gathered up Bill Lawler's notes on the elements. He understood that the classroom dynamics of high schools resulted in dominance by particular students. And those individuals were not necessarily the most able students – but those with the brashest personalities and the biggest mouths.

Chapter 14 – A Hospital Visit and Picketing

Driving back from Curtis High School in his Pontiac, Tom found himself on Bard Avenue across from St. Vincent's Hospital. Feelings of hope, anxiety, and guilt mingled within as he burst into Joanie's room. She had just been wheeled into the room and settled in bed, when Tom rushed over to her.

"How are you feeling sweetie?" He kissed her on the lips, noting more color in her complexion than he had seen in recent visits.

"Actually I feel pretty good, though I'm tired of all the tests. It never seems to end. Did you pray for me?"

"Well, I went to the Harbor to see the plaque they put there for Amon."

"God damn it, Tom. What's so fucking hard about going to St. Roch's and saying a prayer and maybe lighting a few candles for me?"

"I asked Amon to help you. And I felt his presence. I do pray for you – in my own way. You don't necessarily have to be inside a church to pray for someone."

"All right! Actually I've been feeling better lately. Maybe your mysterious friend still has something going , despite the fact he's no longer around with us."

"Remember, this is America. According to Thomas Wolfe, miracles happen all the time in this country."

"Whatever. Only Tom Haley could come up with a weird reference like that.

"You know Thomas Wolfe. I read you some excerpts from Look Homeward Angel."

"I remember. I liked when you read to me. Another thing you don't do anymore."

"I promise I'll read to you when you're back home."

"Did Wolfe also say that life is just a dream," she continued in a teasing tone.

"No, he talked about loneliness and the meaning of life. The life-is-a-dream notion was a philosophic question posed by Bertrand Russell, which he ultimately rejected."

"Well that makes me feel so much better. Even your half-starved white rats know that life is not a dream. It's more like a nightmare for those poor creatures. I'm sure they can't wait until you set them free."

"Soon they'll be set free and soon you'll be home with me. And everything will be just like before."

"I hope so. Come here and give me another kiss and hug."

As Tom left Joanie's room, a young doctor signaled him for a consultation and the former followed the physician to his office. "We have some good news for you. Joanie showed no traces of the brain lesion. It appears to be a miraculous recovery."

"You mean her cancer is in remission?" Tom asked, breathless with excitement.

"The cancer is gone, disappeared, caput. We're not sure exactly why. Her youth, spirit, and attitude may have something to do with it. In any case, we'll do some further testing just to confirm she's in remission. And then your wife will be going home."

"Hurray! That's the best news of all. And I know another reason for her miraculous recovery. My friend Amon Dakota is still working his magic is the world."

"Amon who?" the young physician responded. He was a bit younger than Tom, which amazed the skinny science teacher. Now in his mid-thirties, Tom had reached the age where he encountered people who were younger and more accomplished than he was. He was also starting to run into former students who held responsible jobs in the community – one of rewards of teaching.

Driving from the St. Vincent's Hospital, Tom headed for Richmond Terrace and turned right – following the winding road towards St. George. Coming upon U. S. Gypsum, he observed several men picketing on the sidewalk. They carried picket signs stating they were on strike. Other signs accused Gypsum of foot dragging on the key issues of pay, benefits, and working conditions. Tom saw his cousin Rusty with a sign on his back, talking to a coworker. The latter shook his head with a scowl and headed into the factory, while his red-haired cousin shrugged his shoulders and plodded along the pavement. Tom approached the burly factory worker who was a happy to see his cousin.

"What does your picket sign say?"

Rusty turned around so the skinny Curtis teacher could read it: "U. S. Gypsum is gypping its workers". The bold-lettered message was imposed on a clever sketch of the plant with its big storage silos and tall smokestacks shooting black smoke into the sky.

"I like the sign. You got some talented sign makers in your union."

"United Cement Workers didn't make that sign. Jill and Jennifer worked on it together last night."

"Looks like they got some of that Haley artistic ability that eluded me and you," Tom commented.

"That's for sure. Thank God my wife has a job. She works part time for the St. George Diner. I just hope the other guys can stick it out."

"What about the national union – the A. F. L. – C. I. O. – are they supporting the strike?' Tom asked.

"Sure, U. S. Gypsum has been on their shit-list for a long time."

"Maybe I can ask my union, the U. F. T. to throw their support into the fight."

"I don't think so. What does the teachers' union have to do with factory workers?"

"All working people should stick together. The big shot factory owners never break ranks."

"Now you're starting to sound like your mom. Rumor has it she's a Commie."

"I wouldn't go that far, but she does have some strange ideas," Tom responded, shaking his head.

"She's a tough cookie," Rusty said. It was an observation that Tom was getting tired of hearing.

"Yea. She's a platypus."

"She's a what?" Rusty asked, stopping to stare at his skinny cousin.

"A platypus is a odd duck. You know, a creature that defies classification."

Just then a photographer from the Advocate took pictures of the strikers – including Tom and his cousin.

A newspaper reporter queried Rusty and a coworker about the issues dividing management and the workers. Speaking up, Rusty said that most of them "barely earned $7 an hour, which wasn't enough to put food on the table and a roof over our heads." The other worker mentioned "unsafe working conditions – polluted air and carcinogens like lead all over the plant."

The reporter questioned Tom, who said he was just an impartial observer from the neighborhood. Recognizing the Curtis teacher, the reporter said, "Weren't you the one who hung out with that faith healer – the Mariners Harbor Messiah?"

"Amon Dakota was a friend of mine. He wanted to do good in the world and help people, but I think his powers were exaggerated by the press."

"Would he have supported this strike?" the reporter inquired.

"Absolutely. Amon was always on the side of the workers. He helped the downtrodden, the poor, and those beset with alcohol and drug dependence," Tom replied.

"What about his special powers? It was said that he could heal people and could see the past and into the future?" the reporter inquired, taking out a notepad.

"There were some things he did that defied rational explanation. Not everything in life follows cause-and-effect laws of science."

"So you're saying Amon was some kind of holy man?"

"No. All I'm saying is that he had a gift. He was driven to help people. And you know what? He's still helping people."

With his research on the relationship between nutrition and maze-learning by rats completed, Tom had to find a safe place for his rats to live in the wild. He would keep Mu Alpha, the big friendly male with extraordinary testicles, but the others were destined for the field off Richmond Terrace – not far from the Bayonne Bridge. Carrying the two large cages with the eleven restless rodents inside, Tom trekked along the familiar pathway once traversed by Amon and himself years ago. Arriving at the small wooden shack once inhabited by a scary looking red-haired hermit, to whom Tom had delivered the Herald Tribune as a teenager. Years later, Tom would found him dead in his tiny abode. He had once showed Amon the abandoned hut and the latter was aware of the hermit's tragic ending. Perhaps death leaves invisible traces that are only perceptible to rare individuals. To die alone in that desolate shack was a very sad fate. Surely, this man had a mom, siblings, and friends who would have mourned his lonely death in a city of eight million people.

Opening the cages , Tom waited as the rats cautiously walked around the hut and peered through a large hole in the floor, which led outside. Tom hurried back to his car and soon returned with a large sack of rat food, a gallon of water, and a large plastic bowl. He cut opened the sack of high-protein food and filled the bowl with water. The laboratory rats would have sufficient food and water until they made the adjustment to living in the wild – eating grass, seeds, and roots and drinking water from a nearby stream. Nevertheless, Tom was plagued by guilt. They were smart, friendly critters – with the exception of Miss Feisty who tried to bite him whenever he picked her up. Strangely, this nasty female rat had never bitten Joanie. Miss feisty had bonded with Joanie. Who seemed to get along with all critters. Tom remembered a German shepherd that had gotten loose on Pulaski Avenue. Tom was ready to jump on his old Pontiac when the dog approached them. But Joanie called him over and the wretched cur approached with his tail wagging. Indeed, there was something to be said for girl power. Thinking about Joanie made Tom feel happy and not apprehensive as in the past. With a certitude not experienced before, he was sure she was on the mend. One last time, Amon had demonstrated his power to heal. Of that fact, Tom was certain.

Driving to his beat-up gray Pontiac, Tom headed for St. Vincent's Hospital in West Brighton. Quickly, he walked under the shaded archway, which had finally been repaired. Gone were the criss-crossed twobyfours which looked ready to tumble down on the pedestrians below. Rushing to the elevator, Tom pushed the bottom for the third floor. As the doors swept open, Tom ran to Joanie's room. There she was sitting up in bed beaming at him. Tom was struck by the changes in the young woman. There was a sparkle in her eyes, color in her cheeks, and vivacity in her bearing.

"So you finally did the right thing, Tom."

"Ah. What are you talking about?" he responded, hugging and kissing the pretty invalid.

"You did go to St. Roch's ?"

"Not exactly. But I went to the Harbor and spoke with Amon. Not exactly, but in spirit."

"You're beyond hope. But I am better – no thanks to you."

"You look great Joanie. What did the x-rays show?"

"There's no spots. No lesions. The tumor's gone. And I'm going home!"

"Yippee! It's a miracle. We live in America. Remember? It's the land of miracles – Thomas Wolfe said so many years ago and it's still true today," Tom declared fervently.

"You and your literary references. And don't forget life is just a dream."

"Well, so many things in life seem like a dream and today is certainly a dream come true. Thanks to Amon!"

Chapter 15 – The Bradford Detective Agency

With Joanie back at home, there were unanticipated hospital bills to pay. Joanie was still legally married to her husband back in Indiana. Lacking medical insurance, Tom struggled to pay her medical bills. He only received half his teacher's salary while on sabbatical. Tom 's course of action was clear. He would get back his guard job with the William Bradford Detective Agency. While attending C.C.N.Y., he worked during winter and spring breaks, and in the summer guarding power plants, factories, construction sites, and even a British rock band – the Herman's Hermits. Trekking to the guard company's central office in midtown Manhattan, Tom encountered the same buxom, over-friendly secretary he had known in the past. As in days gone by, the woman was very meticulous in measuring all of Tom's limbs and every nook and cranny of his lanky body. Her warm hands and retractable tape swept over his body with provocative attention to details—prodding and poking everywhere. Trying to distract himself, Tom focused on the laws of physics – especially the third law of thermodynamics. This fundamental principle postulates that mechanical work eventually dissi pates as random heat energy or entropy. Not achieving the degree of separation necessary, he thought a passage in the Bible from Ecclesiastes: all of mankind's strivings and endeavors were mere vanity with with little lasting value. Death and oblivion await us all. But there was a time for work, a time for play, a a time for peace, a time for war, a time for hate, and a time for love. At last, the audacious woman was done with her measurements and Tom left the guard agency with their standard gray woolen trousers, gray long-sleeved shirt, gray visor cap, and green tie – tingling all over. He rushed to the first bar he saw, sat down at a stool panting heavily, and ordered a draft Ballantine to cool off. The bartender noticed his feverish state and queried him about a hot date. Tom replied that he had gone through a uniform fitting that was akin to a session of lovemaking. The gravel-voiced saloon keeper said he was third guy in recent days to register the

same complaint about the William Bradford detective agency. He swore
that he was going to apply for a guard job next door when he finished
his shift.

Ironically, Tom was assigned to sprawling Con Edison power plant in
Travis. Adding to his déjà vu senseTom, was given the graveyard shift
– the least popular time slot. As in his college days, guards still made
the rounds of the large plant with special clocks – but the stations had
TV cameras to record the presence of anyone at each location. The
plant's giant smokestacks still belched black smOKe spewing into the
atmosphere. And upon a phoned signal from the guardhouse, the black
billowing smoke would quickly turn into white smoke. There were fewer
sulfur fumes because the plant burned "clean coal". Of course, of all fossil
fuels – natural gas, oil, and coal – the latter was dirtiest in terms of air
pollution. Tom wondered when Con Edison would get around to using
solar and wind energy to generate electricity. It was a no-brainer for the
power plant to avail itself of the strong winds the Island was subject as a
result of its proximity to the ever-present winds of the New York Bay, the
Arthur Kill, and the Kill Van Kull. Isaac Newton's law of inertia: a body
at rest tends to stay at rest and a body in motion tends to stay in motion,
not only applied to physical objects, but also to people and electric
power companies. Next to the ubiquitous vehicle of American roads and
highways – the private automobile – fossil fuel burning electric utilities
were a major source of air pollution. Eventually, the world would run out
of petroleum derived gasoline and then electric cars would become the
primary means of transportation.

Stepping into the guardhouse he had worked in years ago, Tom noticed
a few changes. In place of the radio was an old television set. Other
innovations were a small refrigerator and an electric coffee pot. These
constituted valued amenities for the Bradford guards confined to the 10-
foot by 8-foot shack for the better part of an 8-hour day. "Well look
who's here! The prodigal son has returned," exclaimed Ralph a gray-haired
guard, whom Tom recalled from his college moonlighting days.

"It's good to see you – Ralph as I recall. Do we still have to write down
the license plates and get the driver's signature?"

"Yup. And if it's somebody from the EPA or the city, we still have to call the plant manager pronto," the veteran guard replied.

"And the black smoke spewing out of that giant chimney magically turns to pure white within minutes," Tom related.

"You're right about that young man."

"Some things never change."

"So what the hell ya doing here. I thought you were a teacher?"

"That I am. But I'm on sabbatical right now. And I need the dough. Girlfriend's in the hospital, etcetera. What's in that cage over there?" Tom asked, looking around the small guardhouse. There was a small chicken wire cage off in a corner, that held a large tortoise.

"That's Jake's. It's a snapping turtle. Don't put your finger in the cage – you lose it."

"So Jake's still here? I thought he was aiming to a cop?"

"Sometimes the best-laid plans of mice and men go awry" Ralph recited.

"That's from the poem – 'To a Mouse' by Robert Burns," Tom replied.

"Yup. Years ago I was into stuff like poetry. I was going to NYU and then I started to drink and my plans went awry," Ralph said, turning to his newspaper.

"Well, it's never too late to go back to school. My mom takes courses at The New School in the city. Not for credit – just for fun."

"You have a smart mom."

Smiling, Tom replied: "I'm glad you made that comment. Every time I mention my mom to anyone, they keep saying she's a tough cookie."

"Well she was that too. She got you through college."

Peering into the cage, Tom was astonished. "Shit! That's one mean looking turtle. Big son of a bitch! Why keep him for a pet?"

"On this job, you need a little diversion."

"I just finished an experiment with laboratory rats. You know the white rats they use for research? Had them running a maze. I was trying to show the effects of malnutrition on learning."

"Did they bite?"

"Only once. There was this nasty female rat – Miss Feisty – I called her. The rest were very tame."

"It's common sense that if you don't have enough to eat, you're not gonna learn very well."

"You're right, but common sense is not widespread in the field of education," Tom replied, observing a plume of black smoke pouring from the plant's smokestack.

Later, Tom went on his prescribed tour of the Con Ed plant, clicking his portable clock at the designated locations. The plant was more extensive then he had remembered and every bit as noisy and dusty as in the past. A new part of his rounds included the boiler room, where the fury of the huge boilers was apparent . As a twentieth century person, Tom realized how vulnerable people were to power disruptions. Interdependence was the fundamental truism in the modern world. The awful fate of that lonely hermit in his shack under the Bayonne Bridge reinforced the basic need for strong bonds with our neighbors.

Chapter 16 – An Angry Snapping Turtle

A few days later, Tom was reacquainted with Jake, a laid-back man around Tom's age, who sought diversions to past the time. He had brought a plastic grocery bag of carrots, celery, and lettuce to feed the snapping turtle.

"You're going to open his cage?" Tom asked nervously.

"How else can I feed him?" Jake replied.

"Can't you slide the carrots and celery through the openings?"

"Nah. Snappy's fine," Jake declared, opening the top of the cage and poking a carrot at the large turtle.

Suddenly the turtle sprang out of the cage, ignoring the carrot and heading for his owner. Tom leaped on a chair as the angry turtle grabbed Jake's boot in his powerful jaws.

"Son of a bitch! Get off me Snappy," Jake yelled, dragging the clinging big turtle across the floor and out the door. Running through the tall swamp grass, the zany Bradford guard was finally able to dislodge him. But the fierce reptile was in mad pursuit of his former caretaker.

Gasping from spasms of laughter, Tom called out, "Run up the hill towards the road."

Jake did as Tom advised, distancing himself from the big turtle. The scary-looking tortoise finally lost interest. Turning around, the big turtle headed for his home in the grassy marshes that surrounded the sprawling Con Ed plant. Tom made a mental note to avoid the swampland adjacent to the road connecting the guardhouse to the power plant.

A few days later, Tom was given another offthe-books assignment covering a general science class for Bill Lawler, who was missing in action.

This time it was a lesson on the atom – familiar territory to Tom. Entering the classroom, he placed the planetary model of the atom of the helium atom on his desk and wrote the aim of the lesson on the blackboard: What is the atom?

As expected, Ronnie fiddled with the helium atom. cranking it harder and harder to make the electrons revolve around the nucleus in ever faster orbits. Sending the rambunctious student to his seat, Tom pointed to his aim, "So what's an atom?"

"It's the fundamental building block of nature," Kelly responded. She was a high-achieving freshman at Curtis, an infrequent occurrence at the school in the 1980s.

"Very good. What's the difference between an atom and a molecule?"

"An atom is the smallest part of an element and a molecule is the smallest part of a compound," Robert answered, adjusting his thick glasses.

"Very good, four-eyes," Ronnie snapped. He was the younger brother of Kenny, with whom Tom had played basketball at the P. S. 21 schoolyard.

"Now that was uncalled for."

"You're right, Mr. Haley. I apologize for that inappropriate remark," the talkative youngster replied.

His apology surprised Tom, but inconsistent behavior was common among teenagers. Backtracking, the skinny science teacher asked the class to define matter.

The red-haired kid in the back of the room called out: "Matter has weight and takes up space."

Through a series of questions and answers, Tom listed and defined the three types of substances – elements, compounds , and mixtures on the blackboard. Element – a pure substance that cannot be brOKen down by ordinary chemical means.

Ex: carbon, hydrogen, helium, iron, copper, sulfur.

Compound – two or more elements chemically united in definite proportions.

      Ex: water, salt, sugar, alcohol, aspirin, ammonia.

Mixture – two or more substances mixed together in variable proportions.

      Ex: salt water, sugar water, sand and water, tincture of iodine.

Looking over his notes, Ronnie raised his hand: "You covered this stuff with us last week."

"That's fine. I'm just reviewing key concepts," Tom replied.

Roy, a heavy-set kid, called out. "I heard you should never mix Clorox and ammonia together."

"That's true. Clorox and ammonia produce chlorine – a greenish poisonous gas," Tom stated grimly.

Ronnie raised his hand. "Isn't there a form of alcohol that is poisonous?"

"That's true. Wood alcohol is poisonous. Rubbing alcohol is for sore muscles. And ethyl alcohol is found in alcoholic beverages like beer and whiskey," Tom declared.

"You seem to be very knowledgeable about alcohol, Mr. Haley," Ronnie observed.

"No more than the average science teacher," Tom responded.

"I think Mr. Haley is a cool teacher. He challenged my brother in basketball and wasn't whipped too badly," Ronnie chipped in.

The class murmured approvingly. Athletic prowess was valued above academic ability In high school.

"Mr. Haley, what is the God particle?" Kelly asked, again showing her keen interest in science.

"There was a physicist, Leo Lederman who went to my alma mater C.C.N.Y. He discovered the ultimate particle of matter, called the Higgs boson, which was referred to as the God particle."

Moving on, Tom asked the class about the three states of matter.

Robert responded, "Solid, liquid and gas. As with water, you have ice, water, and steam."

"What is dry ice?"

"That's frozen carbon dioxide, which is colder than regular ice," Johnny called out from the back of the room.

"Isn't there a fourth state of matter, called plasma?" Kelly asked.

"No plasma is what's in your blood," Roy, the future Curtis footballer, declared.

"Plasma has two meanings: the liquid part of blood and the fourth state of matter. When gas is subjected to very high temperatures, it breaks up into positive and negative charges – called ions."

"Isn't the hydrogen gas inside the sun in a plasma state?" Kelly inquired.

"Yes it is. Plasma is the main constituent of stars. Hence, plasma is probably the most abundant state of matter in the entire universe. An interesting law discovered by guy named Avogadro said the equal volumes of different gases at the same temperature and pressure have the same number of molecules"

Turning to the board, Tom wrote Avogadro's number: 6.02×10^{23} Kelly raised her hand. "Isn't Avogadro's number of molecules referred to as a mole?"

"No a mole is an animal that lives under the ground," Ronnie wisecracked, causing the serious youngster to smile, along with the rest of the class. On that light note , the bell rang – ending the class and sending the freshmen out of the room in a mad dash.

Kelly was a popular girl with a long pony tail. Good looks and athletic ability ranked above academics in high school. She was fortunate to have been gifted with high intelligence and physical beauty. From his high school days, Tom recalled that there seemed to be many girls with brains and beauty. Maybe it was a phenomenon of that era. During the 1960s, kids were more physically active and fast food had not been prominent as it was in the 1980s. Tom was not popular in high school, but he had a certain status as an honor roll student. He might have been considered a minor celebrity – below the social and athletic superstars who possessed the elan that grabbed the spotlight.

Then again if one wasn't attractive in the fool bloom of youth, it wasn't in the cards that he or she would ever be. In the best of all worlds, every person would be endowed with a certain degree of physical beauty and intellectual ability. Tom wondered what philosophers said about unequal endowments. Yet, each individual has something unique to contribute to the world. And It is the duty of a teacher to help each student develop his special gifts in advancing society. Thus, the road to a better world is paved by the teacher-student relationship. From the societal point of view, teachers are worth their weight in gold. Next time he bumped into his union rep, Alan Katz, Tom would make that case to him.

Of course, every generation believes it is the best in the country's history. His mom's generation had endured the Great Depression. Joanie's parents, somewhat younger, had faced the Second World War. His cousin, Rusty, fought in the Korean War, which was a bloody struggle pitting America and South Korea against Red China and North Korea. And the baby boomers (Tom's generation) had fought in or were deferred from the 20-year long Vietnam War, which resulted in 58,000 American deaths plus 1.4 million civilian casualties in the region. Tom's decision to become a teacher was largely a consequence of the unpopular war in Southeast Asia. Unlike his Vietnam-era cohorts, Tom remained in teaching after that tragic war came to an end. If nothing else, the skinny science teacher was a creature of habit.

Chapter 17 – An Unexpected Donation and a Lesson on Motion

Another bright Saturday morning in Claire Haley's kitchen was the setting of a bacon-and-egg breakfast prepared by Joanie for Ton, his mom, and herself. Mother and son gobbled the scrambled eggs, smothered in ketchup, while Joanie picked at her eggs and listened to the rapid-fire morning chitchat. There was a strain between Claire and her son's longtime girlfriend, which time and illness could never dissipate. As a result, Tom worked hard to fill in any conversational gaps. "I drove by U.S. Gypsum yesterday and they're still on strike."

"The workers got to stay together keep the pressure on management. Your President wants to break the unions. That's for sure," Claire replied, rustling her newspaper.

"He's not my President. I didn't vote for him," Tom responded.

"Nor did I," Joanie chimed in, anxious to please Tom's argumentative mother. "They call him the great communicator. Unlike Nixon, Reagan's exudes confidence," Tom observed.

"Nixon was from a working class family. He was a self-made man. Give him credit for that," his mom replied, slurping her coffee.

"Rich folks like the Reagans have a sense of entitlement. The world is their oyster."

"What about you, Tom. Is the world your oyster?" Joanie asked with the hint of a smile.

"To quote my mom, I'm as a happy as a clam. Getting back to Rusty, he must be in a tight place right now. I'm thinking of bringing some food to his house."

"Doesn't your cousin get unemployment insurance?" Joanie inquired.

"Not when you're on strike. Do you want to kick in something or is the pantry snapping shut like a clam shell?" he said, turning to his mom.

"Very funny Mc Gee." Getting up Claire Haley went to the pantry, fumbled around a bit, and then put half-a-dozen cans of soup, peas, baked beans, a jar of instant coffee, and an unopened box of cereal on the table. "You're a Mensch mom." Tom declared, as Joanie watched the proceedings with amazement.

A few days later, Tom was awakened early by a phone call from Curtis principal Low Stout. "I got a job for you. Dick Grimsby's out and I need you to cover his physical science classes. He's doing the laws of motion. One hundred fifty bucks off the books."

"How are you able to do that? I'm curious."

"Principals have certain discretionary funds. The big shots trust administrators, but you not teachers," the wily administrator stated in a matter-of-fact tone.

"That's why you're driving that big Lincoln, while I'm still schlepping around in my old Pontiac."

Walking into Dick Grimsby's s physical science class, Tom was pleased to recognize some familiar faces. Like most teachers, he preferred dealing with familiar faces rather than the unfamiliar. He received a lukewarm reception, which was also preferable to outright hostility. Turning to the blackboard, Tom wrote the aim: What are Newton's three laws of motion? On the front desk Tom placed a metal cart, a rock, a baseball, and some balloons. Kenny, who had had played basketball with Tom at P. S. 21 back in January, grabbed the baseball and tossed it to Hank, who sat in the back of the room.

"All right guys, give it back," Tom said in a firm manner.

Shrugging his shoulders, Hank threw it to Tom, while Kenny feigned indignation.

"Boys will be boys," Lulu declared rattling her silver bracelets and anklets, the latter of which Tom had not noticed before.

Despite her dark complexion and jet-black hair, she reminded him so much of Lora that it was eerie. For teachers , déjà vu phenomena occurred with students, who seemed to be current versions of those he had encountered fifteen years earlier as a rookie teacher. Even Kenny with his loud unruly ways, reminded Tom of Barry who exhibited similar behavior at Curtis back in the 1970s. The time worn cliché – that the more things change, the more they remain the same – is particularly true for teaching.

"Notice that when Hank threw the baseball to me, it traveled in a straight line at a constant speed. It only stopped when I caught it. But if I place the ball on this desk it will remain at rest," Tom lectured.

"No. It actually rolled a little," Kenny objected.

"That's because the desk is not perfectly level. What can we conclude from the ball's motions?"

"An object in motion remains in motion and an object at rest remains at rest," said George, a student who focused on the matter at hand.

"Very good. And this tendency of objects to maintain their state of motion is called inertia."

"Now suppose I gave the cart a push. Notice it moves across the desk. If I give it a harder push the cart moves faster," Tom explained.

"Mr. Haley, you're stating the obvious," Jerry called out, as he turned back to look out the window. Tom hid his annoyance with the pesky student and moved on. "Notice what happens when I push the cart across the desk and then drop this heavy rock into it."

"I think you like playing with those toys. Do they pay you for this stuff?" Kenny asked.

Ignoring Kenny, who was just as rambunctious as Jerry, Tom asked for a generalization of what they had just seen.

"The acceleration of an object increases with the force and decreases with its mass. This is called Newton's second law," Susan answered calmly. She had a serenity that was rare among her peers.

Tom noticed that when Susan spOKe in class, none of the boys made sarcastic comments. They reserved their barbs for the "plain Janes" of the class. Tom also noticed that Susan and George took careful notes of the lesson's conclusions, while the others dawdled.

Next Tom inflated a balloon and then released it. Naturally, the balloon darted briefly across the room before coming to rest on Hank's desk. He repeated Tom's action, sending the balloon to Lulu's desk, who tossed it back to Tom, her silver bracelets and anklets rattling.

"You're supposed to blow the balloon up and send it flying towards the ceiling," Kenny scolded the high strung coed, who continually fiddled with her jewelry.

"So what can we conclude from my balloon rocket?" Tom asked.

George raised his hand. "Action and reaction. The air is forced out of the balloon backward and the balloon moves forward in the opposite direction."

Just then Ethel, the lab assistant, brought in a device that looked like a tin can, with a long wick attached to one end. Aware of Tom's propensity for dramatic classroom experiments, the class became excited.

"Excellent. It's called Newton's third law of motion – action and reaction. Now it's notebook time."

Tom turned to the board and summarized the conclusions of the lesson on the laws of motion.

Newton's Three Laws of Motion

1st Law: An object at rest tends to stay at rest, and an object in motion tend s to stay in motion.

2nd Law: An object's acceleration increases with the force and decreases with the mass.

3rd Law: For every action or force, there is an equal and opposite reaction or force.

"Didn't Newton discover the law of gravity?" Hank called out from the back of the room.

"Indeed Isaac Newton talked about the force of gravity, which makes all objects to fall to the earth. He also stated that gravity holds the moon in its orbit around the earth and the planets in their orbits around the sun," Tom lectured.

"Who was the guy who dropped the two rocks off the Leaning Tower of Pisa?" Jerry asked.

"That was Galileo. In so doing he proved that all objects fall at same rate of speed due to gravity. Isaac Newton was greatly influenced by Galileo's work in physics. Science depends on the discoveries of many people working in different countries at different times."

"Enough with the dumb questions. Set off the rocket already!" Kenny demanded.

Tom cleared his desk set the rocket vertically on a metal stand and light the fuse with a match. As soon as the flame traveled along the fuse to the bottom of the rocket. The can shot upward with a whooshing sound and smashed into the ceiling directly above the front desk. It bounced off the ceiling and landed on the floor. Before Tom could retrieve it, Kenny had grabbed the tin can rocket and dashed out of the class. The class was in pandemonium, but ecstatic over the spectacle. Unfortunately the room filled with sulfur fumes. In the midst of the rocket-induced chaos, the bell rang – ending the class.

At that unlucky moment, Lou Stout, who had been patrolling the second-floor hall popped his head into Tom's room: "I see one of your famous experiments failed again."

Returning from the side windows, Tom replied, "No the rocket went off as planned. We're just opening the windows to disperse the fumes."

"It was awesome, Mr. Haley. I love your experiments – even when they flop," Lulu exclaimed fiddling her silver necklace and rattling her silver bracelets and anklets.

"But did you learn anything today?" the husky principal asked.

"Yes. I learned not to sit in the first row in Mr. Haley's class for my own safety," she replied with a smile. Leaving the room, the jingle-jangle of her silver bracelets and anklets echoed down the long second second floor hallway.

Chapter 18 – Strikes, Turtles, and Connubials

Heading home from Curtis along Richmond Terrace, Tom saw several strikers picketing U. S. Gypsum – including his cousin Rusty, plus some policemen. The picketers appeared to be arguing with the cops and among themselves. Curious , Tom made a left on a side street, parked his car, and approached his unhappy cousin.

"What's going on Cous?"

"Gypsum's brought in scabs to break the strike. I'd like to stop them but the cops won't allow any rough stuff."

"Violence is not the answer. Maybe you should get other unions to join you. There's strength in numbers," Tom said, observing the anger of the strikers.

"Everybody is knocking us – the Advocate, the Daily News, and the politicians are calling us criminals. U. S. Gypsum is going to court to get an injunction. They're pissed because demand for plaster and wallboard is up. There's a building boom on the Island, so the big-shot builders and the businessmen are screaming bloody murder."

"Well, stick to your guns. Workers have the right to strike – thanks to Franklin Roosevelt," Tom stated.

"By the way, thank your mom for the food she sent over. I thought she didn't like me because of that liquor store robbery years ago," Rusty said with a sheepish grin.

"Nah. That's ancient history – you were a kid then. After all, you're family. And family counts in times of crisis."

"Yeah. The family who pickets together, stays together," Rusty proclaimed, giving a policeman standing nearby a dirty look.

"I still think you should get other unions involved. I could ask my teachers' union to picket with you guys."

"The A.F.L.-C.I.O. is sending people tomorrow. So if you guys want to join in – the more the merrier," his cousin replied, shaking Tom's hand and returning to the other picketers.

Tom noticed a man taking pictures of the strikers. Wondering which newspaper the photographer worked for, he questioned the man. There was something familiar about the man that Tom couldn't place.

"What do you care what paper I work for buddy? What about you? Do you work for U. S. Gypsum?"

"No. I was talking with my cousin who does work for Gypsum. Is that against the law?"

"We don't want any outside agitators making trouble here," he scanning the skinny teacher from head to foot.

"I bet you're from middle management." By way of an answer, the openly hostile man took Tom's picture and walked away. Tom resolved to bring his Curtis colleagues to join in the picketing.

A few weeks later, Tom trudged from his old Pontiac to the main gate of the Con Ed power plant in Travis. smelling the sulfur fumes permeating the environs of the sprawling plant. There had been few cars on Victory Boulevard, befitting the late-night hour. Once he adjusted to the midnight to 8 AM shift, Tom enjoyed the quiet and solitude of the small guardhouse. He brought his master's thesis, which needed some editing, especially the review of the literature section. As a college student, Tom liked guard work because it allowed him to study and earn money at the same time. Happily, he opened his nutritional research notebook and perused its contents.

There had been extensive research on the effects of malnutrition on learning in human beings and in rats. The fact that rat physiology was quite similar to that of human beings made them very suitable for such studies. Another advantage was the rapid brain growth of rats. Rats attains their maximum brain capacity within four weeks. Consequently, the rat's vulnerability to stunted brain growth as a result of protein deprivation is most severe during this early stage of life. For human beings, the brain achieves 80% of its weight by age three. The situation with people is more complex because human intelligence depends on a variety of factors – genetic, social, economic, and psychological. In contrast, the white laboratory rat have little genetic variability with regard to physiology. Tom had designed the experiment to control the rats' environment to minimize such factors – with the exception of nutrition. The control group was raised on a diet of adequate protein, while the experimental had been given a low-protein diet. Yet the difference in maze-learning ability was minor between the two groups – barely attaining the 10% significance level. Most educational research aimed for the 5 % significance level. C'est la vie!

On his last tour of the Con Ed plant, Tom was walking back to the guardhouse, when he observed an animal crossing the road which bisected the grassy swampland. It was Snappy, the large snapping turtle that had been Jake's pet. Tom stopped momentarily. Then thinking that no dumb reptile was going to prevent him from completing his rounds, Tom plunged forward. Sure enough, the angry turtle started after him. Breaking into a sprint, he left the turtle behind him on the road. Fortunately, his devotion to schoolyard basketball gave Tom the wherewithal to outlast the stubborn creature. It appeared that the curse of the angry tortoise, Snappy, would threaten the Bradford guards of the Travis Con Ed plant for the foreseeable future.

At the end of his nightshift, Tom walked along Victory Boulevard – passing commuters waiting at a bus stop on their way to work. There's nothing better than leaving work while most people are just starting their work days. Tom could never understand the reluctance of certain individual to obtain gainful employment. The fundamental premise of interdependent societies is the salaried job, which is the basis for all the work that must be done to keep the wheels of the world turning. We need each other's job to be done – whether it's blue collar jobs like plumbing, construction, sanitation, or white collar jobs like sales, clerical work, bookkeeping, store managers, or professions like teaching, law, and medicine. Indeed, working is as natural a propensity in human beings as eating, drinking, sleeping, laughing, learning, laughing, and mating.

Climbing the stairs to his second floor apartment, Tom smelled the pleasant aromas of percolating coffee, sizzling bacon, and scrambled eggs. Joanie, clad in her shortie cotton pajamas presided over the stove. Her dazzling smile was as bright as the early morning sun, filling the small kitchen with a cheeriness that seemed to belie the chilly winter weather. "Wow! A sumptuous dish if I ever saw one," Tom exclaimed, taking off his coat, removing his green Bradford guard tie, and kicking off his shoes.

"Are you talking about me or the breakfast I made?"

"Both! I don't know where to start. With the eggs are with you," he rep[lied, putting his hands on her plump derriere.

"Eat your bacon and eggs first, then you can ravish me," she replied, spinning out of his grasp and grabbing some dishes from the cabinet above the sink. What were you doing at the Plant? Reading girlie magazines?"

"Actually, I was working on my rat nutrition research. The well fed rats did only marginally better than their protein deprived comrades. The results barely reached statistical significance. Maybe the test rats should have been starved."

"No. That would have been animal abuse or rat abuse," Joanie exclaimed.

"All's fair in the name of progress. If rats were the dominant specie, they'd be experimenting on us."

Wolfing down his breakfast, Tom looked up at Joanie smiling at him in the same way she had first smiled at him years before during a softball game with his Elm Park buddies. More than a come-hither smile, it was the age-old call from woman to man that had propagated the human race from the dawn of civilization. Tossing her panties to the floor and turning his chair so it faced her, the sensuous woman mounted him. Slowly Joanie rocked back and forth, breathing rhythmically, and sighing deeply, she kissed her skinny husband. Tom thought about physics of circular motion to calm his excitement and slow things down. Suddenly the phone rang, abruptly ending the couple's relentless climb to an orgasmic summit. Tom ran bare-assed to the phone as Joanie giggled. It was the familiar voice of Lou Stout, "You sound out of breath. What were you doing – screwing?"

"No, no. I just ran up two flights of stairs from the cellar. Working on my maze-running experiment with the white rats."

"Tom's lying. He seduced me in the kitchen before I could even finish scrambling his eggs," Joanie called out from the kitchen.

"You're a horny guy. Joanie better keep you on a short leash. I heard you're moonlighting at the Con Ed plant in Travis."

"Just making ends meet on my meager teacher's salary," Tom retorted. Despite its meteoric growth the past ten years, Staten Island was still a small town – especially the North Shore. If a person sneezed in Mariners Harbor, everyone in West Brighton and St. George knew about it.

"I got a coverage for you tomorrow – $150 off the books. Dick Grimsby's taking a personal day off."

"Is his leg still bothering him?" After Amon's untimely death years ago, Dick's leg deteriorated – forcing him to wear his leg brace again.

"No, he's got bronchitis. Won't give up those smelly cigars," the Curtis principal related. An ex-smoker himself, Lou Stout had little tolerance for smokers.

"What's he doing tomorrow?"

"Circular motion. I'll leave his notes in your mailbox. Just don't set off any of your tin can rockets."

"Funny, I was just thinking about circular motion."

"Now don't get all spooky on me. Like your mind-reading friend, Amon."

Hanging up the phone, Tom called out to Joanie, "Now where were we?" Going into the bedroom, he found Joanie fast asleep in their double bed. Despite the dramatic shrinking of her brain tumor, the young woman was easily fatigued after ordinary household chores. Tom admired Joanie's Mediterranean beauty – her dark brown eyes, long eye lashes, full red lips, tawny complexion, and lustrous black hair. Quietly settling next to her in bed, Tom was soon asleep. Just physical proximity to his high school sweetheart made the skinny science teacher happy. Star-crossed lovers once separated by a thousand miles, their reunion was one of those everyday American miracles that Thomas Wolfe had written about in the 1930s.

97

Chapter 19 – A Lesson on Circular Motion

Approaching Dick Grimsby's physical science class, Tom saw Kenny in the hall, looking to see if he could skip the class. "Mr. Haley would you mind if went to the gym and work out. We got a big game this wee against Port Richmond."

"Would Mr. Grimsby allow you to cut class?" Tom asked incredulously. Dick was the Boy's Dean, in charge of discipline for Curtis's restive teenage boys. As a World War II veteran, the deanship was a job for which he was uniquely suited. Trudging along Curtis's long narrow halls with his idiosyncratic limp and his off key singing, Dick Ryan was well liked by students and teachers alike. Projecting amiable authority, he seldom lost his equanimity. As a rookie teacher, Tom tried to patent his teaching style after the affable pedagogue.

"Ah come on. You're not going to do anything today."

"You know me better than that. I always teach something. There so much to learn and so little time to waste."

"Are you gonna set off one of your tin can rockets?"

"You'll just have to wait and see what I do," Tom replied, going to the blackboard to write his aim on the blackboard: What is centrifugal force? "That's when you're on a merry-go-round and you got to hold on to the bar or be thrown off," Jerry replied, before turning back to the window where a fresh snow fall had whitened the pavement below.

Just then the lab assistant, Ethyl wheeled in a cart with some interesting artifacts for the class: a record turntable, a pebble, and a plastic airplane on a string.

Tom started the lesson by asking the class about Newton's first law of motion.

George, a serious student, raised his hand. "An object at rest tends to stay at rest and an object in motion, tends to stay in motion.'

"That's correct. Not only does a moving object stay in motion, but it maintains its motion in a straight line at constant speed."

"Mr. Haley, you're not telling us anything we don't know. It's just common sense," Kenny complained.

Whirling the airplane on a string around his head, Tom asked the class: "So what's happening here?"

"You just wanna play with toys because you missed all that fun when you were a kid," Kenny snapped.

"What's wrong with that? I still play with my Barbie dolls," Lulu exclaimed, rattling her silver bracelets and anklets.

"I'm sure you play weird games with your anatomically correct Barbie and Ken dolls," Kenny cracked.

"Go fuck yourself!"

"Mr. Haley, send her to the dean for profane language," Kenny replied, thoroughly enjoying himself.

"Gals and guys – can we get back to the lesson? Since objects tend to continue moving in a straight line, there must be a force acting on the plane to keep it moving in a circle."

"And the force is called centrifugal force. Right, Mr. Haley?" Jerry said, focusing his attention on the circling airplane – rather than the doings outside the window.

"No. It's called centripetal force – represented by the string. The tug I feel on the string is the reaction to centripetal force – known as centrifugal force."

"So you can't have centripetal force without centrifugal force?" George inquired, following the lesson closely. Unlike their peers, only George and Susan took notes continually during the lesson. A keen focus on the matter at hand was a necessary ingredient for academic success.

"Exactly. All forces occur in action-reaction pairs. If I strike the desk with my fist, I feel the reaction force of the desk upon my fist," Tom stated as he struck the desk with the side of his fist.

"Then, if I punch somebody in the jaw with my fist, his jaw hits my fist with an equal force," Kenny said.

"That's correct. That's why boxers wear those thick boxing gloves. And baseball catchers have those thick catcher's mitts to protect their hands."

"Don't you need action and reaction to walk?" Hank called out form the back of the room.

"Absolutely. You push backwards against the pavement, which pushes you forward. If there's ice on the sidewalk, you cannot push backward. So you won't go forward. In fact you're likely to slip and fall on icy pavement," Tom lectured.

"Hey Mr. Haley. What's with that record player?" Lulu asked, rattling her silver bracelets.

Plugging in the turntable, Tom placed the pebble on it. Immediately, the pebble shot off the rotating platform. "What just happened here?"

"The pebble flew off the turntable because of centrifugal force. There wasn't enough friction to keep it going around with the turntable," George answered in his precise manner.

"Suppose you put a little car on the turntable. Would it go off in a straight line or circular path?" Kenny asked, suddenly interested in the demonstration.

"Good question. Lulu ran down to the science lab and ask Ethyl for that small plastic car." Lulu dashed out of the room, her bracelets and anklets all jingle-jangling.

Returning momentarily, Lulu placed the car on the turntable. When it was began rotating, the car shot off in straight line – obeying the law of inertia.

"How about trying this?" Lulu asked, placing a jacks ball from her purse on the spinning turntable. Likewise the small rubber ball shot off in a straight line.

"It's clear that inertia is a fundamental property of matter. All objects tend to maintain their state of motion in a straight line and at the same speed – provided that no force acts upon the object," Tom asserted, as the bell rang and the students left the room following their own inertial paths down the school's long dark hallways. The lesson had gone well, provoking the youngster's natural curiosity about the way the world works. The trick in education was to maintain interest so that learning was as natural as breathing, seeing, hearIng and feeling. It would be nice to get them into the science lab and do some of the experiments he had demonstrated in front of the class. The problem was limited space because only the regents classes – biology, chemistry, and physics – had lab sessions. It's no wonder that non-regents students often felt they had second-class status in the New York City public school system.

Chapter 20 – Claire Haley's Quotes

Tom and Joanie spent a chilly Sunday morning reading the Advocate, Staten Island's local newspaper. The sun's rays streamed through the kitchen window of their quaint second floor apartment on Pulaski Avenue, warming and brightening the room. Tom slurped his coffee, while Joanie sipped her tea. Always a fussy eater, she had barely touched the oatmeal she had prepared for them. She had lost some weight as a result of her hospital stay and was struggling to gain it back. She was anticipating the approaching spring weather when she could go for walks with her common law husband. The fresh air and exercise would stimulate her lagging appetite and increase her energy

Miraculously, the lesion on her brain as well as the chronic headaches had vanished. Tom attributed her remarkable recovery to Amon's final miracle – effectuated after his visit to the charismatic young man's abode in Mariners Harbor. Tom had made a desperate plea to Amon in front of a plaque memorializing the self-styled messiah. Joanie attributed her regained health to God. She had been annoyed with him for not praying for her at St. Roch's church. Tom agreed with Pascal, the philosopher-mathe matician, who said that God does not mark his presence in the world with indelible footprints. Pascal proposed the religious wager: Even if the probability that God exists is low, we should live a virtuous life and assume God exists. The religious issue was one of those philosophic differences which the cou ple agreed to disagree about.

Tom was a believer in the age old adage that opposites attract. The fact that they were together was itself a small miracle. Their paths had crossed at a softball game, in which Joanie was a vocal spectator – calling out to him as he patrolled centerfield. Distracted by her vociferous cheers and jeers, he collided with a teammate while chasing a high fly ball. Joanie rushed to his aid applying a perfumed hanky to his bloody nose. An romance blossomed that spring and summer until fate erected a roadblock which devastated Tom similarly to the traumatic separation from his foster parents as a youngster. Joanie's dad was transferred to the distant state of Indiana. Tom continued to write to his former sweetheart, but life has a way of moving on. Joanie seemed to lose interest in being a pen pal and Tom learned through her cousin Jake that she was engaged.

Always a good student, Tom channeled his energy into his studies at C.C.N.Y. – despite his despair.

After receiving his bachelor's degree, Tom got a job teaching physics and general science at Curtis High School. Those were the heady days when there was a shortage of science and math teachers. Pursuing an active social life, Tom dated nearly every available young woman from Staten Island's North Shore – settling on Martha who was a regular at Kaffman's bar on Morningstar Road. Despite certain differences in outlook and temperament, their relationship progressed to the physical level – befitting healthy individuals in the prime of their lives. With the passage of time, Martha sought to legitimize their long affair with the sacrament of marriage. When the skinny science teacher balked, she severed the relationship with hardly a second thought.

Once more adrift in the sea of sexual anarchy in the Age of Aquarius, Tom set about searching for that elusive clone of Joanie. Since one man's misfortune is another man's deliverance, one enchanted evening Joanie magically reappeared at Kaffman's. As fate often confounds star-crossed lovers, the formidable Martha happened to be at that popular Elm Park hangout. As Tom magically sensed Joanie's presence, Martha observed the chance encounter of the ex-sweethearts with a female's fury. As in the past, Joanie was called upon to administer a perfumed hankie to Tom's bleeding nose. An objective observer would note the symmetry of Tom and Joanie's meeting again – after an in terval of seven years. Every couple has a story, a mixture of fact and fantasy, to be transmitted to friends and family over the years. The overcoming of fate-forced separation by young lovers has universal appeal to the romantically inclined among us.

Another Saturday morning rolled around with Claire Haley holding court for Tom and Joanie about the pitfalls and pratfalls of everyday life.

She liked to talk about her formative years during the Great De pression. "On every street corner there were men selling apples and potatoes – doctors, lawyers, businessmen. Millions of people were out of work. Then Franklin Roosevelt came along with the New Deal – putting people back to work in the WPA. He had other programs like the CCC which pro vided work for young people on farms and in forests."

"I read a book about the Dust Bowl in the 1930s," Joanie remarked.

"You're talking about The Grapes of Wrath by Steinbeck," Claire replied, nodding her head in approval.

"The unemployment rate reached 25%," Tom observed.

"It was higher than that – close to 50%. I know. I lived through it. There was a place you could get free shoes. My brother Jack was too embarrassed to go, so I went with him and got shoes for him, myself, and my sister Betty."

"Wasn't the Communist Party very strong in those days?" Tom asked, observing Joanie's discomfort.

"Just about everyone I knew was a Red. It was pressure from the left that pushed FDR to enact social security, welfare for the poor, and pass laws recognizing unions and collective bargaining."

"You worked for the WPA?"

"Yes. I got my first job doing clerical work for the WPA in Brooklyn. That's where I met your father. He was doing construction work for the WPA. Thousands of government buildings were built by the federal government during the 1930s – schools, post offices, power plants, railroad stations, and city halls all over the country."

"Your tax dollars at work," Tom chimed in.

"You're damn right. Not like today. When all Reagan wants to do with our taxes is build more bombs and missiles. That two-bit grade-B movie actor."

When Joanie gasped, Tom grabbed her hand and winked at her. "Mom,

I'm thinking of writing a little book comprised of your sayings – entitled Claire Haley's Quotes – like The Quotations of Chairman Mao. Taking a piece of paper from his back pocket, he commenced to read – to the delight of Joanie and the consternation of his opinionated mother.

Claire Haley's Quotes

1. You either go to school or go to work.

2. You have to live life on the basis of reality.

3. Use your head for more than a hat rack.

4. A car is a luxury.

5. He's crying all the way to the bank.

6. I'm as happy as a clam.

7. You're afraid you might learn something.

8. Love-smove – there's no such thing.

9. Religion is the opiate of the people.

10. You have to die of something.

"Very funny, McGee. Maybe I'm as smart as you. But I was smart enough to go to work and put food on the table, a roof over your head, and clothes on your back," she retorted.

"Absolutely. And I'll always love and appreciate you. My street-smart, no-nonsense, tough-cookie mom," Tom replied, getting up to give his long-suffering mother a hug and a kiss.

Despite her embarrassment with the proceedings, Joanie applauded Tom's rare display of affection towards his mother, with whom Joanie had an uneasy relationship. She had been on the same wave length as her ex-husband's mom, but couldn't abide him as a person because he was a control freak.

"So what are you thinking of doing now that you're feeling better?"

"Well, I'm going to apply for a job I saw in the paper. It's a charitable organization," Joanie said with some hesitation.

"Charity? I don't believe in charity. The government should help the destitute," Claire replied in a strident tone..

"I read an investigation of a well known charity in the Herald Tribune. The reporter said a large portion of their donations go to administration. He called charities the virtue racket," Tom said.

"I'm talking about the Salvation Army," Joanie said, annoyed with Tom's remarks about charity.

"The Salvation Army is an honest outfit. Remember when bought some furniture from them. It was a pretty good deal. I'll even admit to buying a winter coat there when I was in college. And I played for their little league team, the Red Shields, when I couldn't make the other teams."

"So I have your approval, my maverick boyfriend," Joanie responded sarcastically.

"Now don't act bossy, Tom. Let your girlfriend do what she thinks best."

"I totally approve. Thank God, I only inherited your book smarts mom, and not your dominant   personality. By the way there's one maxim that doesn't apply to you: Brevity is the sole of wit."

"Very funny, McGee. With your father I was far from dominant. As far as you were concerned, I made damn sure you did your homework and got good grades. My only regret is not doing the same with your sister. I should have been on her case about school."

"I'll say one thing. You did go after the local saloon keepers for serving Dad."

"You damned right I did. Selling liquor to a hopeless alcoholic is unconscionable. It dirty pool. Blood money was what I called it – to their faces!"

"I remember, mom. It was one of your finest moments."

"So what did the son of a bitch do? He went to bars in Port Richmond and Mariners Harbor. Some times I wonder what brought us together. We didn't even agree politically. East is east and west is west, and never the 'twain shall meet. "

"Love is blind. Ah, the mystery of destiny," Tom commented, smiling at Joanie who had been follow Ing the meandering conversation between mother and son.

"Tom had friends who went to AA and stopped drinking. But he was a hopeless alcoholic – like most of his family."

"It's a habit, a compulsion, an addiction that's very hard to resist," Tom replied, remembering the extreme measures his dad went through to quench his thirst. Tom recalled Thomas Haley taking an iron, a toaster, a radio, lamps, and other household items to the pawnshop to get money for booze.

Chapter 21 –Billy Bumps and Company

Tom got out of his old gray Pontiac on Victory Boulevard and headed for the small guardhouse where the Bradford guards recorded the name and plate number of every car entering the huge Con Edison power plant. An important duty of the guards was to warn the plant manager of the presence of EPA inspectors. Within a matter of minutes the sinister black smOKe pouring from the chimney would turn into harmless white smOKe. The plant still burned coal – clean coal – from which much sulfur and other contaminants had been removed. Nevertheless, coal was the dirtiest of the fossil fuels and trace amounts of sulfur dioxide spewed into the Island's air. The sulfurous odor per meated the entire North Shore of the island.

The burning of coal to run factories triggered the Industrial Revolution, which began in England during the late 1700s. As Tom had taught his students over the years, fossil fuels – such as coal, oil, and natural gas – originate with green plants buried under the earth for millions of years. Since green plants get their energy from the sun, via photosynthesis, fossil fuels represent stored solar energy. Once such fuels are depleted, mankind would have to turn to other energy sources. Work was underway to convert the coal burning plant to natural gas as the fuel for turning water into steam.

Electricity comes from high energy steam rapidly spinning generators .The power of falling water, such as Niagara Falls can also rotate generators to produce electricity. But in the absence of natural waterfalls or the falling water in huge hydroelectric dams, cities must rely on the burning of fossil fuels to provide the electric power people take for granted whenever turn on a light switch or tele vision set. It's an old adage that you can't something from nothing. That energy can neither be cre ated nor destroyed, but only converted into different forms is one of the fundamental laws of phys ics. This basic fact of nature Tom had drummed into his students over the years.

With these esoteric thoughts in mind, Tom trudged towards the 10-foot by 8-foot guardhouse, when he came upon a strange sight. Jake was fending off Snappy, the big snapping turtle with a wooden stick. He struck the aggressive tortoise in the head with his stick, which only made the creature more angry. Tom ran into the shack and grabbed a celery stalk from the small frig. Dangling it before the turtle, he managed to lead the creature back towards the marshes where he dropped the stalk. The turtle turned his attention to the celery, which he devoured ravenously.

"Thanks buddy. You probably saved my life or few toes – if he had gotten hold of my shoe. That son of a bitch is one angry turtle!"

"Try walking on the road and staying out of the marshes when you do your rounds," Tom advised his reckless coworker.

"That friggin' reptile has it in for me. Even a dog knows not to bite the hand that feeds it."

"Maybe Snappy's anger has something to do with your keeping him locked up in that cage. It looked like he could barely turn around in there," Tom replied, looking at the chicken wire cage which was still in the guard house.

"Yeah, but to hold a grudge that long. It must be a female. Snappy reminds me of my ex-wife, She's still mad I had a little fling with her girlfriend."

"Well, nobody's perfect," Tom replied opening up a statistics textbook he was taking in his master's program at C.C.N.Y.

"I'm gonna leave early tonight. Got a date with a hot number from Tottenville. That new kid, Billy Bumps is covering for me."

Tom looked up from his book and nodded.

"Shit! I'm wearing two different socks. I didn't check my socks when I put them on," Ralph said, curs Ing under his breath

"Aren't you going to change out of your uniform?'

"No. This chick really digs guys in uniforms. Kind of turns her own."

"Here's a problem. Supposed you have 10 unmatched socks in your drawer. What's the probability you reach in without looking and get a matched pair?"

"That's easy. One out of ten."

"No. It's actually one out of nineteen, because once you select a sock, there's nineteen left – one of which will match the first sock taken," Tom answered.

"That's why I hate math. It makes no sense."

"But keeping a mean old snapping turtle locked up in a cage does."

"You have a point there. I may regret trying to make a pet out of that nasty reptile."

Both guards were startled when somebody rapped on the door. It was a skinny straw-haired kid who looked from Tom to Jake with a puzzled expression.

"Mr. Bumps, I presume," Jake declared with a grin. "Is that you're real name?"

Billy turned to an invisible companion and replied. "Why would I use a pseudonym? I'm not a movie star."

Jake give Tom a quizzical look. "We got an odd ball here. Bradford and company seems to attract them like flies."

Again turning to his unseen friend, "Me odd? I'm not the one befriending a snapping turtle," Billy replied to his unseen companion.

"How does everything I do here get back to management? Anyway, my buddy Tom here will show you the ropes. I got Teresa from Tottenville waiting for me," Ralph replied, anxious to vacate the guard hut.

As soon as Ralph left the hut, Billy said he'd like to look for that snapping turtle. Tom deicide he would talk to the strange young man as if he was one of his students: "You'll do no such thing. We're respon sible for the safety of this million-dollar plant. I'm going to show you the rounds and the places where you have turn the keys on your guard clock. If you miss a key location, Con Ed will notify Bradford and you'll be out of a job."

"You hear that? I'll be out of a job. No jerking around – OK?" Once again this remark was made to his imaginary partner.

Tom decided the best way to handle Billy was to ignore his idiosyncratic behavior. He had dealt with Curtis students every bit as weird as this Billy Bumps character. They did the rounds together without any untoward incidents. Billy was impressed with the huge generator, which rumbled loudly as it spun at great speed producing sufficient electricity to power most of the Island.

"It reminds me of Dante's Inferno," the kid remarked – to Tom's amazement.

Later when they both returned to the guardhouse, Tom perused his lesson plans. Lou Stout had given him a two-day assignment in which he would teach the metal ores – covering Bill Lawler's general sci ence class. At the same time, Billy Bumps was writing in a marble covered notebook.

Curious, Tom queried the peculiar young man about his perfunctory notebook jotting.

"He wants to know what I'm writing in my notebook," Billy replied to his invisible partner.

"No. It's alright. I was just being nosy," Tom replied in a self-deprecating manner.

"If you really want to know, I keep a diary. Been doing it for years."

"That's cool. Maybe you'll write a bestseller some day."

Turning to his unseen sidekick, Billy said in a sarcastic tone: "You hear that? We'll write a bestseller and hit the jackpot!"

Later, the two guards took a break to eat a 3 AM snack. Tom had his usual peanut butter and jelly sand wich, while Billy had a large bag of peanuts which he shelled – putting the shells carefully into a plastic bag. Intrigued by the strange young man, Tom said there was a trash receptacle next to the frig where he could dispose of the shells.

"Nope. I save them for my compost heap," Billy replied. Then turning to his invisible friend, "Waste not want not."

Sensing that his coworker was truly a weird guy, Tom went back to his lesson plans.

"They said you were a teacher at Curtis – a science teacher," Billy remarked, looking at Tom's jumbled science notes, which had scribbled addendums and crossed out deletions.

"I went to New Dorp. Hated it there – all cliques." Turning to his companion, "Lots of bullying, but we took care of ourselves, Right buddy?"

"That's too bad. Bullying is a big problem in many schools. Right now, I'm on sabbatical this semester – doing research on nutrition with white rats."

"White rats, you say. I used to have a brown rat for a pet. I tamed him – never bit me. Remember Ratso?" The latter question was addressed to his invisible sidekick.

"Anyway, I split them into two groups – a malnourished group and a well fed group. Every day I ran them through a maze and count the number of wrong turns made. And you know what? There was very little difference between the two groups of rats," Tom related.

"When you're done, can I have the rats?" Billy asked, giving his companion a wink.

"I've already let them go. Kept one, a big friendly male, called Mu Alpha."

"Where did you release them?"

"There's a field under the Bayonne Bridge. Follow the footpath to an abandoned hut. They're probably in the vicinity of the shack."

"Shit! I know that shack. I had this uncle, Milton, who was a hermit. He lived there. I think he committed suicide." Again turning to his unseen partner, "Poor Milton went to live on his own – big mistake."

Tom didn't know what to make of Billy's remarks, but vowed to keep silent about his address and do ings. He recalled his mom's sage advice – never volunteer information to strangers.

Chapter 22 – A Lesson on Minerals

A few days later, Tom got another assignment from Lou Stout: covering Bill Lawler's freshman general science class for two days. He was out taking care of personal business. The rumor making the rounds of Curtis was a messy divorce of an 18-year marriage with three children and a roomy Victorian house on the South Shore. Tom recalled his mom's wry comments about a similar divorce with several children. "After twenty years and four kids, they decided that they had nothing in common!"

Walking into the room with a tray full of minerals, pieces of iron and steel, an old nickel, and a horse shoe magnet, Tom was surprised at the friendly greeting. Many of Curtis freshmen were Catholic ele mentary school graduates. Consequently, they exhibited a modicum of respect for their teachers. How long such classroom decorum would last was in the diverse St. George school was uncertain. Often, the role model that most high school students emulated was the bad dude and not the honor student. As usual, Ronny and Roy started handling the minerals on display, before Tom sent them to their seats with the required dose of teacher firmness: "Sit down now or we'll start off with a quiz prepared by your teacher, Mr. Lawler," Tom declared, showing the class a piece of paper with five questions on it.

The two boys returned to their seats. "Yeah, Mr. Lawler is a quiz freak. The guy gives one every friggin' day," Ronnie complained.

Getting into the lesson rapidly before his rambunctious pupils got too antsy, Tom asked the class, "What are minerals?"

"Pieces of metals that come from mines and places under the earth?" Roy, a husky boy, called out from the back of the classroom.

"A compound found in nature that contains a metal," Robert answered. He was a bespectacled young ster who earned high grades and scorn from many of his peers. Unlike the 1960s, Tom's high school days, there was little esteem bestowed on honor students.

"You're such a nerd," Ronnie declared. But upon noticing Tom's annoyance at his remarks, he quickly added, "But being smart isn't a bad thing."

Tom sensed the influence of Kenny, his older brother, a star basketball player at Curtis, on Ronnie. Ken ny was headed for college, via an athletic scholarship – an accolade not lost on the younger sibling. Un fortunately, the vast majority of high school freshmen seldom thought beyond the next five minutes when contemplating their future.

Tom showed the ores hematite and magnetite. He picked up both ores with the magnet. "So what prop erty have I demonstrated here?"

Kelly, a pretty girl with bouncing pony tail raised her hand. "Iron and steel are magnetic."

"That's correct. Hematite and magnetite are iron ores, but magnetite is naturally magnetic. What other elements are magnetic?"

"In addition to iron, nickel and cobalt are magnetic," Robert responded.

Ronnie brought a nickel to the front desk, "Let 's see the magnet pick up the nickel."

Tom tried the nickel but it was not attracted to the nickel. "Why doesn't the magnet pick up the nickel?"

Tom got out an old nickel and showed that the horseshoe magnet picked it up."What happened here?"

Someone from the back of the room said it was magic. "No. I used a very old nickel that was made out of pure nickel. Nowadays nickels are an alloy of nickel, copper, and tin. So they're no longer magnetic."

"So pennies are not magnetic?" Ronnie called out.

Tom tested a penny with the horseshoe magnet – demonstrating its lack of magnetism. Then he tested some iron nails – all of which were picked up by the magnet. Continuing in the same vein, Tom asserted that "the earth itself was a giant magnet. The earth's magnetic north pole is near its geographic north pole and its magnetic south pole is near its geographic south pole."

"That's why compasses point north," said Roy, a husky kid sitting in the back of the room.

"Correct. Compasses are tiny magnets free to pivot on an axis."

"What about the other minerals on your desk?" One of them looks like gold." Kenny remarked.

"That's galena – called fool's gold – which looks like gold, but is actually a lead ore. Sometimes galena is found near deposits of real gold" Tom answered.

Next, he showed the class smithsonite, which was blue-green in color. "Smithsonite is also known as zinc spar."

After Tom showed them a rusted iron pipe, he asked the class: "Why is steel called the backbone of all industrial nations?"

"Because so many things are made of steel – bridges, cars, trucks, trains, railroad tracks, and skyscrap ers," Kelly responded.

"That's correct. Since we are running out of important metals like copper, steel, and aluminum – recy cling has become very important," Tom responded. He recalled bringing newspapers and scrap metal to the neighborhood junkyard as a youngster. Kids would also return soda and beer bottles to the stores to earn spare change.

"OK guys. It's notebook time," Tom declared, turning to the board and inscribing Bill Lawler's notes.

Type of Ore	Name	Chemical Formula
Oxide		
	Hematite	Fe_2O_3
	Magnetite	Fe_3O_4
	Bauxite	Al_2O_3
	Cuprite	Cu_2O
	Zincite	ZnO
Sulfide		
	Iron Pyrite	FeS_2
	Chalcocite	Cu_2S
	Galena	PbS
	Cinnabar	HgS
	Zinc Blende	ZnS
Carbonate		
	Siderite	$FeCO_3$
	Smithsonite	$ZnCO_3$

At that point Lulu entered the room, carrying a long piece of magnesium and some matches. The pretty dark-complexioned senior rattled her silver bracelets and anklets – capturing the attention of the entire class – especially the boys.

"Is it possible to burn a metal?"

"I wouldn't think so. But with Mr. Haley, anything is possible," Ronny cracked.

"Have fun guys. But lean back and brace yourself for an explosion,"

Lulu warned, leaving the class hur ridly to the sound of her jangling bracelets and anklets.

Tom lit the magnesium strip with a match. It burned with a flash of light without any pyrotechnics.

"Ah. That's it? What a letdown," Ronnie exclaimed, as the bell sounded dispersing the freshman to their next class.

Gathering his materials, Tom realized that today's students looked forward to the dramatic and the un expected in the classroom. The humdrum routine was a turnoff to kids raised on television.

Driving home on Richmond Terrace, Tom noticed the workers still picketing U.S. Gypsum. Parking his old Pontiac by the side of the road, Tom found his cousin Rusty arguing with the same manager he had seen awhile back. Happily Tom also noticed two Curtis teachers picketing, Dick Grimsby and Alan Katz, the UFT chapter chairman. Tom picked up a picket sign from a stack on the sidewalk and joined the pic keters. Immediately, the Gypsum manager went over to Tom – venting his anger on the skinny science teacher.

"You and your Curtis friends have no business interfering with this contract dispute," the irate official yelled, attracting the attention of the other men.

"It's a free country. Teachers have a right to support their fellow workers," Tom replied, noticing the blotches on the man's red face.

"You're a trouble maker. I remember you from the Harbor – hanging out with that so-called Messiah fellow – Amon."

"Now I remember. You and your friend jumped Amon and he kicked your asses."

"Oh Yeah?" the manager threw a punch at Tom, who saw it coming and ducked. A better wrestler than a boxer, Tom tossed the picket sign and grabbed the manager in a headlock. Both men tumbled to the ground with Tom on top. Then Tom used his favorite weapon. He began bleeding profusely on the man, who coughed from the blood pouring into his mouth. Quickly Rusty, lifted Tom off the prone U.S. Gyp sum manager, who was hollering and cursing.

"Oh shut up, Bart. You started it. Here, clean yourself up and go home," Tom's cousin handed the red faced manager his handkerchief and dusted off his rumpled suit. Disheveled and embarrassed, the Gyp sum supervisor went home.

Tom's Curtis colleagues, Dick Grimsby and Alan Katz commended Tom on his manhandling of the Gyp sum manager. Tom introduced the teachers to Rusty, who thanked them for their support of the striking Gypsum workers.

"Bart's an asshole. I've been wanting to deck him for years. But it would have cost me my job. I got two kids, Jill and Jen, who go to Curtis," Rusty explained.

"I have them now in my regents bio class – nice girls and very smart," Dick exclaimed.

"You can thank my wife for that. She runs a tight ship around the house and has book smarts. My smarts are streets smarts. That's why I'm stuck in this place," Rusty said, pointing to the big Gyp sum silos looming before him.

"At the UFT we're trying to build alliances with blue collar unions. Nobody likes it when the teachers go on strike, but sometimes it's necessary. The strike is the weapon of last resort – used by workers when they're pushed against a wall," Alan replied.

"I hear you. Especially nowadays with companies trying to break unions. Just let them try to send scab in here. There 'ill be trouble aplenty!" Rusty said, cursing under his breath.

Shaking hands and exchanging pleasantries, Tom headed home for some TLC from Joanie. He noticed some blood stains on his skinny tie, which was out of style – like most of his wardrobe. Joanie had been on his case about updating his suits. He wondered if J C Penney's on Forest Avenue was still open. He had fond memories of their sales girl, Estelle, who had taken extra time to pick out a suit and some sports jackets when he began teaching at Curtis in 1968. She had guessed his jacket size from just a quick glance at the skinny rookie teacher.

Driving along the winding Richmond Terrace in his old Pontiac, Tom wondered why more workers in America weren't organized. His mom had mentioned that the Teamsters wanted to organize clerical workers, but the workers weren't receptive. Of course, Jimmy Hoffa and the teamsters had been investigated by Robert Kennedy in the 1950s. The results of the congressional committee's findings were widespread corruption on the part of that notorious union. The upshot of those investigations was a bloody nose for organized labor in America – not a good thing for the working man. In 1980, the minimum wage was $3.35 an hour, resulting in a weekly salary of $134 – not enough to keep a family of four housed, fed, and clothed.

It seemed that everyone in the good old USA had his price. Did Tom have a price? He hoped he'd never sell out to the establishment. That was a word you didn't hear during the 1980s. There were many such synonyms banded about during the 1960s– Big Brother, the man, the system, the military-industrial complex – no longer in the language of everyday people. America was now ruled by an administration hostile to unions and friendly to big business. Sadly, many blue-collar workers, who were barely a pay check away from homelessness, bought into Reagan trickledown economics.

Chapter 23 – Book Talk and a Botched Robbery

Arriving home at 269 Pulaski Avenue, Joanie was started by the blood on his face, tie, and shirt. Im mediately , she removed all his clothing and shoved in the shower. Tom's protests were allayed when she promptly joined him in the rigged shower, which a neighborhood plumber had rigged up over the ancient claw-feet bathtub. As usual, Tom was startled by his young wife's luminous brown eyes, red pouting lips, perky breasts, and shapely legs. Kissing Joanie, he thought about causality and chance – the profound mystery of destiny. The fact that these former star-crossed teenage lovers had overcome so many obstacles to reunite again was one of those miracles that are everyday events in America.

Resting in bed, Joanie remarked how nice it was to lie down together in that cozy house on that quiet street in Elm Park. Tom concurred: "It's like that Thomas Hardy novel, Far From the Madding Crowd.

Joanie said she preferred Tess of the D'Urbervilles, which surprised Tom. "What? I should give you a good smack. You think you're the only one who has ever read a book? The schools in Indiana are every bit as good as good as the schools in New York."

"I'm sure they are. I remember reading Hardy's The Return of the Native and Dickens' A Tale of Two Cities in high school. We also read Silas Marner, which was actually written by a woman – Mary Anne Evans. In those days I liked English and history as much as science and math. It was all good to me."

"Oh shut up, showoff " she replied, mounting him again.

In the early evening, Tom left their conjugal bed to don his gray William Bradford uniform with the long sleeved gray shirt, green tie, and gray visor cap. He slapped together a bologna-and-cheese sandwich. Then, giving a final loving glance at his voluptuous wife snoozing with a shapely brown leg extended over the side of the lumpy double bed, he dashed down the stairs and jumped into his old Pontiac.

Entering the 10-foot by 8-foot guardhouse, Tom smelled the pleasant odor of coffee and poured himself a cup, adding a dash of cream from the frig. He wondered who his coworker would be for the night. His silent query was answered by the abrupt entrance of Billy Bumps into the small guardhouse, carrying the large flashlight the guards had to carry, along with their portable clock.

"Mr. Curtis High School," the quirky guard exclaimed.

"How are you doing Billy? No critters out there?"

"Nah. It's all quiet on the western front. Kind of boring actually."

"I like boring. Nothing wrong with quiet – right BillY"

"Don't you like a little excitement on the job. When nothing's going on, time sort of drags."

Starting to reply to the eccentric young man, Tom noticed the snapping turtle back in its chicken wire cage. Pointing to the cage, Tom asked, "How did that goddamned turtle get back in the cage?"

"Jake lured it back into the cage with some celery sticks and a carrot. You see what I mean about boring?" Billy replied, winking at his imaginary comrade.

Just then, a car pulled up at the guard house and two men got out and one of them aimed a gun at the two Bradford guards.

"Oh shit. I spoke too soon," Billy replied, as the man with the gun signaled to them to empty their pockets and hold their hands up.

"Anything you want. Take it," Tom declared, trying to remain calm.

The men searched the cabinets, finding nothing of any value. Fortunately, neither Tom nor Billy had much cash, so their take was less than thirty dollars.

"Just don't mess with my turtle over there. He's a rare specimen and I ain't giving him up without a fight," Billy vowed, pointing to the large cage in the corner and nodding at his silent friend.

"Oh yeah? We see about that," the man holding the gun motioned to his unarmed comrade to check out the cage.

Incredibly, this man peered into the cage and stuck his gloved finger inside it – only to have the fierce turtle grab hold of the gloved finger. The foolish sidekick screamed – trying desperately to wrench it from the angry tortoise .

Taking advantage of this distraction, Tom wrested the gun from the armed wrongdoer, as they tussled, the gun went off striking the overhead fluorescent light, which went out with a pop – throwing the small hut into darkened chaos. There was a sound of scrambling feet and by the time Tom had turned on the guard flashlight, the two culprits were out the door heading for their car. Like all getaway cars, it pulled out of the side road and turned onto Victory Boulevard with a roar. Fortunately, the quick-thinking Billy got their license plate number – jotting it down in his marble notebook.

Tom called the police, straightened his tie, and dusted off his gray Bradford uniform.

"We did good today – didn't we?" Billy remarked to his silent companion.

Trying to be humorous, Tom quipped, "Thank your friend for me."

Momentarily, Billy was taken aback. "You realize my friend is imaginary, Tom?"

"If it works for you, it works for me," Tom replied in a conciliatory manner.

"Listen to that one, will you," Billy said turning to his invisible sidekick.

Surprisingly, the police arrived within a few minutes and took down the relevant information from the two guards. The cops were particularly happy to get the perpetrators' license number. In fact, they re ceived a call an hour later by a police sergeant notifying that the two bumbling croOKs were apprehend ed breaking a clothing shop window in Port

Richmond.

"I think those guys wanted to be arrested," Tom observed.

"Listen to him," Billy said to his companion.

"It's called fear of failure," Tom replied.

"Now I've heard it all," Billy said, grimacing at his silent partner.

Noticing a letter written by the Bradford guards supervisor about allowing any pets in the guard house, Tom sighed. "Listen Billy. We have to get rid of this nasty creature. Set him free."

After facing down a man with a gun, Tom was willing to pick up the chicken wire, wood framed box and carry it outside. The worst that could happen was he'd lose a finger or some toes. Boredom was the oc cupational hazard for guards. The yawning late night hours ahead of him gave the skinny science a reck lessness he rarely possessed . On his last inspection rounds of the plant, Tom had noticed two boards leaning on the guardhouse by the door.

"Before we do anything, I'm grabbing those boards outside to place under the cage. Do not under any circumstance put your hands on the cage," Tom instructed his coworker.

"Get a load of him," Billy said to his companion. "He acts like we're a couple of jerks."

Returning with the boards, the two guards carefully slid the boards under the cage while the fierce turtle hissed and snapped at them. Slowly and carefully they carried the cage outside – bringing it to the mar shy area, which had a shallow stream running through it. Using a long stick, Tom opened the door to the chicken wire cage. The angry turtle sprang out and started chasing Tom, while Billy yelled and whistled – trying to distract the fierce reptile. Suddenly, the turtle turned and went after Billy who jumped onto a big rock in the middle of the stream.

"Oh shit! What are we going to do now?" Billy asked his invisible and unhelpful sidekick.

Tom approached the turtle and racked the creature's hard shell with the long stick. Predictably, the turtle turned and pursued Tom who ran onto the paved road. After a short chase, the angry turtle lost interest and plunged back into the marsh. Both guards returned to the hut – laughing and congratulating each other on a job well done.

From that point on, the nightshift passed uneventfully. Time, the ineffable stuff life was of made of, only raced forward when things happened. The morning brought a cheery sunrise. As Billy made ready to leave, the two guards were joined by Jake, who immediately inquired about the whereabouts of his beloved pet. He opened the chicken wire cage, as if the big turtle was hidden under the grass and dried lettuce leaves.

"Orders from Bradford headquarters – dump Snappy,"Tom said, showing Jake the offending letter.

"Who squealed on me?" Jake said angrily.

"They probably got the info from the plant maintenance people, who come in here to sweep up the place. It's a shame because if it wasn't for Snappy we would have been robbed last night. He bit one of the perpetrators, so I was able to grabbed the gun which when off – hitting the fluorescent light. And then the bad guys skedaddled. "

"One of you guys have to replace that bulb, by the way," Billy interjected as he collected his stuff and winked at his invisible companion.

"Holy shit! Maybe you ought to take the police exam for me," Jake said to Tom. It seemed that Jake ignored Billy and the latter directed his comments to Tom.

"No way. I know my limitations. When I get in a fight, my strategy is to bleed all over the guy – like that boxer, Chuck Wepner, the Bayonne Bleeder."

"Chuck Wepner? He used to hang out at that bar in Port Richmond. You know the place on Innis Street," Jake said.

"That's probably the only bar on the North Shore I've never been to," Tom replied.

"Will you listen to these guys talking about saloons? " Billy said to his constant companion, as he left the guardhouse.

"How do you put up with that screwball?" Jake said, as watched the straw haired young man trudge towards Victory Boulevard.

"Eh, he's alright. Actually, he got the bad guys' license plate. And the cops apprehended them with in a half hour."

"Shit! Nothing ever happens on my shift. If I had been here when those guys pulled off their heist , it would have helped me get a police job. Everything in life is based on luck," Jake complained.

"Chance and destiny. Every time you walk out the door it's like rolling dice," Tom replied. No longer dwelling on Bertrand Russell's life as dream question, Tom thought about the effect of pure chance in the sequence of events which constitute a person's life.

"My luck has been very bad lately – except for Teresa. She's hot to trot with a body to die for. What do you say? Help me get that turtle back and I'll bring him home after my shift."

"I'm not messing with that creature again. He's capable of taking your finger off," Tom replied, shaking his head.

"I'll set up the cage so there's a carrot inside with the door open. All you got to do is beat the bushes with that broom over there."

Whether driven by boredom or new found courage, Tom agreed. The sun was rising so the swamp was more navigable than in the dead of night. Facing down robbers and vicious turtles had become routine for the skinny science teacher. It would be something to talk about with Joanie when he returns home.

As soon as the two guards ventured into the swamp, they saw the big turtle, partially submerged in the muddy water. Jake placed the chicken wire cage, door open, with the carrot inside. The crazy reptile must have had a thing for carrots because it headed for the cage, grabbed the carrot in its powerful jaws. As it started to back out of the cage, Jake snapped the door shut, and the two men carried it back to the guardhouse – carefully balancing it on the two boards Tom and Billy had used to haul the cage and turtle into the swamp a few hours earlier.

Back in the guardhouse, the angry turtle seemed content. Strangely, there was some sort of a bond between the reptile and Jake, although the latter was careful not to pOKe his finger through the chic ken wire.

"Well lady luck was on our side, this time," Tom remarked, recalling a statement made by the philos opher Karl Popper that success in life was largely a matter of luck. Popper went on to postulate that there is little correlation between success and merit. Yet Branch Rickey, the Dodger official responsible for bringing Jackie Robinson to major league baseball, asserted that luck was the residue of design.

Arriving in their second floor apartment on Pulaski Avenue, Tom entertained Joanie with a narrative of the preceding night's events. His pretty common law wife was astounded by the lengths Tom went to in transporting the nasty snapping turtle out of and into the guardhouse.

"I didn't know you were so impulsive. At some point your luck is going run out, Tom. For Christ sake, stop playing the hero," she replied, near tears.

Tom responded by referring to Karl Popper's remarks on success and luck. "Years ago, Amon, Mary, and myself were at a diner in Mariners Harbor, when we were held up by an armed robber. Amon hesitated. So I took action, tossing water into the guy's face and grabbing his gun. It may sound crazy, but my good luck in those types of scenarios is a residual effect of Amon."

"Look, Amon was a gifted person – capable of ESP, healing, and kindness. But you act like he was Jesus or a saint."

"Well, he wasn't given the name Mariners Harbor Messiah for nothing. When you got better at St. Vincent's, it was a direct result of my appeal to him in the Harbor," Tom said as he plopped in bed – falling asleep immediately.

Midmorning Tom was awakened by the jarring sound of the phone. It was Lou Stout notifying him of a two-day coverage for Dick Grimsby.

"What's he doing?" Tom answered groggily.

"He's doing food calories and nutrition. He left his lesson plans in your mail box. By the way you sound wasted and you probably look like shit. What were you doing last night? Boozing at Kaffman's til two AM?"

"No. I did some moonlighting at the Con Ed plant in Travis. There was a robbery attempt which I foiled with the help of a big snapping turtle the guards keep as a pet."

"Look, don't be a hero. You're a pain in the ass, but I need you here and the students actually like you. And why the hell are you messing with a friggin' snapping turtle?"

"It's a long story which I'll save for another day," Tom replied wearily.

"Maybe you should go back to bar hopping like in the old days. Go back to bed. I'll see you tomorrow," the grumpy Curtis principal snapped, hanging up the phone.

Chapter 24 – A Lesson on Food Calories and Nutrition

As Dick Grimsby's juniors filed into the class, they greeted Tom with the usual requests for a pass to gym or study hall. Tom ignored their pleas, setting up his materials for the lesson. He had a double-walled calorimeter connected to a DC battery and a slice of bread. Kenny came over to the front desk and grabbed the bread, which Tom took back. Turning to the blackboard, he wrote the aim of the lesson: What are food calories?

"Calories represent the energy content of food," George replied. He was that rarity in the public schools currently – a no-nonsense student.

Tom set up the double-walled calorimeter, placing the slice of bread in the inner chamber and filling the outer chamber with water and placing a thermometer in the water. Then he turned on the electricity,   sending an electric current through the bread, which began burning. He recalled getting a shock from the apparatus in the past, so he was careful not to touch the metal cylinders until the electricity had been turned off. The temperature of the water before turning the electricity on was 240, which Tom had written on the board. After several minutes, he had Lulu record the temperature again. Which she did, jangling her silver bracelets and anklets – commanding the attention of the boys in the room.

"The thermometer says 300 folks," she announced to the class.

"That's colder than it is outside," Kenny called out.

"That's because we're recording the Celsius temperature, not the Fahrenheit temperature. A tempera ture of 300 Celsius is equivalent to 860 Fahrenheit."

"What about the BTU?" George asked.

"The calorie is the metric unit of heat. In this country, heat is often measured in BTUs – British thermal units," Tom explained, turning he wrote the equivalency on the board.

1 BTU = 252 Calories

1 BTU = heat necessary to raise 1 pound of water 10 Fahrenheit

1 Calorie = heat necessary to raise 1 kilogram of water 10 Celsius

"Why don't we go to the metric system, like the rest of the world?" Hank called out from the back of the room.

"I imagine, it might cost industry some money to convert. And people would have to learn the metric sytem," Tom replied.

"They've been teaching us the metric system since we were in kindergarten. It's as boring as hell," Lulu complained, rattling her bracelets and anklets.

Getting back to the experiment, Tom measured the weight of water in the calorimeter as 500 grams.

"How many kilograms as that equivalent to?"

After a long pause, Susan raised her hand. "That would be five tenths or half a kilogram."

"That's correct. The temperature went up by six degrees Celsius. So how many calories would that be? Hint: multiply the mass by the temperature increase."

Once again Susan raised her hand." It comes to three calories."

"Wait a minute. You're telling me that a slice of bread is only three calories? I don't think so," Kenny ob jected.

"A slice of bread is about 70 calories," Jerry, said, turning his attention from the window to the activity in the classroom.

"Back to the drawing boards, folks," Lulu said, rattling her bracelets.

"Well, a certain amount of heat is dissipated to the environment. It's just an approximation," Tom explained sheepishly.

"I'm just glad you didn't work for NASA. The astronauts would have been lost in space forever. It's like your hoOK shot – way off the mark," Kenny snapped.

"How many calories in a Hershey bar?" Lulu asked.

"Approximately 200 calories and a piece of layer cake is 230 calories," Tom answered, after checking the notes prepared by Dick Grimsby.

"Shit! No more sweets for me. If a girl gains a few pounds, she hears it from her boyfriend. But a guy can be as big a hippopotamus and he acts like he's God's gift to the world," Lulu remarked, rattling her silver bracelets and anklets.

"What about a cheeseburger?" Hank called out from the back of the room.

"Those big double cheeseburgers from MacDonald's must be around 500 calories," Tom estimated.

"Damn! All this talk about food is making me hungry. 'Cept that food in the cafeteria is god awful," Ken ny complained.

"Anyway, a person's daily caloric requirement depends on his age, weight, sex, occupation, and the climate. We tend to burn more calories in the winter than in the summer – just keeping warm," Tom read from his notes.

"Doesn't a person's metabolism have something do with how much you eat?" Kenny asked.

"What is metabolism?" Tom asked.

"It's the body's rate of burning calories. We need food energy to move around, build muscles, and grow," Hank answered.

"OK guys, notebook time," Tom announced, turning to the blackboard.

Individual	Calories per Day
Athlete	4,500
Teenage Boy	3,500
Teenage Girl	2,600
Man (desk job)	2,500
Woman (desk job)	2,100

Pam, a chubby girl with dyed red hair, raised her hand. "If a person wants to lose weight, should he eat less or exercise more?"

Tom waited for some wisecracks from the boys, but there weren't any. The reason for their discretion was the fact that her older brother was a bruiser who played for the football team.

"I'd suggest doing both: eat healthy and do aerobic exercise. Even walking is good in the regard."

"How you gonna exercise when there's snow on the ground?" Kenny exclaimed.

"When I was a kid, we'd get a shovel and clear the snow from the basketball court. And then we'd play some basketball. The ancient Greeks used to say – a sound mind in a sound body."

"Playing basketball in the snow is crazy. How you gonna dribble and shoot with mitts? Didn't they have TVs in those days?"

"It's called cabin fever. Sometimes you just want to get outside and frolic in the snow," Lulu chimed in, fiddling with her bracelets.

"I know. Next time it snows, Mr. Haley will take the whole class outside and we'll build a snowman," Pam declared and the entire class cheered in agreement.

"Sounds like a plan," Tom concurred, as the bell rang signaled the end of the class.

Tom no sooner mounted the steps to his second floor apartment when the phone rang. Joanie grabbed the phone, smiled and handed it to Tom. As expected, Lou Stout had another coverage for the skinny science teacher: a follow up lesson on nutrition. "Everything's set up for you – charts on the vitamins and food from the prep room. Just ask Ethel and she'll send the stuff to your classroom. After the les son, you can eat it yourself."

"No thanks. I'll give it to the students. I'm on a diet."

"Yeah sure. If you get any skinnier, you'll be invisible. Doesn't Joanie feed you?"

"I heard that, Mr. Principal. I have you know I'm an excellent cook."

"I'm sure Tom didn't marry you for your culinary art," the school administrator cracked.

"Tom, hang up on the sob," as she grabbed the phone from Tom.

"I'll be there tomorrow," Tom called out. He heard Lou Stout laughing before they were disconnected.

Chapter 25 – A Lesson on Minerals and Vitamins

Tom wheeled in a cart filled with samples of food: an apple, an orange, a banana, an egg, a can of tuna of tuna, a can of vegetable soup, a stick of butter, a pint of milk, a slice of bread, and two slices of bacon. Before Kenny could swipe any of the food, Tom shooed him to his seat and wrote on the blackboard: What is a balanced diet?

"A healthy meal would be a cheese burger, French fries, and a milkshake. It covers the four major food groups – cheese, grains, meat, and milk," Kenny said.

"I don't think so. Cheese and milk are both dairy. You're missing a vegetable," Pam, a chubby redhead, Interjected.

"I forgot to mention pickles. I always ask for a pickle, which is a green veggie. So I'm covered."

"A balanced diet is made up of proteins, carbohydrates, and fats, plus water," George, a serious student, answered.

"That's right. In terms of percentages, a balanced diet consists of 40% carbohydrates, 30% fats, and 25% protein," the skinny science teacher stated.

"Wait a minute. That doesn't add up to 100%," Kenny declared.

"Yes it does. Add up the percentages," Tom said, somewhat annoyed.

When the class added up the percentages, it came to 95%. Tom changed the carbohydrates to 45%.

"Well, Albert Einstein made a mistake with the gravitational constant in theory of relativity. Scientists occasionally make mistakes. So I am in pretty good company.

"That's because you're moonlighting at the Con Ed plant at night. Teachers need their sleep as much as us students," Lulu said, rattling her bracelets and anklets.

Tom wondered how she knew his about his night job with the Bradford guards. If somebody sneezed in Elm Park, the folks in West Brighton knew all about. He now understood why many people like big cities. Growing by leaps and bounds, the Island was no longer the small town it had been in the 1950s. Yet his adventures as a guard at the Con Ed plant seemed to travel through the proverbial grapevine. Turning to the board, Tom wrote down the following uses of the three dietary building blocks.

Proteins – needed for the growth and repair of the body's cells

Carbohydrates – the body's fuel for movement and cellular energy

Fat – provides the body with energy and warmth

"In addition, the body requires two quarts of water a day to function. Water is also found in beverages like milk, coffee, tea, juice, soda, ..."

"Plus those old standbys – beer, wine, and whiskey. Right, Mr. Haley?"

"I wouldn't know about such beverages," Tom replied disingenuously.

"That's not what I've heard through the grapevine. Curtis's favorite science teacher is a loyal customer of Kaffman's bar on Morningstar Road."

Once again, Tom realized that despite Staten Island's meteoric growth in recent years, it still functioned as a gossip mill. As a student, he had little knowledge of, or interest in, his teachers' doings. Teachers seemed to exist on a different plane of existence – as ideal role models.

"Now where was I? Oh yes, the mineral – vital for our health," he said, turning to the board.

Important   Minerals

Iron – red blood cells

Iodine – thyroid gland

Chlorine – digestion

Magnesium – digestion

Potassium – prevents strOKe

Calcium – bones and teeth

Phosphorous – bones and teeth

From the back of the classroom, Hank called out. "What about vitamins? We need them too."

"Absolutely. Vitamins are catalysts – functioning to facilitate ongoing biochemical processes in the body. Where do we get vitamins from?"

"I take vitamins everyday," Jerry said, turning back to look out the window.

"You do? Then why are you so short?" Kenny replied.

Jerry mumbled a curse under his breath and Kenny got up from his seat. "What did you say?"

"Kenny sit down. Don't be so vindictive at the slightest provocation."

"Yeah. We need a little less violence and a little more love in the world nowadays," Lulu chimed in, shaking her bracelets and anklets.

"What the world needs now is love sweet love. It's the only thing there's much too little of," Kenny sang in a high-pitched voice that was actually on-key.

"Not bad. You have something to fall back on if your basketball game goes south," Tom observed, as he turned to the blackboard again.

136

Essential   Vitamins

Vitamin A – promotes vision

Vitamin B – prevents beriberi

Vitamin C – prevents scurvy

Vitamin D – prevents rickets

Vitamin E – antioxidant agent

Vitamin K – helps blood clotting

Niacin –   prevents pellagra

From the back of the room, Hank asked if there were any nutritional benefits of beer, as his classmates snickered.

"Actually, beer has carbohydrates, potassium, and vitamin B," Tom replied.

"Look how healthy Mr. Haley is. He's living proof that booze is good for your health," Kenny wise cracked.

Tom smiled, "That might be a good research paper. Comparing the health of alcoholics to the general population."

"What about cirrhosis of the liver? It's a disease that heavy drinkers are prone to," said Susan, who had been quiet during the lesson.

Susan was a good student who took careful notes and observed the antics of her classmates without comment. She possessed brains, beauty, and serenity. She reminded Tom of Keats' famous line: "Beauty is truth and truth is beauty."

George, another gifted student asked Tom a question: "If you burn paper in a closed container, saving all the ashes and carbon dioxide gas. Would the by-products weigh the same as the original paper?"

"Yes. That's the law of conservation of matter – matter can neither be created nor destroyed. The same is true of energy. Energy can be changed into different forms and utilized to do work. The end product of energy conversion is random heat energy."

"So what you're saying is that there's no death in science, when it comes to matter and energy," Lulu declared, rattling her bracelets and anklets.

"Now that's a poetic way of describing these basic laws of science. You ought to be an artist," Tom said.

"You're a poet and don't know it," Kenny snapped' as the bell rang – ending the lesson and its insight on the immortal nature of matter and energy.

Gathering his materials, Tom listened to the pleasant sounds of the students chattering, mixed with the jingle-jangling of Lulu's silver bracelets and anklets. The dispersion of the students from his class to vari ous destinations in the building could be viewed as a form of entropy. With regard to the laws of chance, entropy or randomness was the most probable state in the universe.

Chapter 26 – Coyotes from Jersey

As Tom entered the 10-foot by 8-foot guardhouse of the Con Edison plant, he saw Ralph stooping over the chicken wire cage feeding a cute looking puppy. The animal growled as it took scraps of meat from the Bradford guard.

"Is that a shepherd mix?" Tom inquired, approaching the cage cautiously.

"it's a coyote. Found it last week in that swamp. Must have been abandoned by its mother, so I adopted It. Just keep mum about it."

"No problem. But it doesn't seem very friendly."

"Yogi just has to get used to people," Ralph replied petting the furry pup.

Tom took a piece of baloney from Ralph and pushed it through the chicken wire. The strange canine to OK it and devoured it quickly.

"It sure seems hungry, but you think it would make a good pet?"

"It'll take some time, but he's friendlier than Snappy," Ralph replied, lifting the brownish coyote out of the cage and holding it up to Tom.

"Well, even a grizzly bear would be friendlier than that reptile you had. Hello, Yogi the coyote," Tom murmured, as he stroked the coyote gingerly.

Tom went out on his first tour of the plant, carrying the Bradford guard clock to be punched at various locations in the sprawling power plant. As he was walking in the area adjacent to the plant's huge gener ator, Tom noticed live steam pouring out of a big iron pipe. Rushing back to the guardhouse, he told Ralph about the situation and called the plant emergency number.

"You better hide the coyote somewhere, in case the Con Ed people come in here to talk to us," Tom warned his comrade.

"I'll put the cage outside for awhile. Those Con Ed people are goddamned nosy.

Within a half-hour, a Con Ed company car pulled up and a man in work clothes entered the guard house. Tom explained what he had observed in the plant. As the two made ready to leave, the coyote pup began to yelp.

"What's that?" the Con Ed inspector asked.

"It's a stray dog that got loose from a nearby neighbor. I gonna return him after my shift," Ralph ex plained.

"You know the rules about pets – right? There was somebody who had a big snapping turtle a while back back," the Con Ed man, whose name was Gary, related grimly.

"The turtle is back in the swamp where he belongs. You don't have to worry about Snappy," Ralph said, trying not to smile.

"You Bradford guys must get bored out here. Back at the plant there's never a dull moment. If anything goes wrong – it's on us."

"Well, we're under orders to notify you when the folks from the EPA come around," Tom replied.

"Yeah, those goddamned EPA inspectors are always snooping around. Everybody wants their power every minute of the day. But to produce electricity, you have to burn fuel – coal or oil – and send smOKe and dust into the atmosphere."

"What about wind and solar energy?" Tom suggested.

"Solar energy would be better if this was Arizona. Wind might work, but the folks in Great Kills wouldn't appreciate seeing hundreds of windmills offshore, instead of sand dunes and unspoiled seashores. "

"That's the way people are. They gotta have their cake and eat it too," Ralph chimed in looking out the window as his coyote pup began to whimper again.

"Well, I'm out of here. Take care of that coyote pup, but bring him home," Gary said with a wink.

Despite himself, Ralph blurted out: "How the hell did you know about the coyote?"

"There's a pack of them in the woods across the street. They probably swam across the Arthur Kill from Jersey . They tend to follow the deer which swim across the same body of water."

"Shit. Maybe we'll be getting black bears from Jersey. Now that would be something."

"With that drought going on, you could practically walk across the Kill. It's only a 450-foot crossing, so you going to find all sorts of critters in these parts," Gary related.

"At one time, Staten Island was joined to New Jersey and not actually an island," Tom said.

"Geography is destiny. Imagine what sort of place Staten Island would be if it belonged to New Jersey, instead of New York," Gary replied.

"The very thought scares me. I can't see myself as a hick from Perth Amboy," Ralph said with a straight face.

"Eh, people are pretty much the same in this region. If you're talking about Texas or California – that's a different story."

Changing the subject, Tom asked, "Why don't they use natural gas instead of oil to generate electricity?"

"Efficiency. Petroleum burn at a higher temperature – up to 3,500 degrees Fahrenheit. The hotter a fuel burns the more efficient the process. You need very hot steam to rotate those big turbine blades which generate the electricity to light up the Island," Gary replied.

"Doesn't most of the energy go up the smoke stack of fossil fuel plants?" Tom asked.

"Absolutely. Coal power plants are 35% efficient. Petroleum power plants are 38% efficient. And natural gas power plants are 45% efficient.

Con Ed is starting to install gas-powered turbines in other parts of the city."

"And coal is the dirtiest. When Con Ed burned coal, you smell the sulfur fumes all over the North Shore," Tom related.

"That's another reason we're converting to natural gas over the next several years. The smOKestack fil ters only removes the particulates but not the sulfur dioxide – a byproduct of coal combustion."

"Yet no matter which fossil fuel you burn, carbon dioxide is a by-product. And the buildup of that gas has been shown to increase temperatures around the world. Entropy is the endpoint of all energy trans formations," Tom continued.

"You're right about that also. You ought to be working for Con Ed. We could use people like you."

"Well, I'm a science teacher at Curtis High School. We talk about energy, fossil fuels, and pollution all the time. My students will face a world that's been contaminated by man's quest for more stuff."

"Maybe we should all go back to growing out own food, burning wood for heat, and using candles for light," Ralph chimed in.

"So, you're gonna trade in your car for a horse?" Tom asked his coworker.

"I wouldn't give up my car for anything. Where would I screw Teresa? Take her into the bushes?"

"You got a point there," Tom replied as Gary gave the two Bradford guards a mock salute and left the guardhouse.

Later on, as Ralph groomed himself for his impending hot date with Teresa, Billy Bumps entered the guardhouse. "Well looked what the cat dragged in."

"Man! That's a cool puppy you got out there. I know it's yours Ralph. Friendlier than that snappy turtle," Billy exclaimed, turning to his invisible sidekick, "How would you like to have a pet coyote?"

Pointing to his head and nodding towards the straw-haired Billy, Ralph left the guardhouse quickly, picked up the chicken wire cage with the coyote puppy, and headed for his car.

"I found one of your white rats near my Uncle Miton's shack. He's very friendly, nicer than Ratso who gives you a little nip from time to time."

"I'm happy he found a good home with you. There's a store in the city where you can buy the white rats," Tom mentioned.

"No, why would I pay for a pet when I can get them free," Billy replied. Then turning to his unseen side kick, "How would you like a coyote pup?"

"I don't think that's a good idea. We just had a visit from Gary, the Con Ed supervisor. He warned us about grabbing any more critters from the swamp."

"You hear that Buddy? No more tramping around in the swamp."

So your invisible friend has a name – Buddy – Tom thought. What a nutty crew they have working for Bradford Detective Agency.

Chapter 27 – Rat Research Approved and Sleeping on the Subways

Having proofread his master's thesis, Tom was ready to hand deliver it to his thesis advisor, Professor Spielman at C.C.N.Y. He wasn't about to trust the U. S. postal service with his 30-page document which he had labored over for nearly a year. Rats were believed to be particularly vulnerable to cognitive im pairment during the first four weeks of life, as a result of protein deprivation. Yet Tom found only small differences in the maze-learning ability of the malnourished rats compared to their well fed peers. The difference in wrong turns in passing through the maze for the two groups of rats had reached only the 0.10 level of significance. The usual level of statistical significance in educational research is the 0.05 sig nificance level. But it is what it is. We live in a quantitative world where data is king. Hopefully, the con genial Professor Spielman would give him a passing grade on his master's thesis , so he could become a proud owner of a master's degree in environmental studies from City College.

Tom met the congenial City College professor in his small office on ground floor of the school's Shepherd Hall. Like most of the buildings on the North Campus, Shepherd Hall with its gothic arches and giant windows, was as impressive as the school's academic standards. As the City University's flagship college, C.C.N.Y. was a pioneer in free higher education for the hardworking offspring of New York's working class. The school's alumni included Jonas Salk, Upton Sinclair, Abraham Maslow, Ira Gerswin, Mario Puzo, Henry Kissinger, Ed Koch, Bayard Rustin, Colin Powell, Barbara Streisand, and Woody Allen – among others. During his undergraduate years, Tom had worked so hard in his classes that he seldom to OK time make friends and participate in extracurricular activities. The two-hour commute from Elm Park, Staten Island to the upper west side of Manhattan was daunting, especially when combined with the long hours of classes and the accompanying homework. Along distance runner, rather than a sprint er, Tom stayed the course – enduring long hour of solitary study to earn his bachelor's degree. Settling into Professor Spielman's office, Tom saw his master's thesis on the desk with the grade of A and what looked like complementary comments on the brown manila envelope.

Smiling at the skinny science teacher, the veteran academic shoOK his hand and congratulated him, "I don't have any wine to offer you. That's the custom with a PhD degree, but I hope you'll go on to earn your doctorate in the future."

"A PhD you say? Maybe someday, but right now I'm very happy to have a master's degree. It means a nice pay raise – when they get around to it," Tom responded. Neither of his parents had a high school diploma, so a master's degree was nothing to sneeze at.

"You did a nice job on your thesis. It was a fine study, nicely written. Your rationale that early protein deprivation affects brain development in rats was documented in the review of the literature section. You also showed that maze-learning ability was a valid measure of rat intelligence. Though it may be a stretch to link human intelligence to childhood malnutrition because there are so many factors that im pinge on a child's academic performance in elementary school."

"Well I did mention some of the factors affecting learning ability in children – like family background, socioeconomic status,, the school itself – in addition to nutrition. But severe malnutrition early in a child's life has been shown to significantly lower his IQ.

"Was that in the review of past research section? I probably should have read your thesis more carefully, but I've been pressed for time lately," the middle-aged pedagogue admitted.

"Anyway I did mention similar studies on the cognitive effects of protein deprivation on poor children who had been malnourished in early childhood. Average IQ scores of such children were boosted by in creasing tary protein. And the results showed that this intervention had to be done at an early age – like one to four years old," Tom explained.

It was unusual for a professor to admit that he hadn't read a document carefully. The more he learned about Professor Spielman, the more he liked him. Tom was fortunate to have had similar professors at C.C.N.Y. They were dedicated, knowledgeable, honest, and very approachable. Tom vowed that when he was remiss as a teacher, he would admit his negligence to his students in the future.

"Perhaps you ought to include some recommendation to augment protein in poor children's diet – like increasing food stamps and expanding the breakfast program of inner-city schools," Professor Spielman suggested.

"That's a good idea. I'll include that in my conclusion section," Tom replied, thinking he would mention a breakfast program for Curtis students to Lou Stout. Realizing he had a bit more to before putting his 30-page thesis to bed, Tom recalled Yogi Berra's axiom that it ain't over 'til it's over.

"I see the light at the end of the tunnel. Just another paragraph or two and then you're done. It's an ex cellent thesis overall."

"Well thank you. It's been fun working with the rats."

"So what are you going to do with your rats – now that your research is finished?"

"Well, I'm keeping one rat, Mu-Alpha, as a pet and I set the rest free in an abandoned shack in a field under the Bayonne Bridge. I left a month's supply of food in the shack with the door open so the rats could move freely in and out of the shack."

Tom was going to mention that an eccentric Bradford guard was going to take custody of the freed rodents, but thought better of it. His mother's dictum of never volunteering information was beginning to make more and more sense to the skinny science teacher.

After his interview with Professor Spielman, Tom took the 7th Avenue IRT local train downtown to 96th Street and then transferred to the IRT express train. Relieved that his master's thesis had passed muster and tired from working the night shift at the Con Ed plant in Travis, Tom feel asleep on the roaring south bound subway train. He had an eerie dream about a train trip through a desolate tundra dotted with fir trees, frozen rivers, and large furry rodents.

Waking up in Flatbush, Brooklyn, Tom was somewhat disoriented. He went outside to get on the Man hattan bound platform. Suddenly, he was confronted by a fierce, heavyset, man who demanded his wal llet. Startled and confused, Tom froze on the spot. Then, a stranger in dark glasses appeared out of no where, grabbed the would-be mugger, and tossed him on the pavement. The burley thug got up and ran down the street – without looking back. Tom turned to thank his benefactor, who looked vaguely famil iar, but seemed to vanish in the crowd. The he heard the same soft moaning sound and observed the same brightening of the sky when he had appealed to Amon to heal Joanie six months ago. She had been in the throes of her recurrent headaches. After Joanie recovered, Tom felt like he was living in a new age of miracles thanks to Amon – the legendary Mariners Harbor Messiah.

When Tom arrived very late at his second-floor apartment on Pulaski Avenue, Joanie was very worried about him. She feared that the submission of his master's thesis may not have gone smoothly or there may have been delays on the subway and ferry. She had been urging Tom to buy a mobile phone, but the skinny science teacher was a notoriously low-tech guy. He explained that he fell asleep on the train – winding up in Brooklyn.

Then, Tom noticed that Joanie was wearing his Bradford guard uniform – complete with the gray woolen trousers, the gray long-sleeved shirt, gray visor cap, and green tie. "Hey what are you doing in my guard uniform?"

She moved a few steps backward and began singing in her appealing off-key manner:

> *"You wander around on your own little cloud.*
>
> *When you don't see the why or the wherefore*
>
> *Don't sleep in the subways darlin'*
>
> *Don't stand in the pouring rain."*

Tom attempted to remove the Bradford shirt, but Joanie moved deftly out of his reach. She ran into the bedroom – tossing off the shirt and pants, singing Petula Clark's famous 1960s song about sleeping on the subways – pirouetting and swaying – displaying her abundant sensuality to her skinny husband. Be fore long, they were kissing, embracing , and panting like the two star-crossed lovers had done in the small cemetery across from PS 21 so many years ago. Habitually awkward and hesitant in most of life's activities, Tom was able and agile in his couplings with Joanie.

Because of the obstacles and uncertainties in their star-crossed relationship, there was an element of the unreal in their romance. The very fact that they were finally living together was another one of those miracles described by Thomas Wolfe that are unique to America. Incredibly their romance be gan with an adolescent girl calling out to a bumbling softball player. Distracted by the pretty spectator's vocal antics, Tom collided with a teammate – bringing Joanie to his side with a perfumed hanky to stem the oozing blood from his beaklike nose. In actuality, she had seen him in her neighborhood for years delivering the Herald Tribune each morning on his rickety red bicycle. She noted his presence on her street precisely at six-thirty – regardless of the weather or season. On Sundays, he was burdened by the voluminous weekend edition of the venerable newspaper – second only to the New York Times in terms of its comprehensive coverage of local, national, and international events.

"What's the matter? You seem distracted?" Joanie asked, pausing to scrutinize her lover.

"Nothing. I was just thinking about my newspaper route – delivering the Herald Tribune to the house next door to your house."

"Honest, I tried to get my dad to order the Trib, but he said it had stale news."

"Stale news, you say? Well it's better than stale buns," he replied, smacking her plump derriere.

"Why you – skinny beanpole. I'll show you whose stale," she exclaimed, jumping on the wiry science causing him to gasp.

Chapter 28 – A Lesson on Renewable Energy

A few days later. Tom was called upon to cover a class for Bill Lawler's general science freshmen on renewable energy. In response to the energy crisis of the late 1970s, the schools were told to teach alternative energy sources, as well as energy conservation. Flexible and adaptable, Tom, dug into his lesson plans and found material on new energy sources. He also utilized material that his absentcolleague had left for him in his mailbox. Having taught this restive group of Curtis freshmen before,Tom was confident he could handle them. It was no secret that students of absent teachers weren't exactly yearning to be learn something new from a sub – preferring to have a "free" period to do home work from other classes, talk with their friends, or skip class entirely. In such situations, you had to hit the ground running.

On Tom's front desk, was a high-intensity lamp, a radiometer, an electric fan, a miniature windmill, a solar cell, a tiny DC motor, pieces of coal, and a can of motor oil. As the freshmen entered the room and began messing with the radiometer and thc motor, Tom shooed them to their seats. However, Ronnie grabbed the tiny windmill and told Hanna, a new student at Curtis, to blow on the windmill – which she did – causing it to spin. But before Ronnie could make a ruckus about it, Tom clapped his hands loudly a held up some pieces of coal – asking them to identify the mineral.

"That's the stuff Santa puts into your stockings when you're bad. Like this chick here," the rambunctious student replied, pointing to Hanna, who was embarrassed by the attention drawn to her.

"Yeah. Why don't you put a lid on it for awhile?" Roy concurred. Ronnie started to say something to the heavy set JV football player, but thought better of it.

Moving on, Tom asked the class about energy conservation.

"It says that energy can neither be created nor destroyed, but it can be converted into different forms," Robert responded. He was becoming a rare breed at Curtis – a serious student who took notes meticu lously, while ignoring the antics of his classmates.

Turning the fan on and aiming it at the tiny windmill, Tom asked: "So what's the energy conversion going on here?"

"Wind energy into mechanical energy," Roy called out from the back of the classroom.

"Very good. Wind energy and solar energy can never be depleted. Scientists refer to them as renewable energy. Power from waterfalls and the energy from rising and falling ocean levels – called tidal energy are other examples of renewable examples," Tom lectured.

"I remember going to Niagara Falls as a kid. They were so loud, you couldn't hear people talking," Kelly, a bright, ponytailed youngster said. Tom recalled these thunderous waterfalls himself on a rare vacation trip undertaken by his own family in the 1950s.

"I don't know about you guys, but I rather rely on oil and gas to heat my house and run my car. What happens to your electricity when it's a rainy day?" Ronnie complained.

"Yeah. Jimmy Carter had solar panels on the White House roof. He used to go around wearing sweaters all the time. When Reagan came in, he took them off the roof," Roy declared, as the rest of the students nodded in agreement. For the first time, Tom understood the appeal of the former movie actor to Amer ica's silent majority.

"Why do we call coal, oil, and natural gas fossil fuels?"

"Because they come from green plants buried under the earth for millions of years," Kelly answered.

"Why are fossil fuels referred to as hydrocarbons?"

"Coal, oil, and natural gas are composed of hydrogen and carbon bonded together in big molecules," Kelly answered again.

"Wow! That girl has smarts," Ronnie chimed in, bowing towards the pretty coed.

"Coal, oil, and natural gas originated with giant ferns living during the time of the dinosaurs," Tom said.

"Where would we be without plants? We should worship plants instead of biblical figures," Roy declared half seriously.

"We'd be in Never-Never Land. The Indians worshipped trees, animals, and rocks – if I'm not mis taken," Ronnie said.

"What's that called? When you worship objects in nature?" Hanna asked.

"It's called paganism, which also existed in ancient Greece and Rome," Robert responded.

"We're getting off topic guys. What is the scientific name of this light windmill?" Tom asked.

"It's called a radiometer and it converts light energy to kinetic energy," Robert again replied.

"Wow! That guy's the answer man. You should go on that new TV show – Jeopardy ," Roy called out from the back of the room.

"Very good," Tom replied, taking a rubber Spalding out of his pocket, holding it up high, and allowing the ball to fall to the floor. "Describe he energy conversion here." Kelly raised her hand. "When the ball is held up high above the floor, that's potential energy. When it's dropped to the floor, it becomes kinetic energy."

Turning to the blackboard, Tom told the class to get out their notebooks. He wrote the following definitions on the blackboard:

Energy – the ability to do work and move objects.

Ex: light, heat, electricity, chemical & nuclear energy.

Potential Energy – energy due to object's position above the earth. Ex: a box sitting on a roof.

Kinetic Energy – energy of a moving object. Ex: a Spalding thrown across a room.

Chemical Energy – energy stored in the bonds of a molecule. Ex: a gallon of gasoline.

Nuclear Energy – energy stored in the nucleus of uranium and plutonium. Ex: an atom bomb.

Heat – energy of a substance due to the motion of its molecules. Ex: a beaker of boiling water.

"People talk about using solar energy and wind energy. But cars don't run on solar energy. They run on gasoline," Roy called out from the back of the room. Tom noticed that these freshmen had a habit of calling out – without bothering to raise their hands.

"Why don't they just drill for oil in places like Staten Island? Shit, there might be oil in my backyard. Then I'd be richer than the Rockefellers. Drive one of those Mercedes, smOKe a Cuban cigar, and go out with some hot chick," Ronnie surmised.

"That guy's got big ideas. I'd keep your feet on the ground," Hanna.

"If there was any oil on Staten Island, it would have been discovered a long time ago," Johnny spoke out. He was red-haired kid who should little interest in the doings of the class. "Someday we'll run out of fossil fuels like coal, oil, and natural gas. And then we'll have to turn to re newable energy sources like the sun and wind," Tom stated, realizing that his students, like most Ameri cans, assumed that there'd always be plenty of gasoline for their cars.

Turning to the board again, Tom wrote the following information on the board:

Solar Constant = 1.36 kwatts/sq meter

Avg. Wind Speed = 10.3 mi/hr

"Now folks, these numbers represent averages for the entire planet — they are global values. For example the average wind speed is 21.3 mi/hr in South Dakota, while in New York it's only 15.4 mi/hr."

"Aw shucks. I was thinking of putting a windmill in my backyard. Now I'll have to move to some God-for saken state in the Midwest, freezing my butt off – just to get cheap electricity," Johnny, a red-haired kid, called out from the back of the room.

Thinking back to his own high school days, Tom did not recall such widespread breaking of the rules for classroom discussions. Maybe the free exchange of ideas benefited from less rigid rules for the class room. In any case, the changes in all walks of American life in the past twenty years was dramatic.

"Another reason to turn away from fossil fuels is the greenhouse effect. Does anyone know what that is?" Tom asked, pushing forward despite his students' indifference to environmental issues.

As Robert raised his hand, the class groaned: "The burning of fossil fuels builds up CO2 levels – trapping the earth's heat and raising temperatures – like a giant greenhouse."

"That's a good thing. Nobody likes winter except those white-boy ice skaters and skiers," Ronnie snapped.

Again Robert raised his hand, to the dismay of the class: "The polar icecaps will melt, causing ocean levels to rise. And coastal areas, like Manhattan and Staten Island could be under water."

"Thanks for your upbeat outlook – Mr. Doomsday," Hanna, the new girl, exclaimed.

At that point, the bell sounded ending the general science class and dispersing the merry freshmen into the long dark hallways – untroubled by the prospect of boiling hot summers and rising ocean levels. As a youngster, Tom was different. He remembered having nightmares about nuclear war with Russian bombers flying overhead – carrying hydrogen bombs ready to drop on the Smith's narrow six-room house, the nearby turkey cage, and the more distant long chicken coop. This was during the 1950s when Cold War tensions between America and Russia put the world under the hair-trigger threat of nuclear Armageddon. From the perspective of nuclear war, the threat of global warming seemed like small potatoes to the current crop of teenagers.

Chapter 29 – A Trip to the Country

It was early April, Tom's favorite time of the year when Joanie began talking about a getting a dog to keep her company when Tom was teaching or moonlighting at the Con Ed plant in Travis."It's lonely around here – especially when you're working the graveyard shift for that Bradford guard outfit."

"The last thing I want to do is walk a dog after a long day of teaching or a hard night at that Con Ed plant with those nutty guards and their snapping turtles and coyote pups."

"Talking about coyote puppies. They're supposed to make good pets," Joanie replied, half-seriously.

"They're wild animals. You might as well adopt a wolf pup. Then I'll come home to find a wolf dressed up in your pajamas waiting in bed for me."

"Yeah. You'd go to bed with it and wouldn't even know the difference."

"Yes I would. You're legs aren't quite as hairy as a wolf's and your teeth are a bit shorter."

Grabbing a frying pan from the cupboard, Joanie began chasing around the house – whacking the skinny science teacher on his backside from time to time. Out of breath, Tom held up his hand and offered the following compromise. They would take a trip to Bloomington, South Jersey and adopt a pet cat from his his faster mother, Granny Smith.

"She has a fertile female that has a litter of adorable kittens every spring. When it comes to pets, I pre fer felines to canines."

"Why's that – teacher man?"

"You don't have to walk cats. Remember – it's not going to be spring all year long. Before long, winter will be rolling along – accompanied by ice and snow. Even with global warming, the cold weather is sure to return. How would you like to climb over snow drifts, looking for a place where Fido can take a steam ing dump."

"Gee Tom. You're so descriptive with your language. You ought to be a poet. I hereby crown you poet laureate of Pulaski Avenue," Joanie proclaimed, bopping him g on the head with her frying pan – a bit harder than she intended.

"Ow ! That hurt. You really clonked me with that frying pan."

"Sorry! Sorry! I didn't mean to hit you so hard," she responded, rubbing his head and smothering him with kisses.

"Wow. With you it's either pleasure or pain – no in-between."

"When it comes to boredom or excitement – I chose the latter," she replied, sitting her husband on a kit chen chair and plopping herself roughly on his lap.

"Well, I don't have any kittens for you. Puss is getting to be an old-timer. She smacks any tomcat that tries to get friendly. Let's see what we have in the chicken coop," his foster mother said, putting on a old winter coat.

As the threesome trekked up the long winding path to the chicken coop, Tom recalled the countless time he had made that pleasant walk. Despite the bright April sunshine, it was a chilly day with a bite of winter in the breeze. Global warming notwithstanding, winter was reluctant to give way to spring throughout the northeast. In recent years, spring weather existed only for a few weeks – giving way to the heat of summer by the middle of May.

As expected, the chicken coop had a room with a mother hen with several fluffy yellow-feather chicks hovering around her – pecking at some grains scattered on the concrete floor. The other rooms were empty except for the last room which emanated a strong porcine odor. Moving around this room were several pink and white piglets, which oinked, squealed, and jostled each other – competing for food in a long trough. In addition to the dry feed in the trough, there were pieces of such vegetables as lettuce, carrots, celery, and potatoes – plus slices of apple, orange, and grapes strewn on the concrete floor.

"Pick one. They make good pets – smarter than dogs and easier to housebreak."

"In other words, you have to walk 'em – like a dog? I was looking for a pet you don't have to walk," Tom said, eying the squabbling pigs nervously.

"As a kid, you used to roam all over this 12-acre farm. Now you telling me you don't like walking?" Gran ny Smith asked, looking from Tom to his pretty wife, who smiled innocently.

"Oh no, walking's good. But right now I'm doing some moonlighting as a guard at a Con Ed plant – the nightshift."

"I thought you were on a sabbatical right now. Doing an experiment with rats for your master's."

"Well, I finished that. But I'm doing some day-to-day subbing at my school for extra money, besides the Bradford guard job at the power plant."

"You'll like the pig. They make great pets. You don't want your wife to be alone all day? Pigs are very loyal. It's like having a watch dog," Granny Smith said, stifling a smile.

"But it's gonna get big. Right?"

"This breed doesn't grow that big. They're bacon pigs – raised to make bacon. Put newspapers down in the kitchen until it's housebroken."

"My mom may not be crazy about the idea of having a pig right upstairs, in her house."

"Pigs don't bark and they don't bite people. She might even grow to like her," his foster mom said, nod ding at Joanie. Clearly, there was no love lost between Tom's two mothers.

"Well, what do you think?"

"She's kind of cute. There was this pig farm I visited in Indiana. Some of them were huge," Joanie said.

"Remember that pig I took care of as a kid? She ate a lot and grew pretty fast."

"If she gets too big, you can sell her to a butcher," Granny Smith said in a matter-of-manner.

"We'd never sell her to a butcher. Staten Island has a petting zoo. They would take her – right Tom?"

Nodding to his pretty wife, Tom asked, "Is this the kind of pet you're looking for?"

Joanie looked over the squealing piglets, "You know what Mrs. Smith? I think we'll take a rain check on the pet pig idea. Tom's got enough on his plate without worrying about walking a pig or even a dog morning, noon, and night."

"The pigs are cute, but they're a high maintenance pet. It's a bit more than we can chew right now. And my mom would have a fit if she saw me coming down the steps to walk porker," Tom concurred

He recalled a few times when the pigs on the Smith farm had gotten loose – brOKen out of their smelly pigpen. Those seemingly ponderous, slippery-skinned animals could move fast when they were freed from their smelly corrals. Cornering the errant pigs and shooing them back into their fenced-in pens was no easy job. But they were fun times for Tom and Cara – a unique excuse for tardiness to school that could not be used when they moved to Staten Island: the pigs had gotten loose.

Chapter 30 – The Rookie Bradford Guard

Back at the Con Ed plant, Tom worked the midnight shift with a rookie Bradford guard, named Rosa. Unlike Jake and Billy, Rosa took her guard duties seriously. Reportedly she put Jake in his place when he started to come on to her. Married with two children, she studied from a high school equivalency exam manual in between her inspection tours of the power plant. When Billy talked about looking for the legendary snapping turtle in the swamp across the road, she told him that to " leave the lizards and turtles alone and stick to your job, man."

Rosa brought her own coffee in a large metal thermos, along with pepper and sausage roll. At one point she was struggling with a word problem, which she read to Tom:

"Bert can paint a room in three hours, while Ernie can paint the same room in four hours. How long will it take the two friends to paint the room together?"

"If you add the times, the answer would be seven hours. But that seems too easy," she declared unsure of herself.

"You're right. Since Bert can paint the room by himself in three hours, if he gets some help – it should take less time to do the room. The right approach is to look at the problem from the rate of work, which is the reciprocal of the time," Tom explained.

Borrowing her pencil time wrote the formula for rate of work:

Rate = 1/Time

"You're going to add the rates of work of Bert and Ernie and set it equal to the unknown cumulative rate."

1/3 + 1/4 = 1/T

"Then to solve the fractional equation, you have to multiply both sides by the LCD, which is 12 T."

Going through the algebraic manipulations, Tom arrived at an answer of 1 5/7 hours.

"The answer is a mixed number, slightly less than two hours. Which, if you think about it, makes sense," Tom said in his didactic tone.

"Oh, yeah. It's as clear as mud. But you're a good teacher. I just have to remember to flip over the time to do the job instead of adding the times like regular numbers."

"A lot of things in math and science don't always follow common sense. If you drop a rock and a piece of paper from a window, the rock falls faster than the paper. But that's due to air resistance and not gravity alone."

Tom took a dime and a quarter out of his pocket, held them above his head and dropped them to the floor. They hit the floor simultaneously. "Galileo proved that all objects fall at the same rate of speed due to gravity by dropping two rocks of different sizes from the Leaning Tower of Pisa." "Yeah. I remember learning about that in school. Didn't Galileo get in trouble for that discovery?"

"Yes he did. During the Middle Ages, there was a conflict between the Church and Science."

"Sometimes the Catholic Church sticks its nose where it don't belong. Don't get me wrong – I'm Catho lic myself. But the priest has no right to tell me what to do in my private life," she asserted, crossed her self.

Tom hid a smile. "Are you Catholic," she inquired.

"Isn't everyone?"

Returning after a midnight stint at the Con Ed power plant in Travis, Tom was given the phone, which had just starting ringing as he slowly mounted the narrow stairs.

"Who is it this time?"

"It's that new math teacher, Miss Green. I need you to cover her algebra and statistics classes for a cou ple of days. Same pay – $150 off the books per diem. But leave the pig home, unless you plan to cook pork chops for the kids."

"No. We decided to forgo the pig. But if you want one, I know where you get a cute piglet," Tom replied wondering how his boss knew about the pet pig idea. Despite its recent growth, Staten Island still func tioned like a small town – especially the North Shore.

"Miss Green said she'd put some notes in your mailbox. So you're all set. Take care of your new pet – make sure it doesn't crap on the sidewalk."

Chapter 31 – A Lesson on Probability

Tom entered the senior math class, carrying the following props: a deck of cards, a pair of dice, a Ken nedy half-dollar, a five-colored spinner wheel, and a Farmer's Almanac. The seniors actually cheered the skinny teacher's entrance – an unexpected warm welcome – which puzzled Tom. But he realized that teenagers were fickle in their likes and dislikes. He would do his job, teach the lesson, and let the chips fall the way fate had intended. Turning to the blackboard, Tom wrote the aim on the board: What is probability?

"It tells when something is unlikely to happen – like a teacher walking a pig on the street," Kenny, the school's star basketball player, with whom Tom had played hoops at the P. S. 21 schoolyard.

"Is that true, Mr. Haley? Do you have a pet pig?" Lulu asked, rattling her silver bracelets and anklets.

"The rumors about a pet pig are without substance. But getting back to the matters at hand, what's the probability of me flipping this coin and getting three heads in a row?"

"It's ½ times ½ times ½ or 1/8," George answered. He was a serious student, who paid attention and took notes carefully. George was a throwback from earlier times when students went to school primarily to learn something.

"Suppose I flipped this coin fives in a row and got five heads. What's the probability that the next coint toss will be heads?"

Again George raised his hand, "It's still ½ because the coin doesn't remember what it did before."

"Good. What if I toss this die. What's the probability of getting a one?"

Hank called out from the back of the room: "It's 1/6."

Turning to the blackboard, Tom wrote the probability formula on the board:

Probability = Favorable Outcomes / Total Outcomes

or: P = F/N

Holding up the five-colored spinner wheel, Tom asked the probability of the spinner landing on red or blue. Again, Hank called out from the back of the room: "It's 2/5."

"Excellent. Notice that probability has range between zero and one. You can never get a probability less than zero or more than one."

"The probability of living forever is zero and the probability of paying taxes is one. So death and taxes are certain events," Kenny replied.

Next, Tom discussed the difference between permutations, where order counts, and combinations, where order does not count – only belonging to the group or not matters. He also wrote the corres ponding formulas for those concepts. He also reviewed the factorial symbol and how to compute it. A student from the back of the room indicated that Miss Green had already covered those topics.

"That's fine, but a little review doesn't hurt. Repetition is the key to mastering concepts in all fields of learning. A good work ethic is critical to success from carpentry to calculus," Tom stated calmly.

"Suppose you had four pairs of socks mixed up in your drawer. You reach in and grab two socks. What's the probability you get a matching pair?"

Susan raised her hand. Like George, she had a genuine interest in learning something new each and every day. " After grabbing the first sock, there seven socks left – one of which matches the first sock.

So the probability would be 1/7."

Tom understood that such intrinsic motivation, the thirst for knowledge, was a rarity in the present era. The million dollar question for teachers was how to ignite that spark for learning in all kids – regardless of their background.

Turning to the board, Tom wrote the two problems for the class to solve.

#1. The probability CVS has flu shots is 0.47, while the probability Walgreen's has flu shots is 0.59. find the probability that (a) both stores have flu shots (b) neither store has flu shots (c) one of the stores has flu shots.

#2. The probability that Joe moves furniture is 0.32. The probability that Joe will hurt his back when he moves furniture is 0.64. The probability Joe will hurt his back anytime is 0.21. Find the probability that (a) Joe moves furniture and hurts his back (b) Joe moves furniture or hurts his back.

#3. Suppose ten people are standing in front of an elevator, which can hold only six people. How many different groups of six people can go into the elevator?

#4. How many different ways can six people line up in front of a candy machine?

#5. How many different meals can a restaurant offer if it serves three beverages, five appetizers, eight entrees , and four desserts?

#6. How many different ways can the letters of the work "success" be arranged?

#7. Only two passengers, Bill and Bob, are left on a bus, with four stops remaining. Assuming they don't know each other, find the probability the two men get off at same stop.

"I'll give you guys 15 minutes to work out these problems," Tom announced.

"Does this count?" Kenny asked.

" Sometimes, two heads are better than one. You can work on the problems with a neighbor. Put that person's name down on the paper, along with your name."

After the allotted time, Tom wrote answers on the board. He allowed the groups to grade their own pa per. He would leave them in Miss Green's mailbox to handle them herself. Each teacher had a different approach with regard to grading quizzes.

#1 (a) 0.277 (b) 0.217 (c) 0.506

#2 (a) 0.205 (b) 0.325

#3 210 groups

#4 720 ways

#5 480 meals

#6 420 ways

#7 0.25

"What about those lottery problems? You can't get into the newspaper store where I live, when they're running one of those mega- lotteries?" Kenny asked.

Before Tom could answer the question, the bell sounded ending the class and dispersing them into Curtis's long dark hallways. Unlike, the outcome of a coin flip or a die toss, the route of the students was fairly probable – they were likely heading for lunch, study hall, or their next class.

On the following day, Tom had the coins, the dice, the deck of cards, the spinner wheel, and the farmer's almanac as on the previous day. Holding the spinner wheel up, he asked the probability of the pointer landing on a particular color.

"That's easy – 1/5. And for two colors, like red or blue, it would be 2/5," Kenny answered..

"What is I spun it three times in a row – getting three reds in a row?"

"Just as easy – 1/5 times 1/5 times 1/5 or 1/125," Kenny answered again.

"Would that be an unusual event?" Tom asked.

George raised his hand. "Yes, because 1/125 is 0.008 which is less than 0,05 the probability of an unusual event.

 "Very good. You guys are on your game today."

"Unlike like you the day I played basketball with you at P. S. 21," Kenny observed.

"Perhaps a rematch is in the works," Tom replied reflexively. "But I'll need time to get in shape."

"Spot him ten points in a game of twenty-one," Hank called out from the back of the room.

"Sounds fair enough to me," Kenny replied.

"Anyway, getting back to the matter at hand. I want to talk about probability distributions. When it comes to data for large numbers of people – like height, weight, SAT scores, IQ scores, even the lengths of driftwood found at a beach. The data would follow the shape of a normal curve, which has a certain symmetry."

"But doesn't some data form an asymmetrical curve?" Susan inquired.

Turning to the blackboard, Tom drew three distributions on the board. "The first one is the normal curve. It's symmetrical – with the mean, median, and mode at the center. The second one is positively skewed – with mean displaced to the right. And the third one is negatively skewed – with the mean dis placed to the left."

As the students, copied the three distributions into their notebooks, Tom asked for examples of the two skewed distributions.

Again Susan raised her hand. "Positively skewed would be income in the U. S. A., where mean income is greater than median income due to millionaires who affect the mean more than the median. Negatively skewed would be income in Switzerland, where median income is greater than mean income."

"Very good. As far as America is concerned, the median income is a better measure of the middle than the mean income. If you earn the median income, it means half the population is below you and half is above you."

"So what is the median income in the good old U. S. of A.?" Hank called out from the back of the class.

"Remember that lottery problem from yesterday. We'll compute the probability of choosing five correct numbers out of forty numbers. Lotteries are combinations because the numbers chosen – not the order counts. So we're talking about the number of different groups of 5 out of 40."

Susan raised her hand. "That would be 40C5, the number of combinations of 40 objects, taken 5 at a time – forty factorial divided by thirty-five factorial times five factorial."

Tom wrote her answer on the board as: 40!/35!5!. He then had the class evaluate it. After extensive computations, Kenny came up with the correct answer: 658,000.

Applying the probability formula; $P = F/N$, Tom wrote the answer on the board:

$P = 1/658{,}000 = 0.0000015$

"Who can read that decimal?"

"It's read as fifteen ten-millionths," Susan answered.

"Why is the numerator one?" Lulu asked, rattling her silver bracelet.

"Because there's only one combination of winning numbers out of the 658,000," Kenny answered.

"You're absolutely right. I think you guys have a flair for statistics."

"I'm ready to go to Atlantic City and play those one-arm bandits and roulette wheels," Hank called out from the back of the room. Several others concurred with his sentiments.

"Remember the odds are stacked against you. The longer you play these games of chance, the more likely you will lose. Given enough time, the house will prevail," Tom declared.

"Suppose you flipped a coin a hundred times and found that heads came up 66 times ? Or you tossed a die a hundred times and found that six came up 30 times?" Susan asked.

"Then, it could be that the coin is not a fair coin and the die is not a fair die. But to be certain, I would repeat the hundred coin flips and the hundred die tosses to see if I get the same outcomes," Tom said.

"You're talking about the law of large numbers. Probability experiments approach the theoretical ratio of favorable outcomes to total outcomes for large numbers of trials," George replied.

"That's true. If I toss a coin five times and get five heads in a row, what's the probability?"

"The probability is ½ times ½ times ½ times ½ times ½ or 1/32," Kenny answered.

"You're absolutely right. Now convert it to a decimal."

"That would be 0.03125 or three thousand one hundred twenty-five hundred-thousandths," Hank called out from the back of the room.

"What would you say about that coin?" Tom inquired.

"I'd say the friggin' coin is crooked," Jerry said. He had been following the class discussion, in lieu of the doings outside the window.

Showing the class the Farmer's Almanac, Tom said it had weather forecasts for each day of the year. "What kind of probability is reflected in the almanac's weather predictions?"

Susan raised her hand. "It's empirical probability – based on past records going back a hundred years."

"That's right. Although it has been shown that the Farmer's Almanac is only 52% correct with its pre dictions. Nowadays, weather forecasts are approximately 75% accurate."

"Most of it is just common sense. Everybody knows it's not going to snow in July and thunderstorms don't happen in January," Kenny remarked.

"You're right. Those are examples of empirical probability – based on recorded data over many years.As I said earlier, you guys have a knack for the notorious science of statistics."

"Why is statistics called the notorious science?" Lulu asked, rattling her bracelets and anklets.

"Because, it was started by a bunch of rich guys in the Middle Ages. You know – noblemen like dukes and princes – who had both the money and the time to spend on gambling."

"Well, much as I like shooting craps and playing cards – I prefer games of skill, like basketball, to games of chance," Kenny said.

"That's right. It's stupid to piss away your hard-earned money on games of chance," Hank concurred.

"Here's a game – called the shell game. I guy has three walnut shells with a diamond under one of them. He moves the shells around quickly. Suppose you play three games. What's the probability of guessing correctly one out of three times?"

Susan raised her hand. "It would be one-third."

"It's an example of a two-outcome problem – win or lose. It's called the binomial distribution," Tom said, writing the binomial probability formula on the blackboard.

$$P(x) \;=\; n!/x! \,(n-x)! \; p^x q^{n-x}$$

"x = 1, the number of correct guesses, out of n = 3, the number of games played, p = 1/3, the probability of guessing right, and q = 2/3, the probability of guessing wrong. Plug in the numbers and tell me the answer you arrive at."

After a few minutes, Susan gave her answer: "12/27 or 4/9"

"That's right. So the probability of guessing right once out of three games is higher than one-third," Tom explained.

"The next time I see the shell game on the street, I'm gonna play it," Kenny vowed.

"Be careful. Those street game players use slight of hand. Remember, the hand is faster than the eye." "Yeah. My fist is even faster than their hand," Kenny responded heatedly.

"Shakespeare once said – these violent delights have violent ends," Tom responded, as the bell rang – ending the class and dispersing the students to the four winds.

Lulu dallied momentarily. "I know another Shakespeare quote that's applies – discretion is the better part of valor."

"That's super Lulu. I'll have to remember that the next time one of my students gets too macho."

Pleased with her teacher's response, Lulu marched down the long dark hall,, jingle-jangling her silver bracelets and anklets. Unknowingly, she was the 1980s version of Lora who had done the same a doz en years before – walking musically through Curtis's hallowed hallways.

Chapter 32 – Aesthetics and Metaphysics

Tom and Joanie decided to celebrate the tenth anniversary of their reunion at Kaffman's bar on a busy Friday in April – the cruelest month according to T. S. Eliot. It was especially cruel to his former girlfriend, Martha, who reacted with the unique fury of a spurned female. In truth, Martha had broken off with the skinny science teacher because of his alleged lack of commitment. The entrance of Joanie to the crowded saloon was followed by Tom magical awareness of her presence and Martha's hot-tempered reaction to their chance rendezvous. The sturdy elementary schoolteacher sent Tom sprawling to the floor with one punch. The females passed each other like two ships in the gray, choppy waters of the Kill Van Kull – Martha storming out the door and Joanie crouching over the fallen science teacher.

As Joanie daubed his bloody nose with her perfumed hankie, Tom remarked that they should stop meet ing like this. She told him to shut up: "Why don't you learn to how to duck when people swing at you?" Tom blamed it on the full moon and the fact that he was an easy target, The passing ten years had changed many things, but their love blossomed – surviving the humdrum ups and downs of working, shopping, paying bills, maintaining a home, and keeping body and soul intact against the ravages of time. The patron of their love, Amon, was no longer around. But Tom felt a his benevolence as surely as a child feels the celestial warmth of a guardian angel.

As the star-crossed teenaged lovers entered, the hazy sweet-sour smelling bar, Rudy Kaffman greeted them as usual. "Well the prodigal son has returned with his better-half. A Ballantine for Tom and what does the young lady want?'

"Just a club soda for me. One of us has to keep his wits," Joanie replied as she looked around the poorly lit saloon. Unlike Tom, she was never comfortable in gin-mills.

Looking around the dingy saloon, Tom noticed Martha sitting at the end of the bar with a guy. "I think we should leave. I just noticed my ex."

"There's no need to leave. We'll take a seat at a table, have a drink, and enjoy ourselves," Joanie said, moving to a table by the window. "You're right. The Haley family's been loyal patrons of Kaffman 's since the 1950s. We've spent a lot of hard-earned dollars on booze.

"Well, I wouldn't brag about that fact. But I get your point. And it's a free country," Joanie replied.

As Tom nursed his beer and Joanie sipped her club soda, Martha got up and walked over to them with a smug expression – as Tom braced for trouble.

"Well, well – look who's here. The playboy of the western world. Has he put a ring on your finger?'

Joanie smiled sweetly and extended her left hand. There was a small, but nicely cut diamond on her ring finger. Martha responded by thrusting her left hand with a sizeable stone under Joanie's nose.

Flinching at the tall young woman's aggressive action, Joanie looked at the proffered ring and oohed – indicating she was impressed.

"I'm getting married in June. What about you guys?" Martha asked with a steely smile.

Before either Tom or Joanie could respond, Harry the Horse walked over to the table and put his arm around Martha. "Hey babe, I think your boyfriend's getting lonely since you ditched him at the bar. You don't want one of the vultures to grab him."

Years ago, when Tom was a youngster, Harry would walk down Pulaski Avenue with a Spalding and a stickball bat. Soon a rousing game of stickball would ensue, which occasionally ended with the ball smashing someone's window – often Mrs. Eggers, who lived across the street from Tom. Always the good sport, Harry would fork over the twenty dollars to fix the window. Granny Schmidt, an alcoholic dowager, was another unhappy spectator of the stickball street games. Presumably, the noisy game woke her from her booze-induced nap. A string of fearsome epithets would issue from her mouth — aimed at Harry and his adolescent cohorts. Never the faint-hearted type, Harry answered in kind the invectives launched at him by the angry women on opposite sides of the street.

Shrugging her wide shoulders and forcing a smile, Martha left Tom and Joanie and pranced back to her stool at the bar.

"I think she was getting ready to punch you out Tom. Hell hath no fury like a woman scorned," Harry re marked, winking at Joanie. Then turning to Tom, "How 'd you like to make some money? I need some extra hands to paint a big Victorian house in West Brighton.

"How much?" Tom asked. The Bradford guard job at the Con Ed plant was losing its appeal. Boredom had driven him and his coworkers to mess around with critters in the swamps adjacent to the guard house.

"One hundred books a day — off the books — plus a couple of beers at the end of the day."

"I get $150 per diem for subbing at Curtis — off the books," Tom replied. But then he remembered that Lou Stout had gone back on his word with regard to paying off the books. He had been paid by check, minus the many deductions for city, state, and federal taxes.

"OK, I'll give it a shot. My dad was a house painter. It's an honest living and you don't have to worry about snapping turtles and coyotes."

"Snapping turtles and coyotes?" Harry asked.

"I did some moonlighting at the Con Ed plant in Travis. Some of the guys there were messing around with the local beasts from the swamp. Boredom is a terrible thing."

"You'll be too busy slapping paint on walls to worry about critters. We work eight hours a day — except for a half-hour lunch break. If you know anybody else who's interested in an honest day's work, bring them along."

"I ran into Willie Worthington from Pulaski Avenue. He got laid off at Sears Roebuck on Forest Avenue and was looking for work. And there's this woman guard at that Con Ed plant who said she was looking to do some moonlighting," Tom mentioned.

"I remember Willie from the stickball games on your block – a black kid. But a woman I don't know about."

"Rosa's a no-nonsense hard worker. Put a stop to all the bullshit with the snapping turtle and the coyote."

"OK, I'll give the gal a shot. It's like a reunion of all the Elm Park kids from the old days. A motley crew if there ever was one."

"Harry was a great stickball player back in the day. He was unbeaten at fast-pitch stickball until Amon smacked a 300-foot homerun on him at P. S. 21."

"Beginner's luck. But that guy was a pretty good hitter. Quick reflexes and very strong. Remember when He lifted that big two-by-four off me in that house in Port Richmond?"

"Amon healed my headaches just by touching my forehead. I can't believe he's gone," Joanie said.

"There are times I feel his presence. He helped when I was mugged in Brooklyn a few months ago," Tom replied, as Harry gave him a funny look.

"My daughter is studying the ancient Greeks. Who was the guy that said that virtue is knowledge?' Harry asked. "Since I didn't go to college, I'm not only ignorant but a bad person."

"That was Socrates, who taught Plato. Plato talked about two realities – the world of objects and the world of ideas. In other words, this wooden table we're sitting at and the idea of a table, which is more real than the physical table itself," Tom explained.

"Is that what you teach the kids at Curtis? If your boss hears you talking about a real table and an imagi nary table – he'll think you're nuts."

"I'm a science teacher. I don't teach philosophy. But maybe it wouldn't be a bad idea to teach the stu dents some philosophy – like the Stoics, who stressed virtue. Or maybe the ethics of Immanuel Kant. Kant proposed his categorical imperative – a universal rule of behavior which applies to all people, in all cultures, over all times."

"We wouldn't need all that stuff if everybody followed the Ten Commandments. The schools should teach practical things that you need to survive – plumbing, carpentry, painting, and common sense," Harry replied.

"Maybe the school should go back to the three Rs – reading, writing, and arithmetic," Joanie chimed in.

"Well, some philosophy makes sense, like Rene Descartes, who said I think therefore I exist," Tom said.

"My daughter said there was a guy, named Hume, who claimed there was no such thing as objects – only what our senses tell us – light, sound, shape, volume, and weight," Harry replied, draining his beer.

"That's correct. Bertrand Russell made the same argument. The only thing we can be sure of is our sen sory data. He said physical objects are just collections of sensory data – mental concepts formed from a lifetime of sensory experience."

Rapping the table and getting up to leave, Harry said: "Maybe I'm crazy, but this table seems real enough to me."

Tom and Joanie followed suit – neither was anxious to have another confrontation with Martha, whose ample physicality brought to mind that mighty race of Amazons who terrorized ancient Greece. Having been on the receiving end of physical violence as a young man, the skinny science teacher had no doubt that physical objects like fists and feet were more than bundled sensory data.

Walking down Morningstar Road and turning down Walker Street, Joanie asked, "What's the difference between physics and metaphysics?"

"Physics explains the laws governing physical objects, motion, and energy. The theories of physics are validated through observation and experiment. Whereas metaphysics has to do with ultimate reality of the universe – concepts like god, ethics, mortality versus immortality. "

"In other words, physics is the how and metaphysics is the why," Joanie observed.

"That's a good way of putting it. A philosopher by the name of Bradley once said that metaphysics is the finding of bad reasons for what we believe upon instinct."

"So what did Bradley believe in – ideas floating in the air like soap bubbles?" "Actually you're right. Bradley was like Plato. He said that the only real things are what he referred to as mental entities or ideas."

"This philosophy seems so removed from the everyday world of jobs, bills, taxes, rents, and the neces sities of life," Joanie commented.

"Now you sound like my mother – food, clothing, and shelter."

"What's so bad about that? Maybe you need some old-fashioned discipline," she replied with a smile.

"Sounds good to me," Tom concurred with a bigger smile.

Tom had picked up Rosa and Willie on the corner of Walker and Morningstar Road at seven-thirty in the morning in his beat-up Pontiac and drove to the West Brighton house, which was located in a nice resi dential area off Forest Avenue. He actually looked forward a day of house painting instead of hassling with the Curtis kids as substitute for their absent teacher. He'd be back as a fulltime science teacher soon enough and teacher burnout was a common phenomenon in public schools throughout the land. Ideally, people should have two different jobs – one utilizing brain power and the other requiring manu el strength.

Chapter 33 – Workaday Rhythm

Harry was already at work in the big Victorian house, sanding and scraping the walls – removing all flecked paint. Soon Willie and Tom joined Harry with the scraping and sanding, while Rosa swept out the accumulated dust and dirt from the floors. The house appeared to have been unlived in for several years. Fortunately, the sinks and toilets worked satisfactorily and no windows were broken. Most im portantly, the roof looked OK and did not leak and the basement showed no signs of flooding. Like most 19th century houses, the walls were made from real plaster and not thin wall boards, And the base boards, window frames, staircases, and floors were made of natural wood – eastern white pine. Upon inspecting the floors, Harry decided that a coat of varnish was sufficient to render them satisfactory. Harry undertook this job himself with the help of Willie while Tom and Rosa cleaned out the attic and the cellar, which had accumulated boxes of old clothes, piles of newspapers , plus stacks of books. The latter, Tom went through – saving some novels for himself and a complete set of encyclopedias for Rosa.

Before long the four-person crew was busy applying a primer on all the interior walls. An old-school workman, Harry would not apply the actual paint until the following day. The second day was spent scraping the outside of the house. Tom and Rosa were given the task of raking the backyard and clipping the hedges. There was also a huge tree limb which had to sawed into smaller pieces and stacked into a pile. Since the house had a fireplace, Harry said it might serve as firewood by a future owner. The job of trimming the front hedge was delegated to Tom. As an Elm Park resident, Harry had seen Tom cutting the formidable front hedge in front of his Pulaski Avenue house over the years. Tom and Rosa worked well together as a team. At one point, he had praised Rosa on her good work ethic.

"What did you expect, sir? We Chicano's know how to work – it's in our blood!"

"So what kind of work does your husband do?"

"He's in California picking lettuce, broccoli, grapes, avocados – you name it," Rosa replied.

"That's back-breaking work," Harry commented.

"Damned right! And you have to know what you're doing. You gotta work fast and careful. So you don't spoil the fruit."

"How are they paid?"

"By how much they pick each day. It's gotten better thanks to the farm workers union – Cesar Chavez."

"I'm not in favor of unions," Harry started to say, but stopped when Rosa gave him an angry look. "But in some circumstances – like coal miners and crop pickers – they're needed."

Eavesdropping on their conversation, Tom was reminded of what so many people had said about his mom : This Rosa woman was one tough cookie. With regard to work ethic, Tom recalled the Brooklyn Dodger , George Shuba, who swung a 44-ounce baseball bat 600 times a day during the offseason.

As with most jobs, there's a certain rhythm you get into and then time flows and the work progresses. With teaching, Tom found this special rhythm midway during the second period. With manual labor, it occurred after the first hour, when his motions became more machinelike and time seemed to speed up magically. An old-school carpenter identified the secret of getting through a long workday, don't watch the clock. Let time work for you. Years ago, Tom knew a man who worked on an automobile assembly line – not the most exciting work. But he was philosophic about his repetitive, routine job. Asserting that you have to put your time in somewhere and a job requiring little thought gave you the time to think about stuff you were interested in. His interest? Old photographs of Staten Island's North Shore, which were eventually published in book that received some acclaim awhile back.

Recently, his mom contacted a roofer to repair some leaks on her gently sloping flat roof. A white man in a business suit came to the house to have the contract signed. The next day two Spanish men in over alls arrived, climbed up a tall ladder and spent most of the day replacing the eroded shingles and sealing the cracks with tar. He could hear them chattering, laughing, and working steadily – taking a short break for lunch – completing the work precisely at four o'clock. The roof job cost $800 – including $100 for materials, which left $700 for labor. Tom estimated that the roofers were paid $10 per hour each, which amounted to $160 for the two men – leaving a tidy profit of $540 for the man in the business suit.

It called to mind the Marxist term "surplus value" in which the capitalist retains a hefty portion of the wages earned by his factory workers. As youngsters, Tom and Cara were lectured by their mom on the fundamental inequities built into capitalism. Yet, the inequities, injustices, and persecutions existing in the Soviet Union were far greater than the economic disparities of the U. S. A. There was something to be said for the Bill of Rights which guaranteed all Americans freedom of speech, press, religion, the security of your home, the right to trial by jury, and most importantly – the right to privacy. With regard to the second amendment – the right to carry a gun – Tom wasn't so sure about. Although Leibniz's con cept of the best of all possible worlds had not been realized anywhere on the globe, it's closest approxi mation had been achieved in the good old U. S. of A.

After two-and-a-half weeks, the Victorian house in West Brighton had undergone a near miraculous transformation—with the rooms freshly painted, the floors varnished, and the siding aglow with pale blue paint. Except for a serviceable kitchen table and chairs, plus two end tables with working lamps, all the furniture had been removed from the house. In addition, there was a small book case that Tom was allowed to take for his own use. The grass in the backyard was trimmed along with an ancient maple tree. In the front yard a rose bush was freed from some strangling vines and an overgrown hedge was cut to a modest five-foot height with rounded contours that invited entry to a freshly painted porch.

Looking over their work, Tom declared: "I'd buy this house myself, if I the money for a down payment." Rosa concurred with the skinny teacher's sentiments as did Willie. The dream of owning your own house was nearly universal among Americans from the working class, to the middle class, to the upper class. Everybody wanted that little patch of grass you could call your own. Under Ronald Reagan's trickle down economics, home ownership had declined. It appeared that the trickle of money from the rich to the poor had thinned to a mere drizzle.

Harry led his motley work crew of Tom, Rosa, and Willie into Kaffman's bar where they grabbed a table near the back and plopped down wearily. "I'm treating guys. As far as eats is concerned, you have your choice between peanuts and pretzels – which is all Rudy serves."

Everybody, including Rosa, requested Ballantine beer. Immediately four overfilled glasses of that popu lar beverage were plopped on the table, along with the usual bowls of peanuts and pretzels by the red faced Rudy Kaffman. For Tom the Elm Park saloon had a special history. It had been the favorite hang out of his alcoholic father. His mom had paid occasional visits to the establishment to harangue Rudy about his serving liquor to Thomas Haley. She used the term "blood money" to characterize this prac tilce. To his credit, Rudy Kaffman had ceased selling booze to his dad, who strolled a few blocks down Morningstar Road where other saloons were happy to take his business. Whether out of guilt or senti mentality, Rudy greeted Tom's initial entry to his place with the words "prodigal son" – dispensing his first beer with the words "on the house."

"So which one of you guys want to buy the house?" Harry asked, as he sipped his beer.

"How much you want for it?" Rosa asked, winking at Tom.

"My asking price is one seventy-five, but for any of you guys – one hundred seventy ," Harry replied with a sly grin.

"That's beyond me," Rosa replied, as Tom and Willie concurred.

At that moment, Tom caught sight of Martha sitting at the bar with her new boyfriend. As luck would have it, she turned and gave him a look that would have scared a grizzly bear.

Marching over to the group, Martha said, "Look who's slumming with the neighborhood playboy – the Pied Piper of Elm Park and his merry gang of street sweepers."

"We were renovating a house in West Brighton," Harry said, a bit embarrassed by the unkempt appear of himself and his work crew.

"I'm doing some moonlighting while on sabbatical," Tom chimed in, trying to avoid a confrontation.

"What does it matter to you – missy? There's no shame in honest work," Rosa asserted in a firm voice.

"Is it honest work or is the city forcing welfare recipients to earn their keep?" Martha replied, hovering over their table and eyeballing Willie, who like Tom, had no stomach for barroom confrontations.

Standing up and moving to within a few inches of the tall elementary school teacher, Rosa answered in a low, but firm voice: "If you don't go back to the bar, I'm gonna knock you on your ass!"

A look of fear passed over Martha's face, which lost its color. Without a word, she retreated to her stool and murmured something to her bar mate who shrugged his shoulders and sipped his drink. "Hey Tom. Remind me never to tangle with this one on any future jobs. Rosa, you're one tough cookie!" Harry said, looking towards the bar where Martha sat hunched over her drink.

"If I hear that tough cookie remark one more time this week, I'll shoot myself," Tom remarked.

"What's that all about?" Rosa asked Tom.

"It's a long story that involves my mom and the saloons of Elm Park," Tom replied.

"I have an idea for this Saturday. Me and Rosa will play you and Willie in stickball at P. S. 21," Harry pro posed, finishing his beer and getting up from the table.

"Your on," Tom replied, as he stood up also. The skinny science teacher didn't want another confron tation with Martha. Getting up from the table, Rosa and Willie agreed to the contest. As the foursome left Kaffman's Tom could see Martha glaring at him out of the corner of his eye. He resolved to steer clear of his old hangout for next few weeks. He could always drop in at K C's, on the corner of Booker Place and Morningstar Road, where Pat McDean greeted him with a similar reference to his dad's legendary drinking prowess. It seems that in small towns, people were continually reminded of their family's peccadilloes – no matter how far in the past they occurred.

Chapter 34 – Work and Play

The stickball game was played with certain ground rules. Harry promised to throw half-speed pitches to Willie who appeared to be new to the game, while Tom did the same with Rosa. She claimed to be a good softball player but was surprised at the thinness of the broomstick bat and the speed of a thrown Spalding. As usual, the game was a low-scoring affair in which the only run was booming homerun off Harry's bat that landed into the cemetery across the street. Always a good hitter, Harry had made con tact with one of Tom's sidearm fastball. Despite his age, which Tom estimated to be well past fifty, Harry could still throw very hard – indicated by the loud thud each time the Spalding bounced off the concrete wall. Late in the game, Tom managed hit a line-drive triple off the fence, but was stranded when Willie flied out to Rosa just in front of the fence. At the end, Harry was happy to maintain his win ning record in fast-pitch stickball – marred only by his defeat at the hands of Amon quite a few years back. It was uncanny that Amon's exploits were part of North Shore folklore after so many years.

After the game, they decided to play some basketball on the 9-foot baskets adjacent to the stickball court. Since Tom and Willie were the most able hoop players, the teams were changed to Tom and Rosa vs. Harry and Willie. A lively game of 21 ensued in which Rosa showed a two-hand set shot that was fairly accurate. Utilizing a similar technique, Harry employed the same two-handed shooting style to even greater accuracy. Since they were experienced playground hoopsters, Tom and Willie agreed to refrain from layups and shots within fifteen feet of the basket. The first two games were split, so it was agreed to play a ty-breaking third game. With the score tied at 20 to 20, Rosa stole the ball from Harry, who claimed he had been fouled. Driving relentlessly towards the basket, the fireplug shaped woman bumped Harry and Willie out of her way and nailed a layup to win the game.

"Hey, lady. You play a rough game of basketball – more like football than hoops," Harry complained, checking the scratches on his arm.

"This is the way we play basketball in Mexico. You're allowed to hack the shooter. And even push him – as long as you don't trip him or knock him to the floor."

"Do they allow the players to run with the ball without dribbling?" Willie inquired.

"Whether you take three steps or four steps, whose counting?" Rosa replied with a shrug.

As the foursome rested on the playground steps, Rosa removed a cup and a ball attached to a string. The string was tied to the cup. "Who wants to play balero?"

"I've seen that game before," Harry replied, taking the cup-and-ball apparatus and attempting to get the ball into the cup, which was somewhat larger than a regular coffee cup. After several unsuccessful at tempts, Harry handed it to Tom who was likewise unsuccessful.

"Let me give it a shot," Willie interjected. On the fourth attempt, he got the ball to land in the cup.

"Pretty good, fellow. You have good hand-eye coordination," Rosa exclaimed.

Harry grabbed the cup-and-ball contraption and nestled the ball into the cup after three tries.

"How about you, Mr. Teacher?" Rosa said, putting the balero into Tom's hands.

Unlike his coworkers, the skinny science teacher could not get the ball to land in the cup. "If you ever had me as a teacher, you'd know that I'm a clutch. I'm known for my botched experiments at Curtis High School," Tom asserted ruefully.

"That's OK. You're a nice guy and that counts more with me. In fact, you're all nice guys. So I'm inviting You guys over for super Friday. I'll make some Mexican food for you – nice and hot," Rosa said with a wide grin.

Harry had another job for his motley crew of painters – Karisi's grocery store. Situated on the corner of Morningstar Road and Booker Place, the neighborhood deli sold basic goods like milk, bread, canned veggies, pasta, tomato sauce, Campbell's soup, and that Elm Park staple –beer. As for less popular items like pickles, tuna fish, and mayonnaise, the buyer had to be wary. There were items on Karisi's shelves which may have been sitting there since the Korean War. Years ago, his mom had returned some dill pickles, along with a big jar of mayonnaise, which had a funny taste. A squabble ensued, but Claire Haley got her money back. The feud deepened when the redoubtable woman marched into Parisis's to belabor him about selling beer to her alcoholic husband. She used the label "blood money" to describe his transactions with Thomas Haley. The "blood money" adjective was also banded about in her subsequent visits to K. C.'s and Kaffman's saloons. Karisi's and the local saloons complied with Claire Haley's demands. Her reputation as a "tough cookie" most likely began with her proscription to this local businesses with regard to selling beer and liquor to Thomas Haley. Of course, the latter solved this problem by walking several blocks down Morningstar Road to drink or venturing further to the sur rounding towns of Port Richmond and Mariners Harbor. Drinking establishments were the economic engine of the North Shore during the 1950s and 1960s and Thomas Haley was a popular patron of most of them.

Walking into Karisi's with Harry, Rosa, and Willie – Tom was singled out by the burly owner, "Harry, this guy works for you?" Turning to Tom, "Does your mom know you're in my store?"

"You've seen me in here before. I bought bread and milk, and a six-pack of Ballantine a few weeks ago. The only thing I stay away from is your dill pickles," Tom replied.

"I never forget your mom and you getting off the number three bus carrying groceries during a snow storm. Probably went to that A & P in Port Richmond – didn't make sense," the eccentric grocer re torted.

"Don't worry about Tom. He does good work," Harry said, carrying paint cans, brushes, and drop cloths.

Eyeballing Harry's crew, Vinnie Karisi exclaimed, "Is that a woman working with you?"

"Yup. She's a damn good worker. And this guy is Willie Worthington – another good worker."

"I know Willie. He's a loyal customer – unlike Tom. What happened – you lose your teaching job?'

"No. I'm on sabbatical – be back in the saddle come September," Tom responded, helping Harry spread the drop cloth on the floor.

"By the way. You're closing the store – right?" Harry asked Karisi, who appeared to be conducting busi ness as usual.

"You mean I gotta close the store today?"

"I'm not working with customers coining in and out all day. We'll be up on ladders and everything has to be covered with drop cloths," Harry replied, staring at Karisi incredulously.

"Alright. If that guy can take six months off from teaching – I'll take a day off. Though it'ill cost me."

"Mr. Karisi, it's a two-day job. I told you that last week," Harry said.

"Close the store for two days? You gonna bankrupt me,"

"My mother would say that you're crying all the way to the bank," Tom snapped. "Your mother says a lot of things – the blabber mouth of Elm Park."

Harry had house painting down to a science so the job proceeded quickly – without any bumps or snags. Karisi wanted the store painted a pale pink, with a white ceiling. The floor had been tiled recently with pink and black ties. So everything sort of fit together. Groceries consisting of canned goods and jars of peanut butter, jelly, mayonnaise, and pickles were placed in one corner so the shelves could be scraped and painted. Tom noticed some ancient jars of pickles but said nothing. Some of the boxes of cereal looked decrepit. And a few of the cans were dented and had torn labels. Shaking his head, Tom stacked the cans and jars in a corner and carried the boxes of cereal and paper goods in the back storeroom

Harry used white enamel for the shelves, which were dusty but in pretty good shape. He had Rosa paint the old wooden ladder with the white enamel. She was very meticulous in her work and never bored by routine tasks. The walls and ceiling were scraped, sanded, and primed on the first day. On the second day, the ceiling was painted white, while the walls got the pale pink picked out by Karisi. Harry and his crew used rollers for the walls and ceilings, while the corners were done with a brush. Rosa brought a transistor radio and played Spanish music to while away the time. As with all jobs, the time passed slowly at first and accelerated as the day progressed. It was just a matter of getting into the rhythm of the job – making time work for you – rather than you working for time.

Tom was amazed how fast the two days of painting Karisi's deli passed. At one point he thought that house painting might not be a bad way to earn one's living. Then the lack of fringe benefits gave him pause. Getting $1,600 for the two-day job, Harry divided up the money equitably. He paid Tom, Rosa, and Willie $320 each, leaving $640 for himself – out of which paints, brushes, rollers, and paint thinner had to be paid for. Tom would have made the same amount subbing at Curtis. However, after taxes and social security was deducted – he came out with a lot less. Besides he had much more fun working with Harry's merry band of painters. The Pied Piper of Elm Park had become the Pranky Painter of Pulaski Avenue. Gathering at Kaffman's to celebrate the completion of their first painting job, the foursome had a few beers, plus pretzels and peanuts. Tom was happy to note that Martha was nowhere to be seen. Noticing Tom searching the place for his old girlfriend, Rosa said, "I don't think your old friend will come around. She knows it would end up with my foot up her big rear end."

Situated next do to Karisi's grocery was Mislicki's bakery and Stan Mislicki's law office on the second floor. Years ago, Stan had followed the doings of Tom and his friends as youngsters in the North Shore little leagues. He had extricated Amon from jail when he was arrested on drug charges consequent to marijuana being found in his boarding house on

Simonson Avenue. When Tom offered to pay the con genial attorney for his services, Stan held his hand up , uttering the seldom legal phrase – "pro bono." Stimulated by his legal acumen and his modest fees, the Mislicki law practice had grown by leaps and   bounds. In Elm Park, the phrase: "I need an attorney" was followed by the name: "Stan Mislicki". Bumping into Tom on his way to his parents' bakery, Stan inquired about Harry's work as Elm Park's premier painter.

"He does good work, charges a fair price, cleans up everything, and has a great crew – myself included."

"I thought you taught at Curtis High School," Stan replied.

"I do. But I'm on a sabbatical right now. So I fill in the time and make some extra bucks painting for Har ry the Horse.""I remember the days when Harry would walk down Pulaski Avenue, toting a stickball bat and a Spald Ing. All the kids ran outside to play stickball," Stan said.

"And sometimes the game often ended with the ball smashing through Mrs. Eggers' window. She'd call the cops on us. And then there was Granny Schmidt cursing us out from her bedroom window when we played in the street."

"I remember Granny Schmidt walking to Dooley's liquor store for her daily ration of booze. She was a character. Those were the days when kids played in the streets – stickball games, punch ball, stoopball, hide-and-seek, jump rope, and hopscotch.

"Speaking of stoopball, that was my first memory of the neighborhood. Seeing Joey Caprino throwing a rubber ball against his front stairs and catching the rebound endlessly," Tom said.

The job of painting Mislicki's one-room office took just one and one-half day. Since the walls were in pretty good shape, very little scraping and sanding was required. Consequently, the first day's prime coat was followed by application of the latex paint on the second day. Flowing Stan's specifications, the ceiling was painted white, the walls painted pale blue, while the door and baseboards were painted a bright red. A large American flag mounted on an eight-foot high pole – completed the patriotic theme of the congenial attorney's office. Harry charged Stan $850 for the job – with the money divided up in the same proportions as with the Karisi grocery store job. Harry next contracted for a job repairing a front porch in a Mariners Harbor colonial house that necessitated only one assistant. He chose Rosa, who had become his valuable worker – highly skilled and fast-paced. So Tom vowed to be more receptive when Lou Stout offered him a substituting gig at Curtis.

Chapter 35 – A Brother Appears

A few days later, Tom and Joanie walked up Walker Street to the little cemetery across from the P. S. 21 schoolyard – the site of romancing so many years ago. It was also the place where Tom learned the bad news of Joanie's impending move to Indiana. For Tom, the mere mention of that Midwestern state brought feelings of dread and melancholia even to the present day. Joanie's parents and younger sister, Dora, still lived there in the city of Bloomington. Ironically, the South Jersey farming town where Tom spent a good part of his childhood bore the same name. As they sat on the familiar bench which bore their carved initials, they were joined by a dark complexioned young man with jet black hair, who looked strangely familiar.

Smiling warmly as if they were old friends, the young man introduced himself as Ziggy Dakota, younger brother of Amon Dakota. Like Amon, Ziggy had the intense brown eyes that burned like a prophet.

"Wow! You're the spitting image of Amon. I didn't even know he had a brother," Tom said, shaking his hand. "This is my wife Joanie."

Joanie smiled and kissed him on the cheek. "You're brother saved my life. He was a faith healer and gifted in so many ways."

"In the short time I knew him, Amon touched people in many ways. He was humble , patient, and kind. Amon did more good in little more than a year than most people accomplish in a lifetime."

"We read about him in the newspapers of Fargo, his home town. The name, Mariners Harbor Messiah, was applied to him. Then, people began to claim themselves as members of his family. Everyday cousins would come out of the woodwork – seeking recognition and advantages."

"How did you know to find us here? Tom   asked, amazed by his resemblance to his old friend.

"Amon mentioned the little cemetery where he had hit a couple of homeruns playing stickball in the schoolyard across the street," Ziggy replied.

"It ain't easy to smack a Spalding with a broomstick bat that far – more than three hundred feet."

"Is Ziggy short for something?" Joanie asked.

"I was named for the Greek god Zeus, but friends call me Ziggy."

"The Greeks stressed virtue and wisdom. You can't go wrong emulating their rational approach to life."

"I've always been head strong. I had a tendency to ignore the advice of my elders, which didn't go over so well in my family," Ziggy explained.

"So what brings you to Staten Island? " Tom inquired.

"Well, the recession has hit us hard in the Dakotas. So I thought I'd try my luck in the Northeast. Amon had written to us about that house he had fixed up for the homeless. I thought maybe I could go there and help out," Ziggy replied in a manner that seemed more like a question than a statement.

"We'll take you the boarding house on Simonson Avenue. His widow, Mary lives there. I'm sure they could use an extra pair of hands. How are you at home repair?"

"I took wood shop in school and did OK. I can paint and even fix leaky faucets and toilets," Ziggy replied.

"I could use you right now. I've been after Tom to fix the faucets and toilets that drip constantly," Joanie chimed in.

It wasn't long before Ziggy was in their bathroom, removing and replacing the washers from the cou ple's old bathroom sink and replacing the guts of their leaky toilet. Since Ziggy refused to take any money for his work, Joanie made him a spaghetti-and-meatball dinner, which he devoured like some one who had been fasting for days.

Tom, Joanie, and Ziggy arrived at the Victorian rooming house in Mariners Harbor. Mary came to the door, looking happy but somewhat frazzled. She identified Ziggy immediately from Amon's description of his younger brother.

"Ziggy! It's great to finally meet you in person — after all those letters. Come on in everybody and have some coffee."

After Ziggy explained his intentions to Mary, she mentioned Jose, whom she referred to as her "right hand man." The short, stocky repairman had been promoted to a live-in companion, which was under standable to Tom. The truism that life goes on — even after death — was a basic fact of the world. Even the stern Catholic philosopher, St. Augustine, said that action — not will — was the essential nature of man. St. Augustine, who was not virtuous in his youth, had famously stated: "Lord, give me chastity — but not yet."

As Tom and Joanie were leaving the house, Ziggy brought up the matter of Amon's death. He had been killed in a drive-by shooting on Richmond Terrace. "I don't think the police were zealous in investigating my brother's death. While I'm out here, I'm going to make a few inquiries of my own."

"Look, it's been ten years. Amon had almost as many enemies as friends. The local folks weren't crazy about the boarding house, there were pimps who objected to his attempts to save some of their wo men from prostitution, and even the police didn't appreciate his vigilante actions."

"If you want to honor your brother, continue his good work among the poor and the homeless," Mary urged the young man.

"We don't want trouble and we don't need to make enemies," Jose added somberly.

"Fine. I'll do what I can to carryon my brother's work," Ziggy said, shrugging his shoulders and looking around the rooming house.

As they left the boarding house on Simonson Avenue, Tom hoped that Ziggy wouldn't act impulsively. It reminded of something he had read recently: "The miscalculations of the world are vast."

A week or so later Tom and Joanie were stirred from a quiet evening by a phone call from Mary: Ziggy had been arrested after a fistfight in Port Richmond. He had been questioning some local toughs ru moured to be drug pushers when he was jumped by a the street thugs. The hot tempered young man had began arguing with the police. Things got out of hand and he was arrested. Tom called Stan Mislicki who accompanied him to the St. George police station. A modest bail was posted and Ziggy was released pending a court date within a few weeks.

As with Amon 's legal miscues in the past, Stan refused to take money from Tom. But the latter insisted, writing a check for one hundred and fifty dollars. "You're a professional and your time is valuable. I sure hope Ziggy has learned his lesson."

"If he's like his brother he'll learn from the experience. By the way, I'm very happy with the work you guys did on my office. My clients are impressed and it will help my practice."

"Stan, your business is growing because you're a straight shooter and you don't charge an arm and a leg for your services," Tom said, admiring the attorney's integrity. In the current milieu, material greed had become the accepted norm for people of every class and stripe.

"I'm just a small-town lawyer – trying to do my job. But like everybody, I've got to pay my bills," Stan replied, pocketing the check.

Chapter 36 – A Lesson on the Planets

After a morning call from Lou Stout, Tom found himself in front of Bill Lawler's general science class teaching a lesson on the solar system. On his desk was a rotating planetary model of the solar system and a 100-gram weight tied to a string. As expected, a few of the freshmen began fiddling with the solar system – cranking it and spinning the planets around the plastic sun faster and faster – until Tom sent them to their seats. The skinny science teacher wrote the aim of the lesson on the blackboard: How does our solar system work?

Kelly, a bright girl with pony tails, raised her hand. "The planets go around the sun in circular orbits – held in place by gravity."

"Why can't you see that both the sun and the moon revolve around the earth? Which what it looks like to me," Ronnie asked .

"The answer is Occam's Razor: the simplest explanation of any event is the best," Tom responded.

"But getting back to the solar system, the glue that holds everything together is gravity. Were it not for the sun's gravity, the planets would fly out of the solar system along a straight-line path due to inertia."

Tom held the string tied to the brass weight and began spinning it around. "The string represents the gravitational pull of the sun keeping the planets, represented by the brass weight in a circular orbit."

"If that string breaks, one of us is gonna rapped in the head," Ronnie, a black kid who was the brother of Kenny – Curtis's high-scoring forward. Like Kenny, Ronnie was outspoken and impulsive, but unlike Kenny – the former didn't grasp the limits beyond which his behavior should not stray.

After many years in the classroom, Tom realized that a gap existed between adolescent girls and boys with respect to maturity. In an ideal world, boys wouldn't start kindergarten until age six – a full year later than their female cohorts.

Turning to the board again, Tom wrote two names on the board: Ptolemy and Copernicus. "How did their theories of the solar system differ?"

"Ptolemy said the sun earth revolves around the earth and Copernicus said the earth and the other planets revolve around the sun," Robert replied.

Like Kelly, he was a good student. In the current unstructured atmosphere of the classroom, the ability to focus on the matters at hand was crucial to learning. Thinking about his own school days, the kids could get out of hand, but there were always limits which restored the equilibrium required for mastery of the material at hand.

"So what is the magical glue or force that keeps the solar system together?"

"It's gravity – discovered by Isaac Newton sitting under an apple tree. The apple fell, hitting Sir Isaac on the head. It knocked him out. Then he woke up and proclaimed the law of gravity," Ronnie said, bowing in response to the applause of his classmates.

"Enough folks. Getting back to planets, does anyone know what the word planet means?"

Robert raised his hand. "Planet means wanderer, because the planets appear to wander in the sky from day to day, while the stars remain in fixed positions."

"Excellent. You guys are very good astronomers. Maybe one of you will become an astronaut and visit Mars someday."

"Do you think there's life on Mars?" Hanna asked.

"Well from the ice caps observed by powerful telescopes, there might be plant life there. The existence of water, plus sunlight, are necessary conditions for plants. What is the process by which plants prod uce food in the presence of sunlight?"

"It's called photosynthesis," answered Roy, a husky kid who was being groomed for the Curtis football team.

Turning to the board, Tom wrote the equation for photosynthesis:

Carbon Dioxide + Water   -----> Carbohydrates + Oxygen

At that point the bell rang, sending the freshmen scurrying out of the class before Tom had time to write Mr. Lawler's homework assignment on the blackboard.

The next day, Tom was back in front of the same group of freshmen giving the follow up lesson on the solar system. On his desk was the same rotating planetary model of the solar system as the day before. And as with yesterday, he had to shoo Ronnie to his seat before he broke the apparatus.

"Someday, man will visit the planets, with Mars the most likely candidate for exploration. Perhaps one of you will be part of a Martian colony – living in a glass-enclosed settlement and growing food and raising cattle like the pioneers did in the old West."

"Not me. I like terra firma. I'm not even that crazy about flying. Give me a car or a train, but don't fence me in," Ronnie answered in an off-key falsetto.

"Oh my God. He's a comedian and a singer," Hanna, a chubby new girl who was not shy.

Someone from the back of the class asked how did the planets form.

"Good question. It's believed that the sun was originally a huge rotating cloud of hydrogen and helium gas, plus trace amounts of other elements. As these gases heated up and cooled, some of the material flew off from the sun to form the planets and the asteroids between Mars and Jupiter.

"You mean we're made up of atoms that came from the sun?" Johnny asked. He was a husky boy who sat in the back of the room who did pay attention to the doings in the class.

"So you're saying we're heavenly bodies. Although some of us are more heavenly than others," Ronnie snapped.

"Well, just listen to him. Talk about conceit," Hanna remarked.

"I'm not conceited – I'm just convinced," Kenny replied.

"The sun is not only the source of all the matter on earth, it's the source of all our energy. When we burn fossil fuels like coal, oil, and natural gas – we're using stored solar energy. These fossil fuels were once green plants that were transformed into coal, oil, and gas by heat and pressure deep inside the earth for millions and millions of years."

In response to a question about black holes, Tom said they resulted from the collapse of stars at the end of their lifecycle. "Black holes have very powerful gravitational fields where nothing can escape – neither light nor gamma rays nor particles can be emitted from them. According to Einstein, black holes repre sent distortions in the space-time continuum of the universe."

"Einstein was one smart dude," Ronnie declared.

"Einstein himself said that genius is one percent inspiration and ninety-nine percent perspiration," Tom responded.

"What's that stuff that gives plants their green color?" Roy called out from the back of the room.

Kelly politely raised her hand: "It's chlorophyll – the catalyst for photosynthesis."

"That's right. And one of the benefits of photosynthesis is that it takes in carbon dioxide and gives off oxygen – which we need for breathing."

"You could say that animals and plants are interdependent," Kenny observed. The verbose youngster had the makings of a good student if he settle down and stop clowning around.

"Exactly. Which why we have to start paying attention to our environment and stop polluting it. If one species becomes extinct, then there's a gap in the food web that affects other plants and animals in the food chain," Tom lectured.

Someone asked about food chains. Turning to the board, Tom wrote some examples.

Seaweed → Trout → Bear

Grass → Deer → Wolf

Carrot → Rabbit → Fox

Ronnie raised his hand, "I have one." He went to the board and wrote the following food chain:

Grain → Chicken → Man

"Thank God we're always at the head of the food chain," Hanna observed.

"You never heard of man eating tigers? In India a food chain might look like this," Roy replied, as he Went to the board and wrote his example of a food chain:

Bread → Man → Tiger

"On that happy note, let's get back to the planets," Tom said, turning again to the blackboard. Reading Bill Lawler's notes carefully, he inscribed the following table on the board.

Planet	Distance from Sun	Year	Day	Moons
Mercury	36 million miles	88 days	59 days	0
Venus	67 million miles	225 days	249 days	0
Earth	93 million miles	365 days	24 hrs	1

Mars	142 million miles	687 days	25 hrs	2
Jupiter	486 million miles	11.9 yrs	9.8 hrs	12
Saturn	892 million miles	29,5 yrs	10.2 hrs	9
Uranus	1.8 billion miles	84 yrs	10.8 hrs	5
Neptune	2.8 billion miles	165 yrs	15 hrs	2
Pluto	3.7 billion miles	248 yrs	6.4 days	0

"Which planet moves the fastest around the sun," Kelly asked.

"Mercury is the fastest – orbiting the sun at 110,000 miles per hour. And Pluto is the slowest – orbiting the sun at 11,000 miles per hour, which is why Pluto takes nearly 250 years to orbit the sun," Tom re plied, checking Bill Lawler's notes.

"You read very well," Ronnie remarked.

"That I do. And you guys are very lucky to have a good teacher like Mr. Lawler, who prepares carefully for all his classes."

"Is there gonna be a test on Friday?" Hanna asked.

"Could be. May I suggest that you guys study your notes for that eventuality," Tom said. With the pre cise timing that only comes after years of teaching, the bell rang immediately after Tom put his chalk down and smiled at the unhappy freshmen. He knew that years from that day, nearly all the youngsters would look back on their high school days with sentimental regret.

In conjunction with master's program in environmental science at C. C. N. Y., Tom had taken several courses in Physics to strengthen his background in that area. On a whim, he applied for a job teaching physics and math at Hamilton Junior College in New Jersey. He was interviewed by two administrators in May – coming away with the mixed feelings. In late June, he was called back to be queried by the college same administrators, plus the Dr. Green, the college president. At the end of the 45-minute interview, the high school science teacher was hired. Relaxing, Tom had mentioned his acquaintance with Amon Dakota, the Mariners Harbor Messiah. The clincher was the fact that Dr. Green had read about Amon's exploits and was a Staten Island native – attending Curtis High School. He even talked sentimentally about the North Shore, going to Clove Lakes Park, and even viewing the Mariners Harbor waterfront with its broken docks, defunct shipyards, decaying ships, and rotting hulks.

Philosopher Karl Popper's remarks that success in life is largely a matter of luck – with little correlation to merit – was evident to Tom. Exclaiming to an elderly man walking by him on Pulaski Avenue, "I'll take whatever lady luck gives me!"

Instantly, Tom recognized the man to be one of his dad's drinking buddies. Before the man could ask him for some money, Tom handed him a ten dollar bill. "Today's my lucky day, I got a college teaching job."

"Your dad would be mighty proud of you. I could use a drink and a meal right now. Thanks son. Do you still play stickball?"

"As a matter of fact I do. Played a game at P. S. 21 just a few weeks ago with Harry the Horse."

"That guy. He curses me out whenever I ask him for a dollar," the old man replied, shaking his head.

"Charity makes me feel good and it brings me luck," Tom replied, realizing that mere chance could have placed the old man and himself in opposite roles in life's complex web of occurrences.

As it turned out, Lou Stout called him for a coverage, "Your union chief, Alan Katz, got a big meeting in Brooklyn and I need to you to cover his classes."

"What's he doing today—the French Revolution? Who was that let 'em eat cake chick whose head they chopped off?"

"How the hell do I know. I taught phys ed for thirty years until the powers that be made me A. P. Any way, I need you to cover his lessons on the Presidents – working your way from Washington to Reagan, the grade-B movie actor. You'll find his notes in your mailbox, courtesy of your truly."

"I don't know what I'd do without you," Tom cracked.

"You'd spend the next four months slopping paint on walls for chump change."

Chapter 37 – A Lesson on the Presidents

Walking into Alan Katz's senior history class, Tom placed a chart on the front wall listing the forty U. S. Presidents. As expected, a few of the students asked to be excused from class, but Tom firmly declined.

"We covering an important lesson on the Presidents – for which you might be quizzed on Friday," Tom stated. He was pleased to observer the students opening their notebooks. God bless seniors – the salt of the earth – as far as high school teachers were concerned.

"How are Presidents elected?" he inquired.

"Not directly by the people, but by the electoral college," George answered.

"That's correct. Each state gets electoral votes – according to the popular vote outcome," Tom said, checking his notes.

"Wait a minute. I thought people all over the country vote for President and the guy with the most votes becomes President," Kenny declared.

"Actually you vote for electors pledged to vote for one candidate or the other. Each state has electors equal to the number of representatives plus senators. So states with a big population have the most electors," Tom stated, perusing Alan Katz's notes.

"No wonder those guys spend most of their time in New York and California," Lulu said, rattling her sil ver bracelets and anklets.

"So if you live in North Dakota, nobody running for President is ever gonna visit you. That sucks," Jerry said, turning back to look at the window – as was his habit.

"Were all the Presidents married?" Hanna asked. She was a chubby girl whose older brother played football for Curtis. As a result, she was treated respectfully by her classmates.

Checking his notes, "Yes. Except James Buchanan, who was known as the bachelor President. He was the fifteenth President – right before Lincoln, when the country was heading towards the Civil War.

"Was he gay," Kenny asked.

"No. He was just ineffectual – doing nothing to stop the southern states from seceding from the Union."

"I heard that Grover Cleveland was elected President twice separated by four years," Hank called out from the back of the room.

"That's right. Cleveland was the twenty-second and twenty-fourth President. In fact he won the popular vote for President three times in a row: 1884, 1888, and 1892. But it's the electoral vote that counts," Tom answered, again looking over his notes.

"What other times was a President elected, who didn't get the most votes?" Susan asked. She was both smart and pretty, which gave her a certain mystique at Curtis.

Checking Allen Katz's notes, Tom recited: "In the election of 1876 – Rutherford Hayes vs. Samuel Tilden, Tilden won the popular vote but Hayes had more electoral votes. So Rutherford Hayes became Presi dent. And in the election of 1888 – Benjamin Harrison vs. Grover Cleveland, Cleveland won the popular vote but Harrison had more electoral votes – becoming President."

"That's messed up," Kenny complained.

"Going back to the election of 1800, Thomas Jefferson and Aaron Burr each had 73 electoral votes. So the election was settled by Congress. Alexander Hamilton threw his support to Jefferson because he dis trusted Burr. The upshot of this was a duel between Hamilton and Burr, in which Alexander Hamilton was mortally wounded."

"Isn't he the guy on a ten-dollar bill?" Hank called out.

"Alexander Hamilton was our first treasury secretary. He set up the banking system in our country and he imposed tariffs on foreign goods to encourage American manufacturing," Tom lectured.

"Here's an interesting fact. Benjamin Harrison, the twenty-third President, was the grandson of William Harrison, the ninth President. Like his grandfather, Benjamin Harrison kept pet goats while President."

"Anyone who has a goat for a pet seems pretty weird to me," Lulu commented, shaking her bracelets and anklets.

"There were three Presidents who had been generals in the Civil War – Ulysses Grant, Rutherford Hayes, and Benjamin Harrison. In fact if you want to be President, you might consider joining the army: George Washington, Andrew Jackson, William Harrison, Zachary Taylor, Ulysses Grant, Rutherford Hayes, James Garfield, Benjamin Harrison, and Dwight Eisenhower were all army generals. Theodore Roosevelt was a Rough Rider, and Franklin Roosevelt and John Kennedy served in the Navy."

"Which president had the most children," Lulu inquired, fiddling with her silver necklace and bracelets. "John Tyler had fifteen children – eight by his first wife and seven by his second wife," Tom replied.

"Now that's a man who knew how to use his dingdong," Kenny snapped.

"You're disgusting!" Pam exclaimed.

Kenny started to say something, but recalled that the chubby red-haired junior had an older brother who was a fierce linebacker for the Curtis football team. Shakespeare's famous line, "discretion is the better part of valor" was suitable in this occasion.

"Which President served the longest term in office?" Tom asked the class.

"George, a serious student, raised his hand."That was Franklin Roosevelt, who was President from 1932 until his death in 1945."

"Very good. Franklin Roosevelt introduced social security, unemployment insurance, rules for regu lating banks and the stock market. His New Deal program to combat the Great Depression also recog nized the right of workers to join unions and to go strike," Tom stated.

"How many people were out of work during the great depression?" George asked.

Checking his notes, Tom responded, "There were fifteen million Americans out of work – representing one fourth of the workforce. The law guaranteeing workers the right to form unions and bargain collec tively was known as the Wagner Act. There was a government jobs program called the WPA, which pro vided jobs for unemployed workers – including artists and writers. Many government buildings – post offices, city halls, schools, and train stations were built during the New Deal."

"If people have the right to go on strike, how come Reagan fired those air traffic controllers for going on strike?" Hank asked.

"Unfortunately, unions don't have the power they once had," Tom replied, thinking of the problems his cousin Rusty had when his union went on strike. After a nine-month strike, his union settled with Gyp sum for a meager increase in wages and scant benefits.

Jerry unexpectedly raised hi s hand," Abraham Lincoln was the tallest President, James Madison was the shortest, and William Taft was the fattest – weighing in at three hundred pounds."

"Excellent, Jerry. How did you learn all that information?"

"My sister has one of them picture books on the Presidents," Jerry replied, turning back to look out the window next to his desk.

Fortunately, no one made a wise crack about picture books and Tom moved on. "There was another President from the Roosevelt family – Theodore Roosevelt – who served thirty years before his cousin Franklin. His program was called the Square Deal in which he broke up monopolies, regulated the rail roads, passed pure food and drugs acts, and conserved forests and wildlife."

"Wasn't he the guy who carried a big stick and built the Panama Canal?" Hank yelled from the back of the room.

"Yes. Teddy Roosevelt spoke softly but carried a big stick." Checking his notes Tom asked about the origin of Arlington Cemetery.

Susan raised her hand: "It was Robert E. Lee's plantation. After the Civil War, it was seized by the gov ernment and used as the burial place for fallen military heroes."

"What happened to Robert E. Lee after the Civil War?" Kenny asked.

"He was arrested and put in jail for a few years," George responded.

"He should have been shot as a traitor," Hank called out from the back of the class.

"Many people in the North advocated the death penalty for the South's top leaders, but the country followed Lincoln's advice for clemency towards the South," Tom replied.

"I remember: With malice toward none, with charity for all, with firmness in the right as God gives us to see the right, let us strive on to finish the work we are in, and to bind up the nation's wounds," Lulu recited, refraining from rattling her silver bracelets and anklets.

"Excellent! When it comes to the Presidents, you guys are experts." Checking Alan Katz's notes again, Tom said: "Presidents have had different jobs before becoming President. There were lawyers, teach ers, farmers, surveyors ,shopkeepers, soldiers, sailors, engineers, mayors, governors, congressmen, and senators."

"You forgot our current dude – Ronald Reagan – who was a movie actor," Kenny interjected.

"The thing I hate about politicians is they talk too much," Lulu complained, adjusting her silver anklet – attracting the attention of the boys in the class.

"You would have preferred a President like Calvin Coolidge, referred to as Silent Cal. A dinner guest made a bet with a friend that she could get him to say more than two words. You lose, he told her."

"That's really funny Mr. Haley. In your next job you should be a standup comedian," Lulu said sarcasti cally, rattling her bracelets and anklets.

"How come you're always rattling your jewelry?" Kenny asked.

"It helps me fend off bad vibes that exist all around me," rattling her jewelry so more.

"Getting back to the matters at hand. Although most Presidents went to college, nine didn't: George Washington, Andrew Jackson, Martin van Buren, Zachary Taylor, Millard Fillmore, Abraham Lincoln, Andrew Johnson, Grover Cleveland, and Harry Truman."

"Wasn't Truman the guy who dropped the atomic bomb on Japan?" Hank called out from the back of the room.

"Yes. Atomic bombs were dropped on Hiroshima and Nagasaki near the end of World War II." Turning to the board, Tom wrote the flowing information down:

Hiroshima – 140,000 killed

Nagasaki – 80,000 killed

"In addition, thousands more died from radiation sickness as a result of deadly gamma rays emitted with the blast. Gamma rays, which cause mutations, can only be stopped by three feet of concrete.

"That's messed up," Kenny observed.

"Yes it is. Albert Einstein's famous equation: $E = mc2$ was the theoretical basis for the atomic bomb. A reporter once asked him what weapons would be used in World War III. His reply: Let's skip World War III. In World War IV, the weapons will be sticks and stones."

"So we'll be living as cave men again. That's really messed up," Kenny commented.

"Who was the greatest President?" George asked.

"Abraham Lincoln, who served during the Civil War and issued the Emancipation Proclamation – freeing the slaves. Lincoln was known for his honesty. They called him Honest Abe. He also was known to walk a couple of miles to borrow a book from someone."

"Wasn't it Lincoln who rescued a pig from quick sand – messing up his only suit?" Jerry asked.

"Shit. I wouldn't mess up my clothes to rescue a dumb animal from mud," Kenny declared.

"What if it was a damsel in distress?" Lulu asked, fingering her necklace.

"Only if she was good looking."

"Would you rescue me?" she asked.

"Yeah. You're not bad."

"Moving on, there were eight Presidents who were born in a log cabin: Andrew Jackson, William Harri son, James Polk, Zachary Taylor, Millard Fillmore, Franklin Pierce, James Buchanan, and Abraham Lin coln. Actually, Harrison was born in a big Virginia mansion, but he used the slogan – log cabin and hard cider— when he ran for President."

"My slogan would be – wine, women, and song – if I ran for president," Kenny asserted.

"Well, Herbert Hoover promised voters a chicken in every pot and a car in every garage. But then camethe Great Depression throwing millions out of work. Homeless people lived in shantytowns – called Hoovervilles ."

Turning to the blackboard, Tom copied the list of U. S. Presidents for the students to transcribe:

George Washington	James Polk
Chester Arthur	Herbert Hoover
John Adams	Zachary Taylor
Grover Cleveland	Franklin Roosevelt
Thomas Jefferson	Millard Fillmore

Benjamin Harrison	Harry Truman
James Madison	Franklin Pierce
Grover Cleveland	Dwight Eisenhower
James Monroe	James Buchanan
William McKinley	John Kennedy
J. Q. Adams	Abraham Lincoln
Theodore Roosevelt	Lyndon Johnson
Andrew Jackson	Andrew Johnson
William Taft	Richard Nixon
M. Van Buren	Ulysses Grant
Woodrow Wilson	Gerald Ford
William Harrison	Rutherford Hayes
Warren Harding	Jimmy Carter
John Tyler	James Garfield
Calvin Coolidge	Ronald Reagan

"Which state can claim the most Presidents as native sons?" Tom asked.

Surprisingly, Jerry raised his hand: "Virginia had eight and Ohio had seven."

"Man. That Presidents picture book of yours sure as a lot of info," Pam observed.

"I'll bring it in tomorrow," he replied, turning back to the doings beneath his window.

"You sure? If something happens to that book, your little sister will beat you up," Kenny chimed in a sing-song, high-pitched voice.

"She has sharp nails and scratches you when she gets mad," Jerry replied.

"What? I'm out of here!" Kenny shouted, as the bell rang ending Tom's lesson on the Presidents. The boisterous basketball star ran out of the class, followed by the rest of his classmates

Lulu tarried a bit, "Mr. Haley, I don't like history much. But you made the lesson interesting."

"Why thanks. Actually, you should compliment Mr. Katz. It was his notes I followed for the class. To tell you the truth, I may be leaving Curtis for a college-teaching job in the fall."

"Ah. We'll miss you at Curtis. My cousin Lora talks about you all the time. She had you for science many years ago."

"I remember Lora. She used to wear a necklace, bracelet, and anklets – just like you. Except they were made out of copper."

"Goodbye," she replied, patting him on the cheek and leaving from the room. As she flounced along Curtis's long dark hallway, Tom could hear the jingle-jangling of her silver bracelets and anklets – re minding him of her cousin's musical exit so many years ago.

Harry's painting jobs required fewer helpers, so Tom gave the William Bradford guard outfit a call. They had a two-day job guarding the elevator entrance of a lobby in a building owned by an up-and-coming real estate mogul named Darren Trupp. One of Tom's duties was to get the signature of each person taking the elevator. A brash six-footer, Trupp stopped to say hello to the skinny guard on his way out of the building one morning.

"It's my practice to get to know everyone working in my organization – from top to bottom. How long you been working as a guard?"

"About six months. I worked for Bradford back in the sixties when I was in college."

"So guarding the rich and famous is not your regular job?"

"No. I'm on sabbatical right now. I teach physics and general science at Curtis High School."

"Never heard of it. I went to a military academy and then Wharton Business School," Trupp replied, turning to ogle a pretty woman passing in the lobby.

"Were you in the service?" Tom inquired, trying to make conversation.

"During the Vietnam War? Do I look stupid? Let me give you some advice – invest in real estate."

"Well, you need capital for that."

"Ask your family to help you. My dad started me off with a stake of a small stake. Now I'm worth a hundred million. To succeed in real estate you need some dough plus a lot of balls."

Tom started to respond but Trupp turned and dashed out of the lobby – wracking the pretty woman on her ample backside with his newspaper as he passed her on his way out of the building.

When she looked at Tom, he shrugged his shoulders. "The next time that son of a bitch pulls that I'm gonna slap his face."

Chapter 38 – A Lesson on Inventions

A few days later. Tom was called upon to cover another class for Alan Katz. Walking into the main lobby of the St. George school, he was given a bundle of notes, plus pictures of early automobiles, trains, by planes, and the printing press by Lou Stout: "It's on inventions – knock yourself out."

Walking into a class comprised mostly of freshmen, Tom grabbed their attention by showing them a large safety pin. As expected, Ronny called out, "Hey Hanna , your diaper's loose – use this."

"Why don't you keep your juvenile remarks to yourself?" Hanna retorted angrily. New to Curtis, she had quickly learned that turning the other cheek didn't work in high school.

"The safety pin was invented by Walter Hunt, a New York City mechanic in 1849. He sold the rights to his patent for $400. Hunt also worked on early versions of the fountain pen and sewing machine.

"Only $400 – that was a mistake," someone called out from the back of the classroom.

"Speaking of the sewing machine, it was conceived of by Barthelemy Thimonneir, a Frenchman, in 1830. Thimonneir was killed by a bunch of angry tailors – afraid of losing their jobs. In America, a guy by the name of Elias Howe patented a sewing machine in1846," Tom read from Alan Katz's notes.

Robert, a serious student raised his hand. "The book credits Isaac Singer with inventing the sewing machine."

"Yea. When I think sewing machines. I think Singer," Barbara chimed in.

Checking his notes, Tom concurred: "Isaac Singer improved upon Howe's version. The Singer sewing machine is widely in use to this day."

"Somebody hasn't prepared for today's lesson," Ronnie snapped.

"You're right. It was a last minute coverage. I'm using Mr. Katz's lecture notes, which I didn't study. I was remiss. What's that old adage? Don't do as I do – do as I say."

"Going back further into history, when was fire first used by mankind?"

"Fire goes back to the caveman to keep warm and to keep the saber-toothed tiger away at night," Kelly answered. Her cute pony-tailed appearance belied the freshman's sharp mind.

"To build a house, you need nails. Who invented the nail?" Johnny inquired. He was a red-haired kid sit ting in the last row, who asked good questions.

"Let's see. The first nails, which were made of copper, came into use around 3,400 BC by the Egyptians."

"What about Bronze?" Johnny asked from the back of the room.

"Bronze is an alloy of copper and tin. The Bronze Age ran from 3000 BC to 1000 BC. It was followed by the Iron Age, which lasted until 100 BC," Tom read from his notes. "The wheel has been called the most important mechanical invention of all time. When did the wheel come into use?"

Raising her hand, Kelly answered: "The people of Mesopotamia used it in chariots around 3400 BC."

"China was the first civilization to use the compass as a navigational device – around 250 BC. And China was the first to use paper – around 100 BC."

"What about printed books?" Robert asked. Unlike Kelly, Robert was often teased for his academic acumen. Somehow in the years since he was in high school back in the sixties, the country had become anti intellectual.

"The printing press was invented by Gutenberg in Germany in 1439. Once books were massed produced, rather than hand-written, literacy was expanded throughout Europe," Tom stated.

"I love reading. Don't you Robert?" Ronnie exclaimed in a high-pitched voice.

"Who invented saltpeter – better known as gunpowder?"

"That was also China. The chemical name for gunpowder is Potassium Nitrate," Kelly responded.

"Watch out for her, Mr. Haley. She's making a bomb at home for her science project," Ronnie snapped.

Ignoring Ronnie's non sequitur, Tom continued. "The ancient Chinese are credited for inventing the rocket. In modern times, the American engineer, Robert Goddard made the first liquid-fueled rocket. On a happier note, who invented penicillin?"

Robert answered: "That was Alexander Fleming in 1928. Penicillin comes from a mold and it is used to combat bacterial infections."

Raising her hand, Hanna contributed: "The steam engine was invented by James Watt in 1763."

"Excellent Hanna. Another thing I want to mention is that units in science are often named after famous scientists. The watt is a unit of power, the volt is a unit of electric force, the amp is a unit of electric current. Someday we'll have the Ronny – a unit of chaos."

"Ha Ha. Very funny. Just like Haley's Comet, which signals the end of the world," Ronny retorted.

"Talking about electricity. Who invented the light bulb?'

"Thomas Edison," several called out.

"That brings us to our favorite invention – the automobile. Who invented it?"

"Two German inventors in the 1880s – Karl Benz and Gottlieb Daimler

– using the internal combustion engine, which burns gasoline," Kelly answered.

"Very good. We're almost done folks. Except for the airplane."

"I know," Ronnie called out. "That was the Wright brothers around 1900 in Kitty Hawk. The plane was made out of light-weight wood and canvas to keep it light. And it only flew a hundred feet for about ten seconds."

"You're absolutely right."

"Now give me extra credit for my answer," he said half seriously.

At that moment, Ronnie's older brother looked into the class and pointed at him. "Is that guy behaving himself?"

As Ronnie sat hunched over in his seat and his classmates laughed, Tom responded: "Yea, he's OK for a work in progress."

Mercifully the bell rang, dispersing the students – including Ronnie. The latter adroitly avoided a playful punch from his older brother and skipped down Curtis's long dark hallway. The leading scorer on Curtis's basketball team, Kenny Forde was grooming Ronnie to fill his shoes upon graduation. Realizing that his younger sibling liked to play the classroom clown, Kenny monitored Ronnie's behavior from time to time.

Chapter 39 – Another Walk to Mariners Harbor

On a mild Saturday morning in May, Tom and Joanie decided to walk down Morningstar Road. Reaching Richmond Terrace, they turned west – strolling towards the Mariners Harbor waterfront once marked by rotting docks, rickety warehouses, rusted hulks, and abandoned ships . Tom recalled the refurbished tugboat where Amon had converted to a makeshift home. Now the area had been turned into an urban park and a marina for fishing boats and yachts. Tom felt that gentrification, which turned picturesque neighborhoods into bland, cookie-cutter locales, was vastly overrated. Ambling on the Terrace, they passed a newly constructed condominium that had replaced the twelve-room Victorian house where his mom and dad once lived back in the 1950s. Tom recalled spending e few weeks there, watching the cargo ships, oil tankers, garbage barges, and tugboats churn through the choppy gray waters of the Kill Van Kull.

Turning on Simonson Avenue, they walked up to the refurbished Victorian rooming house where Mary, Amon's widow, lived. She had a live-in companion – Jose, who helped her maintain the sprawling 18th century building. As the saying goes – life goes on. Ziggy, who occupied a room in the house, pitched in with home repairs and backyard maintenance. After a brief unhappy attempt at vigilantism, Ziggy had opted for more productive activity. Yet, he still appeared to be looking for his niche in life. Some of his youthful cockiness had left the young man. When speaking of Ziggy, Mary had quoted the maxim that pride goes before destruction and a haughty spirit before a fall. Remembering his own youthful pratfalls, Tom was optimistic about Ziggy finding himself and doing good things.

"It's so good to see you guys. I'm busier than ever and if it wasn't for Jose I'd be at my wit's end," Mary said, nodding toward Jose, who could be seen through the kitchen window raking the backyard.

"Are you still teaching at St. Mary's ?" Tom asked.

"Oh yes. The money's not great but it's steady."

"I hear you. Have you heard from our mutual friend, Martha?"

"I don't know about mutual. She's still pissed at you, Tom."

Let's not go into that. She's had plenty of time to move on. Do you mind if I lie down for a few minutes. I feel a bit woozy after our walk from Elm Park."

Mary led Joanie to a couch in the living room where she put a pillow under her head and a blanket over over her. Within minutes, Joanie was in an uneasy slumber.

Ziggy came in with a large black dog of uncertain pedigree. "Meet Duke, the newest member of the household." The good natured dog went over to Tom who petted him cautiously – wary of his substan tial size.

"So what are you up to Ziggy?" Tom asked, as the friendly canine went over to Mary, who hugged him.

"I'm working in a vet's office over on Van Name Avenue. Dr. Buena thinks I have a way with animals. I'm able to communicate with them," the young man replied.

"Who was that saint who tamed a wild wolf," Tom paused momentarily. "He was born rich, but after an epiphany went around in rags. It was St. Francis of Assisi. He used to preach to animals – converting fierce animals to tame God-fearing creatures."

"Anyway, Dr. Buena says I have a magic touch – a gift for healing."

The remark gave Tom pause, since Ziggy's older brother had the healing gift in spades – for people, as well as animals. Although near the end of his life, Amon's gifts of healing and clairvoyance seem to fade. Looking back, his diminishing popularity as a local wunderkind appeared to presage his untimely demise. So far, Tom had not observed in Ziggy his brother's uncanny ability to discern events of the past, as well as those of the future. As for Amon's wonderful compassion for the downtrodden,

Tom sensed that Ziggy acted impulsively. He had gotten into a hassle with a Port Richmond landlord that had been evic ting tenants who had fallen behind in their rents. In the beginning Amon had acted as a vigilante, but after the police intervened – he chose lawful methods of righting wrongs .Whether or not Ziggy would exhibit Amon's heightened perception of the past and future – only time would tell. As the Danish exist tentialist once said, "the grip of time seizes everything finite."

Just then Joanie awoke, calling to Tom. "I have a god-awful headache."

Tom cradled his wife's head on his lap, while Mary got her some aspirin. Swallowing two aspirin with a gulp of water, Joanie smiled weakly at Tom.

"Don't worry. It'ill do the trick. Aspirin works for me within a matter of minutes," Mary said, stroking Joanie's head gently.

"Let me give it a try," Ziggy declared, going over to the young woman, placing his hand lightly on Joanie's forehead and murmuring some words from a childhood prayer:

"Grandfather Great Spirit

Fill us with light

Give us the strength to understand

And the eyes to see."

After a short nap, Joanie woke up – smiling. Ziggy came over to the couch and patted her cheek gently. "Whether you're a person or a cat, there's nothing better than a catnap."

"I guess everyone tells you how much you remind them of Amon,"

"Actually, at home I was constantly reminded about our differences – physically, mentally, spiritually. Amon was a recipient of the Purple Heart for bravery in Vietnam. He was a gifted athlete, a skilled car penter, a good fisherman, but he didn't care for hunting. Amon was a very tough act to follow."

Mary spoke up, "I have something for you to do. The steps on the back porch I started to rot. Maybe you can look at them?"

Joined by Tom, Ziggy grabbed some tools in the panty and headed out of the back entrance. Soon the sounds of sawing and hammering resounded from the backyard. Meanwhile, Joanie helped Mary with dinnertime it's preparations. Tom had brought over large quantities of chop meat, potatoes, and asparagus – sufficient to feed a dozen people. The roster of boarders in the twelve-room house had decreased recently with the pickup in jobs on the North Shore.

However the housing situation was prone to ups and downs – depending on local and national economic factors. Even in good times, the number of poor people in the world's richest country increased stead dily. In America, the existence of untold wealth coexisted with grinding poverty, notwithstanding the political affiliation of those running things. Tom's mom, an inveterate Marxist, believed America's eco nomic woes could be settled by a more equitable distribution of goods, services, and wealth. Tom more or less agreed, though a classless society appeared to be unattainable in the current money-obsessed era of the 1980s. Instead of Herbert Hoover's chicken in every pot, the government should guarantee a decent paying job for every person able to work.

Chapter 40 – A Rude Tycoon

The following week, Tom and Rosa were sent by the Bradford guard outfit to patrol the first and twenty eighth floor of Darren Trupp's building in midtown Manhattan. There was a stipulation to prevent news paper photographers from snapping pictures of the impudent magnate. There was also a ban on all folks from the media in the lobby of his luxurious building. The tall fair-haired business man had a love-hate relationship with newspapers. At times he sought the limelight and at other times he avoided it with a vengeance. Once after a photographer snapped a picture of him on the arm of a voluptuous woman, Trupp reportedly had smashed the shutterbug's camera on the pavement. He was married to a blue blooded socialite who had given him a pair of tow-headed sons. Nevertheless, Darren Trupp regarded his marriage vows in the same way as his business contracts – as mere legal mumbo-jumbo to be broken when personally or financially advantageous.

As Tom and Rosa stood before the elevator in the lobby, Trupp burst out of its sliding doors with an en tourage of dark-suited men, he stopped upon observing the two Bradford guards. Recognizing Tom, "I see you've got a helper today. What's your name, senorita ?"

"It's Rosa Torres, a proud American citizen."

"I'm happy to hear that Bradford is careful who they hire to do guard work. But to be honest half of the domestic staff in my hotel are illegal."

Not knowing what to say to the rude magnate, Rosa shrugged her shoulders.

"I get them on the cheap – but who's checking?" Trupp gave once of his oft-photographed smiles, which was akin to a tiger flashing his teeth to a rival carnivore.

As the two guards nodded, Trupp turned away, but then quickly turned back – whacking Rosa on the butt with his newspaper.

Turning red with anger and embarrassment, the chubby woman yelled, "Don't ever do that again!"

Taken aback by Rosa's angry remarks Trupp scrutinized her for the first time. Again flashing his synthetic smile, the brash magnate hustled out of the building – followed by his blue-suited assistants.

Typical of business tycoons of that era, Darren Troop was vain, venal, corrupt, nefarious, and depraved. 1980s epitomized greed – the reckless pursuit of the almighty dollar. No one considered John Kennedy's axiom: "Ask not what your country can do for you, ask what you can do for your country."

An attractive young woman in a business suit went up to Rosa. "He pulls that shit all the time with women. If they reacted they way you did, maybe he'd stop."

Before either Rosa or Tom could react, a man in a trench coat came up to them. "I caught the whole thing with my camera. It will be on the six-o-clock news tonight."

"I don't want my picture on the news !" Rosa exclaimed.

"Troop is talking about running for mayor. This will put a big dent in his man of the people campaign ," the man replied, packing his TV camera into a big valise and running in the opposite direction from that Darren Troop and his entourage.

Fortunately, Tom and Rosa were sent to familiar terrain the next day – the sprawling Con Ed power plant in Travis. It had been several months – Ralph had retired and Jake had moved to the NYC police depart ment. Billy Bumps, the straw haired eccentric who conversed with an invisible companion, had been promoted to sergeant. It was a classic example of the Peter Principle, in which a fairly competent indi vidual is promoted to a level where he's unable to do perform satisfactorily. Tom recalled that Billy and Ralph had kept a large, nasty snapping turtle in a cage – more out of boredom than any concern for the welfare of the aggressive animal.

Tom had once climbed on a chair when the angry turtle broke out of its chicken-wire cage. After a Bradford supervisor heard about the caged tortoise, the guards carefully returned it to its home in a nearby swamp. There was also some tomfoolery when the reptile was re captured and brought back into the 10-foot by 8-foot guardhouse – only to be released again when the Con Ed folks got wind of the recurring turtle nonsense.

Walking into the dusty guardhouse, Tom noticed few changes: the same black-and-white TV, along with the noisy frig and the tarnished coffee pot. One innovation was the paved walkway in place of the dirt pathway leading to the meandering road, which in turn lead to the power plant with its adjoining park ing lot. In addition, the tall weeds and thick shrubs that once grew in the swamp were cut back. Cutting back flora and eliminating fauna may have represented progress to mankind, but not necessarily for the plants and critters which coexisted on planet earth.

Rosa made the first round of the power plant, while Tom made some coffee and watched the news on the twelve-inch screen TV. The newly elected Reagan administration was unveiling its budget – feature ing a huge increase in defense spending, accompanied by a corresponding decrease in domestic spend ing. There would be cuts in food stamps, welfare, Medicaid, mass transit, and education. Tom worried if the proposed cuts would affect his new job at Hamilton Junior College. Also Reagan's antiunion rheto ric had an intimidating effect on blue collar workers throughout the land. America was subject to wide pendulum swings politically. After four years of Jimmy Carter's moderate policies, the country was ready for an Old West cowboy promising prosperity on a credit card.

Hustling back from her rounds, Rosa said there were more stops in which she had to punch the clock with the designated keys. "We now have to go to a new station on the outer perimeter fence."

"Yeah. I noticed that on the guard notes written by Billy Bumps – our new boss," Tom replied.

"By the way, I bumped into your ex-girlfriend Martha a few days ago on Morningstar Road. She gave me this phony smile so I says to her: "I haven't seen you in awhile, but I want you to know I still think you're a piece of shit."

"Remind me never to get on the wrong side of you," Tom said, shaking his head.

Coincidentally, entering the guardhouse at that moment was the eccentric Billy Bumps himself, car rying a glass bowl with pebbles, grass, and a small green turtle. "Don't worry guys. I got clearance from the big shots to have Greenie as our mascot."

"Whatever you say, Sergeant Billy. You're the boss," Rosa declared giving Tom a wink.

"Get a load of her winking at the teacher," Billy said to his ever present companion.

Supervisor or not, was the same weird guy. Having dealt with countless odd behaving students, Tom was never bothered by Billy's eccentricities. In fact, he found the high strung young man a pleasant dis traction from the dull routine of guard work. Tom noticed that Billy still carried around his old marble covered notebook.

"You still keeping a diary?" Tom asked.

"Yup. The lady guard is taken aback by the diary," Billy remarked to his companion.

"Not at all, Billy. I should do something like that to keep track of all the stuff that's happened in the past few months. Me and Tom have been painting for an Elm Park guy – they call Harry the Horse.

"Well nothing much happens around here," Billy replied, looking through the front window of the shack. Then doing a double take, the odd young man exclaimed, "There's a ghost out there!"

Rosa peaked out the window and screamed. Peering through the same window, Tom observed a phan tom-like creature that gave him pause, "What the hell?"

Tom and Rosa ran outside of the hut to get a better look, while Billy stayed inside – paralyzed with fear.

The phantom took off with inhuman speed, running out to Victory Boulevard, where it jumped into a waiting car which sped off.

"Well, it seems that the ghost has friends who drive a fast getaway car," Tom said, peering down the road. Returning to the guardhouse, Tom asked Billy if he had made any enemies recently.

"No. But there's a bunch of guys I went to school with at New Dorp. I thought they were my friends. They heard about my promotion from my mom. She's always bragging about me."

"Friends should be happy that you're doing good. They're not your friends," Rosa commented.

"When you advance yourself in life, some people can't deal with it. You might have to make some new friends," Tom advised.

"That's why I like animals – turtles, rats, dogs, even coyotes. Remember Ratso?" he asked his invisible friend, who was named Buddy. "I had Ratso for a year. One day I put him in the backyard. He got out of his cage and an alley cat grabbed him. Turning to his invisible friend, "We buried him in the backyard with a proper funeral."

Chapter 41 – Black and White Smoke

Billy had gone to the field under the Bayonne Bridge where Tom had released his white rats after finish ing his master's thesis on nutrition. The eccentric young man had found Ratso peacefully sunning him self on a large rock. How he had eluded the cats that prowled the field was a small miracle in itself. Tom kept one of the rats, Mu Alpha, a big friendly, well-endowed male who lived to a ripe old age of five years. Tom wondered if there were a population of tame light brown rats, descended from those lab rats which flourished in that vacant field. He hoped they hadn't fallen victim to feral cats from the neighborhood. Like people , animals lived in an unpredictable world filled with friends and enemies.

Things were quiet for the rest of the shift as Tom and Rosa went on their alternate rounds of the Con Ed facility. Tom noticed that the plant's huge smokestack emitted black smoke from time to time. Back in the 1960s, the guards were required to call the plant people if EPA inspectors drove up to the guard house. Within minutes of receiving the phone call, the billowing smoke had turned to a gray-white hue. Apparently, there was a filter able to absorb the most visible, and hopefully, the most noxious gases. The reason for the relaxed smokestack policy was that the Reagan administration no longer hounded utilities about their atmospheric emissions.

"So they're letting these guys put all the stuff they want into the air for people to breathe?" Rosa asked.

"It sure looks that way. Guess what? Rich folks breathe the same air as poor folks. I knew something was up when I started smelling that Sulfur Dioxide."

"They don't care if their kids smell bad air?" Rosa asked, screwing up her face."

"I read in the paper that the federal government is also relaxing its water quality standards"

"I was better off in Mexico where we had clean air and clean water. And better food – home grown,   without all those chemicals in it."

"I think all that stuff about pesticides is overplayed. When I was a kid in South Jersey, the planes used to dust the crops with pesticides. Back in the 1950s, the trucks would come around and spray the bushes with DDT to kill the mosquitoes on Staten Island."

"What did you do? Run out and play in DDT spray?"

"As a matter of fact we did. It was a lot of fun."

"When you die of insect poison, I'll go to your funeral," Rosa said.

"Another thing that bugs me is all this malarkey about bottled water. When we were thirsty, we just took a drink from the garden hose."

"So what kind of flowers do you want at your funeral?" Rosa inquired, getting a pencil and pad.

"We used to play in the poison ivy vines with no ill effects. Kids today are like hothouse flowers. If the slightest exposure to weeds results in a rash, the parents panic and send their kid to the doctor."

At that point, Billy returned to the guardhouse from his rounds of the power plant, holding his hand out For inspection. "Guys is this a rash or what? I was walking by the plant perimeter and tried to pull some tall weeds by the fence. And now my hands are real itchy."

 "Not to worry, Billy Boy. I got some stuff for you," Rosa said, taking a bottle out of her knapsack and applying some of its contents to hands.

"What is that stuff? It feels pretty good."

"It's witch hazel. It works for anything from pimples, measles, rashes – even the clap," Rosa replied.

"I swear. I've never had the clap," Billy replied blushing.

"That I'm sure of Billy," Tom responded. "There was this guy who must have been some sort of neigh borhood Lothario. Every time he walked into Kaffman's the folks would clap."

"Well, nobody ever clapped for me," Billy muttered.

"You know what? I'm cooking Mexican tonight. I want you and Tom to come over my casa. Bring your long suffering wife Joanie too."

"She's inviting us to dinner, what do you say Buddy?" Billy asked his constant companion.

"Only yourself – not your magic friend," Rosa said. Then observing Billy's crestfallen face, she quickly added, "Just kidding – your friend is welcome too."

A true member of the working class, Rosa was down-to-earth, hardworking, honest, and tolerant. Like Tom, she lived in Elm Park. And like most immigrants, she wasn't afraid of hard work. When Jesus re ferred to people who were the salt of the earth – he had folks like Rosa in mind and not the likes of Dar ren Troop. In today's world, the value of physical work had been denigrated in favor of paper shuffling and legal wrangling. Rosa's common law husband was supposedly in California – picking crops. She had referred to her long gone spouse as a "free spirit" – a bit too free for his own good. Thus, it could be said that Rosa's marital status was uncertain at best. In the current era of fragile marriages, Heisenberg's Un certainty Principle was more applicable to American marriages than to subatomic phenomena.

Rosa's small apartment on Winant Street was cozy and neat. There were various bric-a-bracs and snap shots of her family, including her itinerant husband – looking roguish with a dark moustache, a red ban danna, and a sombrero tipped at a rakish angle. There was also a picture of the two of them posing to gether – Rosa with a demure smile and her beau smiling like a wolf. Pointing him out, "That's Alejandro – the wandering pistol. Remember that TV Show – Have Gun Will Travel? My husband's motto is: have pistol will use it."

Billy started to make a remark to his ever present companion, when Joanie kicked him under the table. Like Rosa, Joanie wore a colorful dress – looking better than she had in weeks. "I brought a desert which I baked myself – a chocolate layer cake – Tom's favorite."

"Anything chocolate is my favorite. Right Buddy? I mean Tom," Billy chimed in, anxious to make a good impression. The young man was dressed in a light blue collared shirt with a bright yellow tie.

"Once I gave Mu Alpha some chocolate and he devoured it in five seconds. That rats would eat anything. He especially liked Chinese food – those bean sprouts," Tom said.

"Chocolate is not good for rats. Would you give chocolate to a dog? Table food is not good any pet. Right Buddy?" Billy chimed in. Then realizing his faux pas, abruptly stopped talking.

"It's OK. Habits are hard to break. Alejandro used to fart at the table. He said it was a complement to my cooking. Each time he let one go – I'd elbowed him in the gut." "Tom's pretty vocal when it comes to anal chatter. Did the elbowing work?" Joanie inquired.

"Did it work? Hell no. Wherever he is now, he's probably letting go with los pedo – his awful farts."

Turning to his invisible sidekick, Billy said: "We used to call them fluffies. As in, Buddy did a fluffy."

Sensing that they had exhausted the topic and were getting grossed by it, Tom changed the subject. Billy, did you ever play stickball as a kid?"

"I played table tennis in high school. Couldn't play basketball because of a heart murmur – congenital. I have a table-tennis setup in my basement."

"I used to play it at a place in Port Richmond. Had a girlfriend who was very competitive. The one time I beat her, she got so pissed she threw racket at me."

"So what did you do?" Billy asked.

"I ducked. After that I made sure she won all the table tennis games."

Joanie had joined Rosa in the kitchen. Before long, the two women brought out the food – steaming Bowls of rice, black beans, chop meat, spicy red peppers, browned onions, and veggie-filled tamales. Once the food was served, there was a lull in the conversation as the ingestion of food took occupied everyone's full attention. The men folks ate the heartiest and the fastest, but Rosa was no slouch in the eating department. Though short in stature, Rosa had the strength and stamina of a man. And she was a good housepainter – neat and patient.

Tom was pleased to notice that Joanie ate with a rare relish. Unlike, Martha who ate and drank like a man, Joanie had an appetite like a sparrow. Tom was happy to notice that Joanie cleaning her dish and going for seconds . Never a big eater, his pretty wife had lost weight as she dealt with recurrent head aches. He hoped that Ziggy's incantations had a similar positive effect on the young woman as Amon had done – so many years ago. The gift for healing, found in doctors, nurses, was a special calling. But the so-called faith healers seemed to be a rare God-given trait – not widely dispersed in the human race.

Chapter 42 – Food for Thought

As a man of science, Tom wasn't a big believer in faith healing, but after witnessing Amon's uncanny ability to heal – he was no longer dubious. Perhaps the efficacy of faith healing was attributable to a placebo effect in which the patient's belief in the healer promoted rehabilitation. The psychological as pects of the sickness-health continuum could not be ignored. Often miracle cures from dreaded dis eases were rooted in the patient's particular outlook on life – optimists trump pessimists in the game of of life. Sigmund Freud talked about the two fundamental forces: the life-force and the death-force. The former represented drives like sex, hunger, thirst, and pleasure. While the latter represented drives like aggression, violence, and suicide. Aggression appears to be innate in human beings who can be catego ized into two broad groups: active-aggressive and passive-aggressive.

"What are you thinking about?" Rosa inquired. "Sometimes you act like you're in outer space – a million miles away."

"Tell me about it. When he was a teenager, everybody said Tom Haley was an oddball, a deep thinker, neither fish nor fowl." Joanie remarked.

Coming to Tom's defense, Billy said: "I'm the same way. I avoid anger and hostility by focusing on my own thoughts. That's why I carry a notebook wherever I go."

"There's nothing wrong with introspection. I'm like the ancient Greeks. I'm a rationalist. A person who dwells on facts and principles – rather than emotions and violence."

"Wasn't it Plato who talked about a real chair and the idea of a chair – claiming the idea of a chair is more important than the chair itself?" Billy inquired.

"You're right. Plato proposed the dual theory of reality — the realm of physical objects versus the realm of ideas. The latter was ultimate reality because ideas are real. perfect, and eternal," Tom stated.

"So if I'm tired and want to sit on a chair, I should sit on the idea of chair because a real chair is not per fect. That's the difference between women and men. Sometimes m en make no sense at all," Rosa de clared as Joanie nodded while Tom frowned.

"I propose a toast to Rosa, who's got smarts and looks and muscles too," Billy said, lifting up his glass of sangria.

"By the way. This sangria is great. What's in it?" Joanie asked, taking a long sip of the purple -hued sangria.

"I made it myself. Mixed orange, lemon, and grape juice with some red wine. Not too strong. And it tastes good. And presto — instant buzz!" Rosa proclaimed proudly.

"I got something in the mail about rehabilitating a house for the poor. Jimmy Carter uses volunteers to fix up houses. Everybody pitches in — including the family who will occupy the house," Tom said.

Billy said he would help out with the construction and Rosa concurred. "It sounds like fun. And it's nice to some good in the world. What's that saying? No man is an island."

Turning to his invisible companion, Billy said: "We're all peninsulas — joined at the hip."

"Now don't get weird on us Billy," Rosa exclaimed, patting him on the back.

Ironically, that night Tom got a call from Lou Stout. He would be covering some lessons on philosophy for Curtis's union honcho, Alan Katz.

Chapter 43 – A Lesson on Philosophy

Walking into the class, Tom noticed some familiar faces in the senior class. He placed pictures of four philosophers on the front board: Plato, Immanuel Kant, Soren Kierkegaard, and Bertrand Russell. Recognizing the Curtis teacher known for his dramatic, but sometimes errant experiments, the students cla mored for something his match-head tin can rocket.

"No fireworks today folks." Today we're going to go back in time more than two thousand years go to ancient Greece – the land of Socrates, Plato, and Aristotle."

"Who cares about some weird Greek guys who walked around in those gowns. What do they call them?" Kenny asked his classmates.

"Togas. The Greeks and the Romans wore togas," Pam, a chubby red-haired girl responded.

Realizing he was in for a strenuous lesson, Tom turned grimly to the blackboard and wrote the four aims of philosophy:

1, To understand the world.

2. To determine the purpose of life.

3. To grasp the meaning of reality.

4. To understand God.

George, a serious student, raised his hand. "There was this guy Pythagoras, who devised the Pythago rean Theorem. For right triangles, the square of the hypotenuse equals the sum of the squares of the other two sides."

"Very good. Pythagoras had some interesting ideas outside of math. He believed in a strange form of re Incarnation. He said people would come back as animals and animals would come back as people."

"I'd like to come back as cute bunny rabbit," Lulu offered. She was a cute Spanish girl wearing a silver necklace, bracelets, and anklets which she continually rattled.

"Then I'd comeback as big old wolf and gobble you up," Kenny replied with a fierce grin.

"Who said the unexamined life is not worth living?"

"That was Socrates who took his own life by swallowing hemlock, which is poisonous," George replied.

"Socrates most famous student was Plato, who postulated that reality was twofold – the world of every day objects and the world of ideas. He called it the dual nature of reality. Cab anyone elaborate?"

Susan, a student who combined beauty and brains, answered the question. "Plato's metaphysics said that the world of objects was imperfect and changing, while the world of ideas was perfect and eternal. In other words, the idea of a desk is more important than the physical desk itself."

"That's crazy. I can't put my books on the idea of desk or sit on the idea of a chair. If you can't see it, hear it, touch it, or taste it – it ain't real," Hank responded from the back of the class.

"What about Xrays? You can't see them, but they pass through body. Doctors take pictures of your lungs with Xrays," Tom replied.

"Whatever. Those ancient Greeks don't make sense to me," Pam complained.

"This material on philosophy is in your textbook and you guys are responsible for it," Tom said grimly.

"There's more to life than book learning. We should be learning practical stuff like how to get a job and what to do to keep it,"

"You've got a point there. Nevertheless, Mr. Katz said there would be a quiz on this material next week," Tom said, looking through the lecture notes given to him by Lou Stout.

"I bet some of those ancient Greeks didn't have the smarts to get out of the rain," Jerry said. He sat by a window – spending most of his time looking out on the street below.

"Anyway, there was a group of ancient Roman philosophers, called Stoics. The most famous Stoics were Zeno, Epictetus, and Seneca, who advocated an austere life, the endurance of suffering, and belief in a life of virtue."

"Not exactly your kind of guys," Kenny said, looking directly at Lulu.

"Go fuck yourself!" she yelled, shaking her bracelets and anklets.

"That outburst was uncalled for Lulu. The whole idea of philosophy is make us more rational and less violent in our responses to the world," Tom observed. The world had changed since he was in high school. He had seldom been witness to the verbal spats which were commonplace in all walks of con temporary life.

"Moving on. There was a famous philosopher named Immanuel Kant who had an analytical approach to ethics. He proposed the categorical imperative – a universal rule of behavior valid for all people, across all cultures, and valid for all times. What would be an example of a categorical imperative?"

Susan raised her hand. "Thou shall not kill. Thou shall not steal."

"Thos shall not screw," Kenny chimed in.

"We can always depend on you to bring the discussion down to the level of the gutter," Pam replied. With a big brother on the football team, the chubby red-haired coed spoke her mind to everyone – no matter their status at Curtis.

"Kant also believed that a person's happiness should be in proportion to his virtue. If that didn't happen in life, then God would provide a reward in the afterlife."

"So if someone steals your money, you have to wait until the afterlife for him to be punished?" Hank called out from the back of the room.

Checking his notes, Tom continued. "Then there was a man named Karl Marx who said ultimate reality w was the material world. He was a determinist stating that history was a dialectic process in which antag onistic classes – peasants versus landowners and workers verses capitalists – would struggle until an ideal classless society was achieved."

"That will never happen. You're always gonna have the poor, the rich, and most folks in between," Lulu said, rattling her bracelets and anklets.

Perusing Alan Katz's notes, Tom continued. "Marx labeled his theory dialectical materialism, in which an Idea – thesis – is followed by its opposite – antithesis – and the ensuing conflict leads a better idea – synthesis."

Noticing many of the students had that familiar dear-in-the-headlight look, Tom wrote on the board:

Idea (Thesis)   +   Opposing Idea (Antithesis)

→Better Idea (Synthesis)

"Marx is a bad dude. He's responsible for communism," Jerry exclaimed, turning away from the window he constantly focused on.

"Actually, his ideas led to socialism as well as communism," Tom interjected.

"Ain't they the same thing?" someone called out from the back of the room.

"Countries like Sweden, Norway, and Denmark are socialist. They have democratic governments. Russia, China, and Cuba are communist. They are run by dictators with no political opposition permitted."

Hank called out from the back of the room. "What about that guy Nietzsche? Didn't he say that God is dead?"

"When he's ready to croak – he'll change his tune," Kenny said grimly.

"Nietzsche said there was no such thing as universal morality. Marx agreed – asserting that morality was a class concept. Each economic class has its own values, customs, and truths," Tom lectured.

"Didn't the Nazis follow Nietzsche? He said stuff like the will to power by the master race," Hank said.

"In certain ways, Marx and Nietzsche were similar. They both stated that truth and morality are subject tive. Nietzsche went so far as to say that there are no objective facts. There were only interpretations. Next, we arrive at the existentialists – Kierkegaard and Sartre. The existentialists said that existence precedes essence, in other words the individual person and his actions determine his destiny."

"So, they're subjective – compared to the Greeks and Romans – who were rationalists " Susan said. Like George, she followed the lesson closely.

"Exactly. Kierkegaard was very religious, he had an inner-world focus – believing that the modern world was corrupt. He described religious faith as an irrational leap beyond reasonable justification. Similarly, a person discovers his true purpose in life through an irrational leap in faith."

"So if you believe that Jesus Christ is our savior, you're irrational? That's messed up," Kenny asserted.

Rechecking his notes, Tom plunged forward. "Well, Kierkegaard said some provocative things. We can not derive an ought from an is. In other words, morality isn't derived from objective facts. The realize tion that we might die at any moment results in dread or what Kierkegaard called angst."

"What's that?" Lulu asked, fingering her necklace.

"It means fear or dread," George answered.

Kenny raised his hand as Tom waited for the inevitable putdown. "Man I got to hand it to you, George. You do know a lot of those ten dollar words." The class responded by cheering George, who blushed deeply, looking at his notes.

Jerry was stirred from his side window staring. "I have a quote from that guy Kierkegaard: Life is under stood backwards but is lived forwards."

"That's awesome Jerry," Kenny exclaimed.

Raising his hand again, Jerry said "I got another quote: Literature gives form to life. It was made by a person named Joyce Carol Oates."

"That's also awesome Jerry, but off topic," Kenny commented.

Tom talked about deduction and induction."In math deduction is used, whereas science uses induction. Just about all the laws of science are cause-and-effect statements. Who can give me an example?"

Susan responded: "If you heat up a gas, it will expand."

"Isn't that how a thermometer works? When the temperature rises, the mercury inside it expands – showing a higher temperature," Hank called out from the back of the room.

"That's right. Sidewalks have spaces between the concrete squares – called expansion joints. In the sum mer, the concrete expands. Were it not for those spaces, the sidewalks would buckle," Tom stated.

Noticing that time was running out, Tom mentioned Jean Paul Sartre. "He was a twentieth-century exist entialist influenced by the Nazi occupation of France during the second world war. He denied the exist ence of God – stating that man is condemned to be free and responsible for everything he does. There is no reality except in action."

"So you can't say the devil made me do it," Pam responded.

"So then Sartre is asserting that man has free will," Susan.

Referring to Alan Katz's notes, Tom mentioned Bertrand Russell. "During the 1960s, Russell was known as a peace activist and advocate for nuclear disarmament. He was called the father of analytic philoso phy, which emphasized language and the meaning of words."

"That's because words are the lenses through which we observe the world," Susan said in a matter-of fact manner.

"Man! That girl is scary smart," Kenny commented.

Checking Alan Katz's notes once more, Tom mentioned the poet T. S. Eliot. "He spoke like an existential Ist: Everyday is the day we should fear from or hope from. One moment weighs like another. The critical moment that is always now and here."

"That's about as clear as mud," Jerry said, turning back to gaze out the window. Tom shrugged and moved on.

"Twentieth century philosophy philosophers emphasized language and logic – instead of theorizing about metaphysics and ethics. They separated statements into empirical propositions and analytic propositions," Tom lectured, turning to the board to write out some definitions.

> Empirical Proposition – statements about the world. Ex: The notebook has a red cover.

> Analytic Proposition – necessarily true statements. Ex: A baseball is round.

"These modern philosophers asserted that if you cannot verify a statement analytically or empirically, Then it is meaningless. So they removed metaphysics, ethics, and aesthetics from philosophy." Turning to the board, tom wrote out some more definitions.

> Metaphysics – statements about the nature of ultimate reality.

> Ethics – statements about one's behavior in terms of right or wrong .

> Aesthetics – statements about beauty in art, music, and literature.

"What about determinism?" Hank called out from the back of the room.

The bell had sounded, but most of the students remained seated. "Determinism is the doctrine that every event has a cause. In other words, each action can be traced to a chain of causes. Determinists like the Roman stoic Zeno and the Dutch stoic Spinoza stated that free will does not exist, Determinists assert that everything that happens is the result of absolute logical necessity.

"Isn't determinism really cause-and-effect? I can see that determinism applies to science – physical ob jects, but when it comes to people – free will governs our behavior," Susan commented.

Tom agreed as the students closed their notebooks and slowly filed out of the classroom – thinking about the lesson. Lulu came up to Tom's desk and complimented his lesson. "You made this stuff kind of interesting. With all the peer pressure in high school, there isn't much free will."

"To be honest. You should thank Mr. Katz. I just followed his lecture notes, which were awesome."

"Well your awesome too," She said, walking down the long dark hallways of Curtis – jingle jangling her silver bracelets and anklets all the way.

Tom was on his way out of Curtis when Lou Stout buttonholed him, "I need you tomorrow to cover Dick Grimsby's physics class."

"What's he doing?"

"It's right up your alley – the laws of motion," Stout replied. Noticing Tom's hesitation, "What? You have something better lined up. You're painting Kaffman's bar in exchange for a year's worth of free booze."

"Would that I had a painting gig. Can I set off one of my match head tin can rockets?"

"So long as you don't blow yourself up and the school with it," Stout said, eyeballing Rosie Murray. The femme fatale of the Curtis faculty, she attracted lecherous stares from students and teachers alike – despite the added pounds that middle age often brings to the fairer sex.

"Will you look at that ass. How would you like to screw her?" Lou confided.

"I never allow my reach to exceed society's constraints," Tom said, glancing at the woman's bouncing gluteus maximus as she flounced down the hall.

Chapter 44 – A Lesson on the Laws of Motion

Walking into Dick Grimsby's physics class, Tom noticed several of the same students he had taught the day before on behalf of Alan Katz. He was upbeat about the lesson. Familiarity was a high teacher's best friend. Tom pushed a cart laden with the following items – a glass tumbler, some index cards, a couple of balloons, a cart connected to some weights via a stringed pulley system, and a match-head filled tin can. The last item intrigued the students who congregated around the cart until Tom sent them to their seats, while he wrote the aim of the lesson on the blackboard: What are the three laws of motion?

"You're talking about Isaac Newton. The guy who dropped two rocks from the Leaning Tower of Pisa," Jerry called out with a smug grin.

"No sir. That was Galileo. He proved that all objects fall at the same rate due to gravity," Kenny said.

"That's right. Newton discovered the law of gravity sitting under an apple tree – watching an apple fall towards the earth. He said that the same force of gravity keeps the moon orbiting around the earth and the planets orbiting around the sun."

Tom stated the lesson by placing a card with a quarter on it over the glass tumbler. He snapped the card with his finger and the quarter fell into the tumbler. As the students cheered vociferously, Tom asked: "What happened here?"

"The quarter stayed put. An object at rest tends to remain at rest," Jerry said, focusing on the demon stration – rather than the doings below his window.

Next, Tom pushed a cart across the desk. It continued to move until it struck a stack of books on the opposite side. "And what happened here?"

"An object in motion tends to remain in motion," Jerry replied once more.

"Very good, Jerry. We've just demonstrated Newton's first law of motion – sometimes called the law of inertia."

"So inertia is an object's resistance to changes in its motion. Like when a school bus stops suddenly, the kids are thrown forward," Susan said.

"You don't need Newton's laws to know that. It's just common sense, girl," Kenny chimed in.

"For the most part, the laws of science correlate with everyday experience. What we call common sense is actually Newton's classical mechanics," Tom stated.

Next, Tom set up the cart, which was connected to a pulley by means of a string – at the end of which was a suspended weight. Upon releasing the cart, it accelerated until it collided with the pulley. Then, Tom increased the size of the suspended weight pulling the cart, which made the cart accelerate faster.

Then, Tom kept the force acting on the cart the same, but increased the mass of the cart by adding weight to it. When he released the cart, it moved at a slower rate.

"What's going on here?"

"The increased weight represents a force acting on the cart. As this force increases the cart accelerates faster, but when the mass of the cart increases the cart accelerates slower," Lulu answered, fingering her necklace.

"Very good. We've just demonstrated Newton's second law of motion: the acceleration of an object in creases with the applied force and decreases with its mass."

Reaching into for the balloons, Tom blew them up and released them from the front of the classroom. Naturally, some of the students jumped out of their seats to retrieve the balloons, fill them with air, and shoot them at each other. After a time, their pent up energy was released and the discord subsided.

"So what happened here?"

Kenny raised his hand. "It's called action and reaction. The air leaving the balloon is the action and the balloon being pushed forward is the reaction."

"Excellent. This is Newton's third law of motion. For every action there is an equal and opposite reac tion. Suppose I'm on a boat that's not tied to the dock and I step out of the boat. The boat will go back ward as I step forward and I'll wind up in the lake."

Turning to the blackboard, Tom wrote out Newton's three laws of motion for the students to copy in   their notebooks.

Isaac Newton's Three Laws of Motion

1st Law: An object at rest tends to remain at rest, and an object in motion tends to remain in motion.

2nd Law: The acceleration of an object varies directly with the force and inversely with its mass.

3rd Law: For every action or force, there's an equal and opposite reaction or force.

From the back of the room, Hank called out. "Can't Newton's second law be written as an algebraic equation, force equals mass times acceleration?"

Turning to the board again, Tom wrote the following equations: $F = M \times A$ or $A = F/M$.

"In fact, let me give this problem. Find the acceleration on an object with a mass of two, subjected to a force of twelve pounds."

"That's easy. Its acceleration is six," Jerry called out.

"Hey! What about the rocket? Are you gonna set it off or not?" Kenny exclaimed.

With time running out, Tom lit the fuse with a match. The tin can rocket seemed to shake momentarily before zooming upward. It veered towards the blackboard – striking it, bouncing off the ceiling, and landing on the front desk – almost exactly where the rocket was launched. The students cheered and applauded loudly, as the room quickly filled with smoke. Tom rushed to the rushed to the windows and opened them – with the excited students assisting him.

As the bell rang, the students happily left the class. Lulu approached him with a big smile, "You made my day, Mr. Haley. This is one lesson I'll never forget," she exclaimed, giving the skinny science teacher a pat on the cheek.

"Well, I'm glad I made your day. Whenever you see a Fourth of July rocket, think of Newton's third law of motion."

"I wish my other teachers would do stuff like this. It was the best science lesson ever," she replied. Then leaving the room and walking down Curtis's long narrow hallways, Lulu jingle-jangled her silver bracelets and anklets merrily.

Lou Stout entered the room and shook Tom's hand. "You ended your Curtis career with a bang and not a whimper."

"How do you know I'm leaving Curtis?"

"This guy from Hamilton College, Dr. Green, called me. I said you were a great teacher when sober."

"What?" Then realizing the amiable administrator was joking, he shook Stout's hand.

"Who will I call when I need a somebody in a pinch to cover a class?"

"Rosie Murray."

"I said somebody in a pinch – not somebody to pinch."

"Bill Lawler. "

"Lawler's not flexible. You think he'd do a lesson on the Presidents or philosophy? No way. Anyway, come to my office with me for a second."

They entered Lou Stout's office where he gave Tom a package. "Here you go. Share it with your wife and don't drink it all in one night."

Tom thanked the burly principal – his eyes tearing up.

Slapping the skinny science teacher on the back, Stout said: "Don't forget us . You're part of the Curtis family. Comeback and visit us anytime."

Chapter 45 – Reflections on Past Events

Leaving the front entrance, Tom looked at the school's façade with its formidable limestone gargoyles. Those scary stone creatures had frightened him when he first walked into the St. George school years before. He had gone through some rough times as a novice teacher. He spent too much time in places Kaffman's and K. C.'s – seeking comfort in booze and idle chatter. The marriage of his high school sweet heart in faraway Indiana left him with despair. He searched unsuccessfully for a "new Joanie" in the myriad of bars and dance halls that can be found in New York City.

Burdened by overwhelming melancholy, Tom thought about a electroshock therapy – the application of electric currents to the brain. He knew a colleague at Curtis who had confided in him about his experi ence with such therapy. He had read about a similar approach – insulin shock therapy – utilized by some practitioner in the field. ECT treatment involved the application of 240 volts to push 0.8 amps of electric current through the brain for a few seconds. Tom was concerned about the effects of electro shock treatments – particularly amnesia . He learned that the memory gaps for people and events at the time of these treatment were short lived. The research indicated that retention of ideas and con cepts, acquired over long periods of time, was unaffected. But forgetting the names of his students in the middle of a semester would not be a good thing. Curtis students would attribute his amnesia to ex cessive drinking. And the rumors about his heavy drinking had persisted long after he had ceased his bar hopping in the gin mills of Elm Park.

Consulting with Dr. Atlas, his family doctor of many years, Tom was given the name of an excellent Korean psychiatrist, Dr. Kwonk. Tom did a five-year stint on Dr. Kwonk's proverbial couch, learning much about himself, his childhood, and his handling of the curve balls thrown by fate. From habits that origi nated in childhood, he tended to turn minor setbacks into catastrophic events. Over the years, through trial and error, he mastered the techniques of teaching – the forty-minute lesson plan, classroom con trol, student discipline, and backfilling idle moments with information that grabbed the students' inter est. He especially enjoyed the opportunity to cover classes outside his field – teaching lessons in math ematics history, and philosophy. Now he viewed those experiences, the good times and the bad times, with rueful melancholy and sentimental regret. For better or worse, we are the products of the hodge podge of experiences and people which constitute our lives. Tom believed that teaching was a noble profession. Indeed, the name give to Jesus by his disciples was "Rabboni" – meaning teacher.

When he looked at his life, Tom discerned a certain pattern: an initial period of struggle, then an interval of painful adaptation, and finally a time of mastery of the challenge at hand. He went through that failure-then-success cycle with his Herald Tribune paper route, in high school where he barely made the honor roll to reaching the acme of academic distinction, and at City College where he felt lost and alone to the point where he earned the regard of his professors for his strong work ethic. As a youngster, Tom had been a fan of Robin Roberts, the durable hard-throwing ace of the Philadelphia Phillies. A work horse, Roberts won twenty games between 1950 and 1955 for a weak-hitting club, while pitching 300 innings, averaging 160 strikeouts and 50 walks. Like Tom, who was asked to cover classes for absent teachers, Roberts was often called upon as a relief pitcher between starts. There was something to be said for the American work ethic which had been passed down to us from our Puritan forbears.

Of course, Puritanism with its stress on sobriety, discipline, thrift, and religion can be overdone. Pulling up to Kaffman's in his old gray Pontiac, Tom decided to have a couple of beers. Embarking on a new juncture in life necessitated a drink or two. Sitting at a stool in the hazy, sour-sweet smelling saloon, Tom, saw Willie Worthington sitting at the end of the bar. Moving to a stool adjacent to the congenial young black man. Willie's family had lived on Pulaski Avenue near the abandoned railroad tracks for as Tom could remember. He had been part of Harry the Horse's painting crew, but left for a job at Waller stein's factory in the Harbor.

Rudy Kaffman placed a Ballantine beer next to Tom. Following Tom's nod towards his companion, the red-faced bartender did the same for Willie. Years ago his dad was a regular customer of Kaffman's , along with K. C.'s, until his mom visited those establishment – demanding they stop serving an incurable alcoholic. She used the term "blood money" to describe the proceeds which went into their coffers in stead of the Haley family budget. When Tom began frequenting Kaffman's and K. C. 's as a young man, his first beer was on-the-house, in recognition of the debt owed the Haley family.

"I'll be starting a new job in the fall. Teaching math and physics at Hamilton Junior College in Jersey," Tom said to the former P. S. 21 stickball enthusiast and basketball player.

"Wolstein's is moving me to the graveyard shift next week. There's a big demand for Bosco since they came out with a new strawberry flavor – which I hate," Willie said, sipping his beer.

"They ought to try a vanilla-flavored mix. The best thing about the midnight to eight shift is going home when everyone else is heading for work."

Rudy refilled Tom's glass and started to likewise with Willie, but the latter shook his head. Years ago,   Kaffman's had been a favorite haunt of his dad – a hard-drinking house painter.

"Are you still working with Harry and Rosa?"

"Yeah. When he needs an extra pair of hands. Painting is hard work," Tom said finishing his beer and signaling refills for himself and Willie.

"Remember the days when Harry played stickball on Pulaski Avenue with us? Some of the neighbors didn't appreciate it. Who was that old lady – used to curse us out from her window?" Willie asked.

"That was Granny Schmidt. She would trek to Dooley's for her daily bottle of whiskey."

"You know that guy they called the Mariners Harbor Messiah? He's got a brother – I forget his name."

"Calls himself Ziggy, for the Greek God Zeus," Tom replied.

"Well he was beaten up by some pimps in Stapleton. Trying to talk to the working girls – convert them to upstanding citizens," Willie said, shaking his head.

"He's on a fool's errand. Amon tried similar vigilante stuff, but soon learned it was a losing battle. It re minds me of something T. S. Eliot once said – the last temptation is the greatest treason. Doing the right deed for the wrong reason."

"Amon is a tough act to follow – that's his problem. Doesn't he work for a vet?" Willie asked.

"Dr. Buena. He seems to have a gift for healing, like his brother. But to be honest, his efficacy pertains to animals rather than people," Tom replied, finishing his second Ballantine.

"Then he ought to stick to healing animals and not mess with pimps and prostitutes."

"Have you noticed that things are changing so much and so fast nowadays?" Tom said.

"Reminds me of what Satchel Paige once said – don't look back, something might be gaining on you," Willie replied.

"And with Reagan running the country, there's a lot of anger. Not good vibrations like the Beach Boys used to sing about but bad vibrations," Tom remarked, looking around the poorly lit bar nervously.

"I don't pay attention to politics. Just focus on what I got to do to get by," Willie took a final gulp of his beer, shook Tom's hand, nodded at the bartender, and left the dingy bar.

Sitting in the hazy, sour-sweet smelling bar, Tom thought about the changes the country had undergone in the past years. Back in the fifties, everyone who worked at Wolstein's factory was white. The first black cabinet member, Robert Weaver, was appointed by Lyndon Johnson in 1966. Weaver was the head of the Department of Housing and Urban Development (HUD). The first black person invited to the White

House was Booker T. Washington, by the maverick Teddy Roosevelt in 1901. There was such an uproar, that the second black person, Jessie De Priest, wasn't invited until 1929 by Mrs. Herbert Hoov er. America's most influential evangelist, the Reverend Billy Graham had preached to segregated audi iences back in the 1950s. With the advent of Dr. Martin Luther King's civil rights movement, Graham had dramatically torn down the ropes separating whites from blacks to signal his acceptance of racial in tegration. He even scolded a group of white southerners: "We have been proud and thought we were better than any other race . . . but we're going to stumble to hell because of our pride."

Chapter 46 – Joanie in Distress

Returning to the house, Tom found Joanie in bed with an icepack on her head. "My head aches so bad. It's must be a migraine."

"Did you take some aspirin?" Tom asked, kissing her on forehead, which felt feverish.

"I've been taking two aspirin every few hours. Doesn't help at all,"

Joanie had been experiencing headaches for many years, but there was something different about her appearance. "Joanie get dressed. I'm taking you to the hospital."

At first she declared it wasn't necessary. Then, a surge in pain nearly overtook the young woman and she relented. Joanie quickly dressed and Tom drove her to St. Vincent's Hospital on Bard Avenue in West Brighton. She was given a room where Dr. Sibley, a tall gray-haired physician saw her immediately. A few years back, Tom had taught his Sibley's son at Curtis – giving the hardworking youngster an "A" in physics. Despite its growth in recent years, the small town nature of the North Shore was a blessing.

"We're going to do a CAT scan and see what's going on. Then we can decide upon a treatment," he told them, after examining Joanie.

Once Joanie was settled in the room and they were alone she made him promise that he'd would pray for her at St. Roch's. They had occasionally attended the church on special holidays like Christmas and Easter. Unlike a few years back, Tom immediately agreed to do so. But he would also pay a visit to Mar iners Harbor, where a plaque had been placed on a utility pole in memory of his old friend, Amon Dako ta. After praying in the nearly empty church in Port Richmond on a drab, overcast day, Tom drove to the Harbor and pulled next to pole in question. It was the very pole from which Amon had fallen when Tom had first met the charismatic young man.

"I'm sorry for not visiting you more often or even helping Mary at the Simonson Avenue house. You know how it is – we get busy with our petty affairs. I think it was Wordsworth who said the world is too much with us late and soon. Getting and spending we lay waste our powers. I need one more favor from you – Joanie is very sick. She's too young to die. Please help her my friend."

As Tom headed back to his old gray Pontiac, he saw Harry's painting crew working on dilapidated house on the other side of the Terrace. Shrugging his shoulders, he waved to them and jumped into his car and drove off. It could have been worse. Had he been observed beseeching the utility pole by Martha or by a Curtis student, he really would have been embarrassed. He had once seen a homeless woman urinating in a parking lot. The poor woman had reached the stage where embarrassment was no longer part of her emotional repertoire. When she finished, he gave her a five-dollar bill unsolicited.

Unlike many people, Tom was disconcerted when observed unawares doing the right thing or the wrong thing. The incident motivated Tom to think seriously about guilt. The idea of undeserved guilt is connec ted to the Christian concept of original sin. At City College, Tom learned about Sigmund Freud's ideas concerning guilt, which he linked to society's constraints on the id, which propels us to fulfill our basic drives, urges, and needs. The nineteenth century Viennese psychiatrist introduced the notion of the un conscious mind, which is the storehouse of our instinctual needs and psychic actions. Hidden messages from the unconscious provide a form of inner communication that people are unaware of. The uncon scious can be thought of as a repository of socially unacceptable ideas, wishes, desires plus traumatic memories and painful emotions that have been suppressed. Many neuroses originate with childhood traumas which are suppressed under peer, parental, and social pressure. Freud said that unconscious thoughts can be tapped by random association, verbal (Freudian) slips, the interpretation of dreams, and examined through psychoanalysis.

Sigmund Freud differentiated between suppression and repression, in that the former involved denying impulses at the conscious level, while the latter was the denial of impulses at the unconscious level. Freud defined alienation as the separation of different parts of the ego. The alienated individual is out of touch with himself and with society. Often the socialization process is lacking in dysfunctional families . If institutions like the public schools and churches don't do their part — drug addiction, crime, and alien ation inevitably result. Despite his abstract theorizing about Freud, Tom was not oblivious to the bloom ing of flowers and the bursting forth of blossoms from trees befitting the arrival of spring on the North Shore. The pleasant odor of honey suckle, dandelions, lilies, sunflowers, and even wild blueberries was borne by the mild spring breezes. Feeling energetic, the skinny science teacher decided to walk south on Morningstar Road, crossing Forest Avenue towards Graniteville. He was headed towards the little league baseball field — now overgrown with weeds — where he first met Joanie.

It had been a balmy spring day when he had played that memorable softball team matching a group of Park Elm players — including Joey Caprino, Mike Palermo, Gene Munski, plus others against Graniteville guys in a high scoring game. Among the opposing players was Jake Giardello, Joanie's cousin. Befitting the small town nature of the Island, everyone knew each other. There were several cute girls watching the contest — one of whom made her presence felt. Joanie took an interest in Tom's outfield play – di- recting a stream of remarks both flattering and derogatory towards the skinny centerfielder. At one point, Tom was so distracted by the vocal teenager's impudent rude chatter that he collided with an other teammate chasing a fly ball in right center. Instantly, Joanie ran onto the field and began dabbing his bleeding nose with her fragrant hanky. Tom made a remark about dying and going to heaven, to which she reprimanded him: "Oh shut up! Why don't you look where you're going?"

Actually, the provocative teenager had seen Tom in her neighborhood for years. He had delivered the Herald Tribune every morning to Joanie's next door neighbor. The skinny kid riding his rickety red bike, with a canvas bag of newspapers, had been a fixture in the Port Richmond-Mariners Harbor-Graniteville area for many years. He earned a meager stipend of roughly twelve bucks a week for his efforts — except for

Christmas when tips ballooned his proceeds to thirty or forty dollars. Delivering papers seven days a week all kinds of weather paid dividends with regard to hardy health and a good work ethic.

During the five years he was in the employ of the New York herald Tribune, Tom never caught a cold, came down with the flu, or even experienced a cough or sore throat. There were also dividends paid in terms of physical endurance, shoulder and leg strength, plus the tenacity to stick to a job – even if not well paid. A comprehensive newspaper second only to the New York Times with regard to local, nation al, and international news, the "Trib" was far superior to the Staten Island Advocate, which focused on   local news and gossip. Years ago, the Advocate had a story about cousin Rusty robbing a liquor store and leaving a bag of money at Claire Haley's house. When the police arrived, his mom was already at the front door – shoving the paper bag, brim full of dollar bills, into the policeman's hand: "I work for my money – there are no freebies in this world."

The teenaged romance between Tom and Joanie was affected by her family's move to Indiana. Most star-crossed romances do not survive the buffeting of fate. Random events can be the enemy, as well as the friend of romantic alliances. The adage "absence makes the heart grow fonder" has less validity than what common sense tells us – that propinquity contributes mightily to attraction and even ro mance. The blossoming of love is nourished by the sensory information – sight, sound, touch and tactile feelings – which cannot be conveyed over large distances. Tom had written romantic letters during his years at C. C. N. Y. with Joanie responding initially. After a few years, her letters arrived less frequently until the dreaded "Dear John" letter arrived during Tom's senior year at college. His moonstruck plans of moving to that distant Midwestern state and getting a teaching job upon graduation were dashed.

Joanie's unexpected return to Staten Island, nearly a decade later, was so stunning that their first meeting in Kaffman's bar had a surreal, dreamlike quality. A couple of times, Joanie caught Tom pinching himself. And the skinny teacher told her exactly how he felt. Their reacquaintance after so many years confirmed what Bertrand Russell discussed years ago – the idealist notion that life is a dream. Tom went on to explain that philosophers like Bishop Berkeley and David Hume asserted that we are given only sensory impressions – hot, cold, color, shape, texture, sound, odor and taste – material objects exist on ly in our minds. At that point, the earthy young woman placed Tom's hand on her breast: "Is my boob just an idea floating in the air or is real human flesh."

These sentimental reflections and philosophic musings had brought Tom back to Pulaski Avenue where he saw Joey Caprino sitting on his front porch. Tom's first memory of Elm Park was Joey's relentless games of stoopball – throwing a Spalding against the concrete steps and catching the rebound endlessly. Tossing Tom a yellowish baseball, he told him to get a glove. After Tom hesitated, Joey called out; "Come on. You're not that old. Go get your glove and will have a catch."

The two old friends who had played hundreds of stickball, softball, baseball, and basketball games to gether played an earnest game of catch. Joey threw a variety of fastballs, curve balls, and even knuckle balls to Tom, who exchanged his fielder's glove for a catcher's mitt. When his fast began to pop and his knuckleball started to dart up and down unexpectedly, Tom put a catcher's mask to "protect his Holly wood looks." After forty-five minutes or so, the two men, no longer in the prime of youth, began huffing and puffing. Tom ran into his house and returned with two cans of Ballantine beer.

"So how's Joanie doing?" Joey asked, momentarily catching Tom off balance. But he realized that their moms spoke regularly as longtime neighbors are wont to do.

"Well, she has theses recurrent headaches. They're doing lots of tests . It's mostly wait and see," Tom replied, his voice trailing off.

"I'll pray for Sunday at St. Roch's," Joey replied, pounding the old baseball into his worn glove.

Tom was surprised by his old friend's remark. Though a former altar boy, Joey Caprino was not a dutiful Catholic . He probably outranked Tom in the irreligious scale – if there was one. Years ago, Joey had been compelled by family pressure to marry a girl he had gotten pregnant. Tom remembered Joey cursing out his "old man with his Guinea-Catholic values" who had pressured him to marry Mary Rose. They were still married with a daughter who was doing well at Port Richmond High School and would be attending Wagner College in the fall. All in all, this was one shotgun wedding that turned out as well as could reasonably be expected.

Tom was distracted by a sparrow that flew right over their heads as they sat on the Caprino front porch. He recalled the biblical saying that not a single sparrow can fall to the ground without God knowing it. "Remember that passage in the Bible that a sparrow cannot fall without God's knowledge?"

"Yeah sure. Every time I pick up a newspaper, there's a story about some dumb son of a bitch getting shot or stabbed for ten dollars. Or a dead baby left in a garbage bin – like a bag of dog shit!"

"I think you need a another beer," Tom said, getting up to get some more beer.

"Nah. I'm good. I'm gonna putter in my garden – like my old man used to do."

"That's what happens in life. We start acting like our parents," Tom observed, draining his beer.

"Well then go easy on the beer. If you know what I mean," Joey snapped with a wry grin.

Chapter 47 – Joanie Departs

Walking over to his house, Tom saw that his mom's face was wracked with grief. She ran to him, hugging him and weeping profusely. Tom understood immediately. While he had been on his sentimental jour ney of Graniteville, Joanie had died. As when he was a youngster, his mother's fierce hug left him numb and breathless. "I'm so sorry Tom. She was too good and too young to die like that."

Overwhelmed by grief, shock, and numbness, Tom was speechless. He recalled his father's death from a heart attack on the street – amidst one of drinking binges. Coming from school, Tom had learned about his dad's awful death from the upstairs tenant, Mr. Taglia. His sister Cara, arriving a few minutes later, had been informed of the terrible news by Joy Eggert, the rude teenager who had tormented them upon their arrival in Elm Park from South Jersey. Trying to console his sister, Tom said their dad "was watching them from heaven." Cara would have none of it: "No! He'll be six feet under with the insects and the worms. Don't give me those dumb fairy tales."

Now, with Joanie dead, Tom sought desperately to console himself with thoughts of a sweet hereafter where Joanie and himself would reunite in a state of eternal bliss .There must be a sanctuary outside   of this vale of tears we call life. Plato said the existence of perfect, eternal ideas demonstrates that the soul is immortal and God exists. Kant asserted that if anything at all exists in the universe, then an abso lutely necessary being, God, must also exist. And Jesus, the ultimate authority on heaven, said that he was the resurrection and the life. Everyone who believes in him would have life – even after death.

Originally, Tom had opted for a memorial service at the Methodist church in Port Richmond which he and Cara had attended years ago, but Joanie's family demanded a memorial mass at St. Roch's. Tom relented –

realizing the differences between the dominations were minor. The priest commended to God his servant Joanie. Her soul was transmitted to heaven as her body was committed to the ground – earth to earth, ashes to ashes, dust to dust, forever and ever, amen. Notwithstanding Catholic tradition, Tom spoke for a few minutes. Gathering his emotional resources and summoning his teacher's disci pline, he talked about his first job delivering the Herald Tribune to the house next door to where Joanie lived. They had exchanges glances through her front window.

That cursory glance had moved something inside the both of them which altered their destiny forever. Tom went on to relate the story of their first encounter on the ball field in Graniteville and their result Ing puppy love as idealistic teenagers. But theirs was a star crossed romance consequent to Joanie's move to Indiana. Then, her unexpected return to Staten Island and their rekindled love after years of separation. I t was one of those modern day miracles that can only happen in America – the wondrous land of miracles.

"Meeting Joanie, falling in love with her, and reuniting with her after so many years shaped my entire life. Our enduring love, despite the obstacles that fate imposes on everyday people, was miraculous in deed. How fortunate we are to be Americans. We live in a country born out of ideals: freedom, justice, brotherhood, and the pursuit of happiness. We are judged by what we do – not by where we come from. Wherever I go in the world and whatever I do in life – Joanie will be with me. Blaise Pascal, known for the binomial expansion, said that we know the truth not only by reason but also by the heart. And my heart tells me that I'll surely meet Joanie again."

There was a dispute over the final resting place of Joanie. Tom opted to use Sam Dabinski, the son of Ray Dabinski, who had handled his dad's funeral years ago. Her family wanted to transport her back to Indiana. Unlike Tom's mother, the Gardello s never really accepted their common law marriage. But Tom was adamant that she would be buried in the small cemetery across from P. S. 21, where the two of them had spent many hours talking, kissing, hugging, and even consummating their relationship. He re called amusing Joanie with chatter about waxing and waning moons, Henry Hudson's ship, the Half moon, first entering New

York harbor, and the old Dutchman, Peter Stuyvesant, buying Manhattan from the Lenape Indians for $24. As the years went by, Tom and Joanie would return to this special place place where they had gotten to know each other spiritually, emotionally, and physically As the site of Joanie's permanent resting place, the little cemetery was truly sacred ground. Years later, whenever Tom retrieved a Spalding smashed from an opponent's stickball bat, he knelt by her grave, shed some tears, and prayed for this tragic young woman.

Since Joanie's death, Tom and his mom had resumed their Saturday morning coffee klatches. Having both suffered the loss of a spouse, mother and son had suffered were drawn closer by common views regarding a person's fate in life. They were both fans of Thomas Hardy, whose novels reflected the de terminist view that a person's fate is subject to psychological, familial, and socioeconomic forces be yond his control. Despite the ups and downs fate has thrown at Claire Haley, she cherished the little comforts of life – a cup of coffee, a plate of scrambled eggs, and a newspaper. With the Staten Island Advocate spread out on the kitchen table and a view of her neighbor's backyards and the morning sun Light diffusing through the small old fashioned kitchen, the sixtyish woman was content. Or express it in her own words – she was "as happy as a clam." Her thirtyish son, not yet recovered from the loss of Joanie, was muddling along.

"So when do you start your new job at Hamilton Junior College?" she asked, rustling through her news paper.

"I start in September. But there are some orientation meetings in late August I have to go to," he said, looking at the Caprino's backyard where Joey was watering some flowers with an oversized pitcher. "Why doesn't he use a hose. Who has the patience to water each flower and bush with a pitcher?"

"He's just like his dad. Mr. Caprino never used a hose. He once said something about the pressure from a hose can harm flowers. So how much are going to make as a college professor?"

"Well. There's a slight pay cut. But eventually I'll do better."

"So. It's not exactly a promotion. It's not a step up – it's a side step," she replied, slurping her coffee.

"Mom. It's something I've been wanting to do for awhile. Curtis isn't the same school that it was ten years ago. I'd like to spend more time teaching rather than hassling with my kids."

"So what are you doing in the mean time?" She went to the stove, refilled her cup, and slurped some of it down noisily.

"Mom. Will you stop slurping your coffee so loudly. I don't know. Putter in the backyard. Go for long walks. Hang out at Kaffman's – just kidding!"

"I think you should get back with Harry the Horse and his painting crew. It will get your mind off things."

"Mom. He hasn't been called Harry the Horse in twenty years," Tom replied, remembering the days when Harry played stickball on the street with the neighborhood kids. The other dads of Elm Park were too busy working, puttering around the house, arguing with their wives, or hanging out in the gin mills for street games.

"And stay away from those damn bars. It was the rumination of your father. May his soul rest in peace."

However, Kaffman's bar was the place where Tom walked – climbing the gently sloping hill of Walker Street to enter the dingy sweet-sour smelling bar. As luck would have, he found Harry perched on a stool near the door. Rudy Kaffman made his usual remarks about the return of the prodigal son. He even laced a brimming glass of Ballantine beer "on the house". The free beer custom had ceased in recent years, but understood why it had been recently reinstated.

"Tom, I'm sorry to hear about your wife. She was a classy dame – I mean a nice woman – the best," Rudy exclaimed, wiping down the bar with a soggy cloth that must have been used when his Dad was a regular at Kaffman's.

Tom nodded as the other patrons mumbled similar condolences. Of all the human emotions, grief was the one people could not relinquish because it was so tied up to our memories and our regrets. What could we have done differently to have changes the awful course of events?

Harry uttered similar sentiments. He also congratulated on his new teaching job in New Jersey. Despite its meteoric population growth, Staten Island was still a small town in which gossip, chatter, good news and bad news spread faster than the speed of sound.

Anticipating Tom's request for work, Harry said he was rehabilitating a shack in a vacant field under the Bayonne Bridge. "We're gonna enlarge it. Add some rooms and fix the roof. Redo the kitchen and bath room They also want us to pave walkway which leads to the Terrace.

"I know the shack. I used t deliver the Herald Tribune to a guy who lived there. He had this long red beard – kind of scary looking."

"Yeah. The cops found him dead inside the hut. It was in the Advocate: the mystery of the red-bearded Hermit," Harry related.

"Is Rosa still working with You?"

"Yup. I got you, Willie – when he's available – and a new guy, Connor – my concrete man.

"Who's Connor? " Tom asked , not recognizing the name. There was a time when he knew everyone his own age living in Elm Park.

"He's from Brooklyn. We're getting a lot of people moving to the Island from there. He was trying to start a paving business here, but construction has slowed down," Harry said, downing his beer and get ting ready to leave. Tom was finishing his beer when he noticed his old girlfriend Martha sitting at a table with Wayne O'Toole, the erstwhile neighborhood bully who had once slammed his red bike to the ground bending the front wheel. Even as an adult he tried to steer clear of the man, who always said hello whenever they met. Like many former bullies, Wayne seemed to have no memory of his earlier depredations.

Martha came up to Tom and hugged him. "I'm so sorry about your loss. But she's in a better place now – free from pain and suffering.

Tom thanked the tall woman and got up from his stool. Wayne swaggered over and shook his hand with a vice-like grip "Ditto. Hang in there man. Things 'ill get better ."

Chapter 48 – Ghosts from the Past

Tom nodded and got up rather too quickly and felt dizzy. Wayne reached out and steadied the skinny teacher, who did a double take. Momentarily, he saw a middle aged man downing a whiskey through the haze, who looked eerily like his father. Through the haze, he could see his intense blue eyes. Blink ing, he looked again. But the man had vanished magically before his eyes.

"Man! You look like you seen a ghost," Wayne exclaimed.

"I think I did," Tom replied, shaking his head and rubbing his eyes. Nodding to the unlikely couple, Tom walked out of Kaffman's and headed down Walker Street carefully – as if he was treading on ice. Across the street, he saw his foster parents giving two familiar-looking kids some sandwiches, while talking to them with comforting words. A newspaper boy on an old red bike nearly barreled into him.

Approaching him in the opposite direction was Granny Schmidt. Years ago, the grumpy dowager made daily trips to Dooley's liquor store on Morningstar Road for a bottle of cheap whiskey. When the kids played their rollicking games of stickball on the street, Granny would open her bedroom window and rant at them. If Harry was there, he'd give the old woman what for – to the amusement of everyone.

"Hey Granny. You stick to your boozing and I'll stick to my ball playing. And never the twain shall meet."

Then Mrs. Eggert, from the other side of the street would open her window – telling Harry and the kids to take their ball games to the schoolyard. Once, Tom had sent a Spalding through her parlor window. Her verbal threats to call the cops were muted when Harry, got a glass pane from the Perry's junkyard and repaired the broken window pronto. A similar emergency repair of an Eggert window had been also been done by Amon, who also fixed a leaky faucet for the cranky woman.

"What are you staring at – wise guy? You look like just saw a ghost," Granny cried out in her raspy voice.

"I thought you were long gone, Granny. I must be going off the deep end – I'm seeing ghosts," Tom said out loud, as a passing stranger looked at him incredulously.

"Don't you remember? You once saved me when I passed out on the street," she screeched.

"I just need a some sleep – a reprieve from these unearthly torments," Tom said rushing to his house on Pulaski Street, fumbling with his keys, running up the stairs, and flopping on the couch.

He had left the TV on. Not bothering to turn it off or even shut off the light, Tom plopped onto the couch. Soon he was in a deep, but troubling sleep. He was riding his red bike, delivering the Herald Tri bune midst a snowstorm. Suddenly, a strong wind blew his newspapers on to the sidewalk. He jumped off his bike to gather the scattered papers, Joanie magically appeared and began helping him. When he turned to thank her, she had disappeared.

Chapter 49 – A New Day

On a balmy May morning, Tom followed the winding dirt pathway on the weed-filled field below the Bayonne Bridge. The sea breeze from the Kill Van Kull, along with the smell of honey suckle, dandelions, and other wild flowers made the walk pleasant. One's view of the world is affected by our surroundings. It's difficult to remain gloomy when mother nature presents us with such a bright sunny face. Tom was familiar with the hut once occupied by the red haired hermit. Years ago he had delivered the Herald Tri bune to the reclusive man who had died alone – a tragic ending to a lonely life. The hut became a hang out for teenagers hanging out, drinking beer, smoking pot, and carrying on sexual assignations.

Harry, Rosa, and Willie were already at the site cleaning up the hut and its environs. There was a ton of trash – newspapers, paper cups, beer cans, wine bottles, trojans, garments, sneakers, dog poop, auto mobile tires, a rusted bicycle frame. Tom and Rosa were given cleanup duty, while Willie helped Harry remove the broken door and busted windows. Soon Connor, a short muscular man, arrived via his pick up truck which was emblazoned with "Connor Concrete Corps". With the help of Willie and Tom, he re moved to big iron vats, some sandbags, and a bag of concrete mix from his pickup truck. Soon everyone was busy doing their assigned tasks – getting into that work rhythm where time flows and the work pro ceeds at a steady pace.

Clearing the surrounding area of weeds, shrubs, and miscellaneous debris Tom and Rosa worked well together. She was a tireless worker who alternately hummed off key and chattered about the doings at the Con Ed plant, where she worked part time. "By the time they get though taking out taxes and other stuff – I got nothing left. So now I'm mostly working for Harry, OTB, off the books."

"How's Billy Bumps doing?" Tom inquired. He had remembered the eccentric young man who was always conversing with his invisible companion.

"He's alright. We went out for awhile. I didn't mind him talking to his invisible friend, but when they made him boss at Bradford – it went to his head."

Walking through some dense underbrush, they saw a light brown rat that went up to them. Rosa froze on the spot, but Tom took a piece of carrot he had been nibbling on and extended toward the rat. Cau tiously the rat took the carrot in his paws and began chomping on it.

"Man. You have a way with animals. It took the carrot like it knew you.," Rosa observed.

"There's a story behind it. A few years back I did a research project with white rats. After the project was done, I set them free – except for one rat – Mu-Alpha. He was the friendliest of them all."

"What happened to him?"

"He died. Rats only live for two or three years. Mu-Alpha lived to the ripe old age of four years. So this guy must be his great-grandson."

"So what did you do with the rats?"

"I had them running a maze. They were separated into two groups – well fed and malnourished."

"That's cruel! How would you like to be malnourished?"

"It was a research project. I was trying to show that malnutrition impairs learning. In other words, kids with inadequate diet don't do as well in school."

"Everyone knows that. If you don't have a good breakfast, you don't give a shit about what the teacher is saying. I can tell you that from personal experience," Rosa said, shaking her head.

"That's the trouble today. Pointy-headed scientists doing experiments to prove what everybody already knows. Instead of curing diseases like cancer they keep building bigger bombs to blow up more people."

"You do have a point there. Maybe you should go into politics. This country needs people who are down to earth – with common sense.

"I'd rather be a prostitute than a politician," she replied, raking the debris which Tom gathered and put into a large garbage bag.

"Here's a joke. How are prostitutes and lawyers alike?"

"I don't know. They charge a lot of money," she guessed.

"You're close. They both charge by the minute."

"Oh my God! If you're students could here you know," she exclaimed, glad that she had distracted the skinny teacher from his woes.

"Not so long ago, a student in one of my class mentioned Paul McCartney. And someone else said that was the guy from Wings," Tom related.

"Well he is from the group Wings."

"So you never heard of the Beatles?" Tom inquired half seriously.

"Of course I heard of them. My favorite song of theirs is Help."

She began singing the words in a winsome off-key manner that reminded Tom of Joanie.

"Help me if you can I'm feeling down

And I do appreciate you being 'round

Help me get my feet back on the ground

Won't you please, please help me?"

After the group's hard work on the wooden hut with the tragic history, they congregated at Kaffman's bar on the corner of Walker Street and Morningstar Road at the end of the workweek .The smoke-filled, grimy saloon was crowded with weekend celebrants in accordance with the Friday night setting of their meeting. Harry bought the first round of drinks – beers for Tom, Willie, and himself, wine for Rosa, and scotch on the rocks for Connor. The half-acre of weeds, bushes, gingko trees, and debris had been pret ty much cleared, the bathroom sink and toilet repaired, boundary boards were set up for the 250-foot long sidewalk which lead from the Terrace to the tiny house, and the concrete foundation for the two room addition had been completed. Once the foundation dried, two-by-four framing for the two-room addition would proceed. Surprisingly, the roof wasn't in bad shape – requiring the replacement of a few loose shingles, but the redbrick chimney needed some work.

"Listen up folks. Once the house is done, I want to make a Mexican dinner for everyone. You too, Connor. You're now part of the family."

Connor nodded. "Will do. I've got to admit it. You folks from Staten Island are very friendly."

"Of course we are. You don't have to worry about someone putting a knife in your back like those crazy people from Brooklyn," Harry replied.

Tom started to say something to the effect that he wasn't up to it. But Rosa, who sat next to him, wasn't having any of it. "Tom, I want you to come. It'll be good for you."

Harry chimed in, "If you come I'll give you another chance to whip me in stickball."

Willie also chimed in, "If you come I'll play you one-on-one at P. S. 21."

"You're both on. We'll play a stickball game and then some basketball next Saturday. I need a week to get into shape."

"I want to play too. Can I come?" Rosa asked.

"Of course. Where would Harry's crack home-repair team be without you?" Tom said with a certitude he hadn't felt in a long time.

Then Rosa squeezed his hand and bestowed him with a beaming smile that lit up the whole room.

The End

ALL ABOUT THE AUTHOR

The author taught science and mathematics for many years on the high school and college levels. His approach to teaching is to make abstract principles concrete by connecting to real life experiences. The students should come away with facts and ideas, the ability to solve problems, and the ability to make ethical decisions. The book is about a close-knit group of people of different backgrounds fixing up old houses. They learn the secret of blue collar folks -- focus on the task and not the clock. There are five books in the Tom Haley saga: 1950s-1960s Fable, 1960s-1970s Fable, The Mariners Harbor Messiah, Blue Collar Folks, and The Pulaski Prowler.